A Roar in the East

Steven Lusk

First publication: Llumina Press, Tamarac, Florida 33319 December, 2005

ISBN 10: 159526552X
ISBN 13: 978-1595265524

First Revision August, 2011

ISBN 10: 0983989419
ISBN 13: 978-0983989417

To my mother and father who created my humor and

for my wife for putting up with it

PROLOGUE

The jungle was darkly thick and seemingly impenetrable with a myriad of strange bushes, trees and exotic flowers. The air was thick with water and cloying with odd and unreal scents. Monkeys scampered in the upper branches of the trees, chattering to each other, and unseen birds gave loud hooting calls. In the near distance a loud drumming sound could be heard.

Through this dense forest a figure slowly moved, his image barely seen, the darkened hands reaching out to carefully move a bush or branch to allow the figure to slip eel-like through the foliage. The man crept silently forward until suddenly the jungle ended at a clearing filled with rough huts constructed of woven branches and grasses, strange conical shaped buildings with small black objects hanging from the eaves. Unseen beyond the huts the drumming continued.

Between two huts a circle of stone could be seen confining a low burning fire with wisps of smoke that climbed lazily into the thick air. Rough clay pots and dishes lay near the fire. A spear with a stone point leaned against one of the huts.

Still moving slowly the man emerged into the clearing. He stopped for a moment and peered around. He was clad in a jump suit imprinted with a green, black and brown pattern that blended almost perfectly with the surrounding jungle. In the clearing of hard packed tan dirt and tan huts, he stood out like a belly dancer in a Baptist church.

In one hand he carried a black crossbow and across his back was a small black carryall. A floppy bush hat covered his head and his face was streaked with green and black camouflage paint. Small bugs tugged desperately to free themselves from the colored goo. With a darkened hand the man reached up and scratched at one of the twitching insects, squishing it and adding a slight red tinge to the surrounding green.

Moving stealthily from hut to hut the man worked his way deeper into the village, his eyes constantly on the lookout for the people of this primal town. A small pig grunted at him and wild chickens strutted across his path. As he moved deeper into the village the drums became louder.

Silently he crept through the empty village, sliding smoothly from hut to hut. At the third hut he started to peer past the curve of the wall when something brushed his forehead. Still looking outward he absently brushed at his hair. His hand struck a rubbery hard object and he casually glanced upward to see what it was. With a loud, "Ahhh," he jumped away from the hut and turned around to stare, his hands brushing rapidly at his hair.

His wide round eyes were focused on the small dark objects hanging from the edge of the huts roof. Each of the balls had hanks of black hair drifting from their tops, Deep indentations showed where eyes used to be and each shrunken head had a Mona Lisa smile formed of threads through the lips. The shriveled ears looked like raisins stuck onto prunes. The heads bounced slowly up and down, giving them an evil sense of life.

He turned and started to run to another hut but tripped over a pot and fell part way into the fire. With a low, "Wow," the intruder scuttled from the fire and quickly looked around before darting to the side of another hut after first checking that there were no dark balls of former life dangling from the eaves. With a soft "woof" through his teeth the man waited for a moment for his heart to slow down before again traversing the village, moving carefully around huts, chickens and pigs.

Reaching the farther edge of the village without encountering any of the residents, he peered around the last hut and found the natives. A semicircle of women knelt with their backs toward him. Their black hair was daubed with reddish colored mud and leather cords were wrapped around their brown upper arms. Other than that, they all seemed to be quite naked. Fat and thin buttocks pointed at him, reminding him of the chorus line from the nude rock musical "Hair." Two men squatted at the edges of the circle, their hands slapping down onto a pair of large wooden drums. The instruments had rough hide stretched taut across the top and the side were decorated with stick figures carrying two poles that supported a circle marked with red and green.

In the center of the semicircle of women the men of the village were lined up in two ranks swaying slowly back and forth to the beat of the drums, their feet pounding down into the dirt with each step. Sway, thump "Uh," sway, thump, "Uh," like a primeval line dance. Like the women they were devoid of clothing except for the mud daubed hair and leather cords on their arms. White chicken feathers sprouted from the mud on their heads and their faces were streaked with red clay in jagged lines. As they moved they waved their arms up and down in the air like a wave at a football game, only more coordinated.

Beyond the dancers the invader could see two natives standing with their backs to him, bright red plumes dangled from their foreheads and white streaks ran down their backs. The two stood with their hands in the air and he could hear the soft murmur of some pagan chant. Occasionally the native on the left would reach up and flip the drooping feathers out of his face.

While the whole scene was picture perfect for "National Geographic", it was the item on a stone pillar beyond the two natives that drew the man's attention.

Seated in this place of reverence was a gleaming metal cylinder with a blue stripe around the top portion. Alternating red and green lights blinked on and off within the stripe. The cylinder stood almost a foot tall and was about seven inches in diameter. Under the sound of the drum the man could hear a low hum emanating from the object. The native's chant and the drumbeat matched the cadence of the hum.

Ducking back behind the hut the man dropped the carryall and unzipped it. He extracted a dart with a thin, almost invisible string attached to it. Working carefully he laid out a loop of the string on the ground and pulled back the cocking handle on the crossbow, then set the dart into the tray being sure that the string would not catch on the framework of the bow. He then mounted a telescopic sight to the bow. Or, rather, he tried to.

The sight mounted with a simple slide that slid over a track on the top of the crossbow. It had worked perfectly before the mission began, but now absolutely refused to go together. The man rested the front of the bow on the ground and tried pushing the sight on. He grunted slightly from the effort. The dart fell onto the ground.

When this pushing did not work he placed the sight into position and tried hammering down on it with his fist. This earned him a cut on his palm and a lance of pain. He muttered an almost silent, "Ow!"

He brought the bow up to eyelevel and examined the track and could see nothing that would cause the problem. Carefully he aligned the sight and pushed slowly with his fingers. It wouldn't even begin to go on. "Blasted thing," he muttered angrily as blood dripped from his knuckle.

By this time the dart on the ground had mixed with the coil of string, making the string look a bit raveled. The line had come loose from the dart and lay loose in the dust.

He tried again to force the sight onto the track without success. In a rage he threw the bow onto the ground and held the sight up to his eyes. It was then he noticed the arrow on the side of the viewer. He had been trying to put it on backward.

"Well you dumb twit," he muttered.

He picked up the crossbow, checked the direction of the arrow and smoothly slid the sight onto the track. "Duh, if all else fails, follow directions, stupid," he whispered to himself.

He grabbed the dart from the ground, wiped the dirt off on his pants and then noticed the string was gone. Searching in the dirt he found the end of the string and reattached it to the dart. Setting down the bow he carefully repositioned the coil of string.

Blowing a breath through clenched lips, creating a blubbering sound, and wiping sweat off his forehead the man in black peered stealthily past the hut to see if the natives had noticed his antics. With relief he saw that they had not changed position.

Stepping back from behind the hut he knelt down and pulled the bow stock into his shoulder and looked through the sight. He carefully steadied his arm on his knee and sighted in just above the cylinder. As the dancers swayed out of the way, he pulled the trigger.

The dart flashed through the air between the swaying hips of two of the natives, barely missing one dancers bouncing equipment. As the dart flashed over the cylinder, the man pulled a second trigger and the loop of the string flowed free to settle around the gadget. With a light tug the man pulled the string tight to the artifact.

He tossed the crossbow behind the hut and yanked on the string, rapidly pulling it toward himself. The cylinder jerked off the stone and fell into the dirt. It began a jerky shuffle past the two-feathered natives and then through the dancers. A cry of alarm rose from the women as one of them jumped to her feet and screamed while pointing at the cylinder that seemed to be skipping across the ground all on its own.

The dancers drew back and stared at the oddly moving object. Then the two "priests" cried out and fell to the ground, their hands and bodies extended toward the moving cylinder. At their cry all of the villagers fell down with hands pointed toward the careening object.

The man continued to pull on the string until he could reach down and scoop up the gizmo. Quickly he pulled off the string and tossed the cylinder into the carryall. He hurriedly yanked the zipper closed and grabbed the straps. Turning he started running back through the village toward the wall of jungle. A perfect escape until he stepped on the chicken.

As his foot connected with the scrawny bird, the fowl let out a horrible squawk and started screaming in Chickenese. The man fell down and landed on the pig, who promptly added his voice to the protest. One of the native dancers looked up to see what was going on. He spotted the man and jumped to his feet while yelling in some obscure native tongue.

The other natives scrambled to their feet as the man ran into the jungle and promptly tripped over a protruding root and landed with an "oomph" in the sodden and reeking humus of the forest floor. With a howl the natives dispersed through the village to grab spears and stone axes. They then took chase after the man, the women yelling encouragement after them.

Scrambling to his feet while spitting out rotten leaves and dirt, the man resumed running through the jungle, leaping over branches, roots and the occasional semi-seen animal. Behind him he could hear the shouts of the natives as they followed his broken path.

The man was panting and sweating from the heat. His lungs labored to supply enough of the thick, damp air to his to his rapidly air-starved body. Between gasping breaths he muttered, "I knew, pant, huff, I should have, pant, huff, spent, pant, huff, more time, pant, huff, in the, pant, huff, gym."

Behind him the yells of the natives were getting closer. A spear whistled past him to thunk into a tree. He was rapidly running out of energy when he spotted daylight through the trees. A second spear whizzed past his head. Ahead of him the trees began to thin and he could see a blue bag near a tree.

Reaching down as he ran, he snagged the bag and pulled it to his chest. A moment later the trees ran out and so did the ground.

The man's feet were still moving as he sailed out and off the cliff. Twelve hundred feet below him a river could be seen meandering through the trees. Huge rocks lifted their faces from the water. AS he started failing he failed to appreciate the majestic view of the spreading jungle with its glorious vista of greenery and towering trees, the natural beauty of the sparkling river steaming in the bright sunlight.

Struggling with the two bags, the man frantically worked to pull the straps on the blue bag around his arms so the bag would sit on his back. It seemed to take forever before he finally had the thing in position. With a grunt he yanked the front straps together and snapped them closed.

As he fell he was slowly twisting and he looked up to see the natives standing at the edge of the cliff. With an evil grin the man raised his left hand and pointed his middle finger at them. With his right he yanked on a strap attached to the blue bag. He could feel the bag get lighter and he waited for the pull of the paraglider. And he waited. And he waited.

Above him he could see one of the natives holding a second blue bag. With a jerk the native did something and a bright yellow mass slipped from the bag. The wind caught it and the yellow resolved itself into the rectangular form of a paraglider.

With rising fear the man looked above his head to see a pair of blue polka-dot boxer shorts drifting down. Near it a green sock swayed in the wind. A tube of toothpaste kept pace with him as he dropped. A pair of pants, a shirt, a disposable razor and jock strap followed him down. An MRE rushed past him in an attempt to be the first one to the river.

His fall rotated him so that he faced the rising canyon floor, the rocks growing larger and sharper as he neared them. With a muttered, "Oh crap", the man fell into darkness.

CHAPTER ONE

Abu Al Raini laughed with glee as he pressed the big red button on the console in front of him. The sound of his laughter echoed hollowly through the dark, poorly lit cave, the vibrations knocking loose small stalactites that thumped to the ground and clanged off various machines. He stabbed the button again, turned suddenly toward his faithful follower, Sidi al Down, and slapped him on the ear. "Stop already with the American jokes," he yelled in Arabic. "I can't get any work done with you telling jokes and messing up my concentration!"

Sidi put one chubby hand to his reddened ear and the other over his mouth while mumbling an apology.

Abu turned back to the controls and stabbed again at the big red button. Nothing happened.

Grabbing a screwdriver he removed two screws and lifted the console in front of him. Peering inside he spotted a red wire hanging loose. Muttering a curse that had something to do with a genie, a rabbi and a catholic priest, Abu grabbed the wire to reconnect it. His eyes popped open and his beard went straight out from his chin. His body started doing a hootchie kootchie dance.

1

Sidi slapped his hand on a red Emergency Stop button, cutting the power and watched as Abu fell off his chair and dropped to the ground. His turban fell off and rolled under the console.

Shaking his head, Abu looked at the scorch marks on his fingers. He stuck them in his mouth to try to cool them. It didn't work.

Grabbing his turban, Abu righted the chair and sat back down. With a glare at Sidi he very carefully flicked a finger at the wire. Nothing happened. Growing bolder he tentatively touched the wire and, with a sigh of relief, connected it to a metal post and twisted it tight. Using a soldering iron he firmly attached the wire so it wouldn't come loose again.

After closing the console and replacing the screws he again stabbed at the big red button.

This time, without the laughter blocking the sound, he could hear a tiny click as the button was depressed. Behind him a spark flashed between two giant condensers, the arc momentarily suffusing the cave in a blue glow. The air began to vibrate with a low hum that gradually built up, getting louder and louder until it was almost impossible to hear. Abu grinned as the noise increased. Sidi took his hand from his mouth and put it over his other ear.

Suddenly, with a loud pop, a large black wire snapped free and swung down to strike a metal table behind Abu, creating a massive blue flash. A samovar setting on the table momentarily lit up like a Christmas tree. The lid blew off, soaring through the air to just miss striking Abu in the head. Dark brown coffee bubbled from the urn, soaking the table and dripping onto the floor. The loud hum quickly dropped to a low whine and stopped.

Sidi muttered something about the coffee being done as Abu yelled, "Blasted Arab mechanics! If it isn't camel dung, they're useless!"

Throwing his hands in the air Abu stabbed at the red button again. The blue spark continued to light up the room. Muttering Islamic obscenities about pigs and Japanese trained mechanics he stalked over to a black power box and jammed a switch down into the off position. The lights in the cave went out, creating an inky darkness lit by a blue haze of sparks. "Blast it," muttered Abu as he pushed the switch back up again. The lights came back on. Turning to a second box he slammed that switch to off. The blue sparks suddenly quit.

Turning to Sidi he growled, "Have those blasted engineers fix the machine. This time it had darn well better work right or they all go to Iran with Bibles in their pockets. And tell them to move that bloody light switch to a different place. I'm getting fed up with the lights going off." With that he stalked from the room through a small tunnel. Turning back for a moment, he yelled at Sidi, "And have those idiots make these tunnels larger. I'm also getting tired of walking stooped over in these small tunnels. I have to see a chiropractor once a week and my HMO won't cover much more. Bloody useless socialized medicine."

Abu had been born Ibrihim al Rashid, destitute and uneducated in a Palestinian refugee camp. His father had been a camel dung sweeper and his mother was a stamper at the camp gate. While dad pushed a broom, mom would put a red stamp on the papers of everyone entering the camp. Visa, red stamp. Passport, red stamp. Newspaper, red stamp. Toilet paper, red stamp. She got paid by the number of red stamps. Why? Haven't a clue. Bureaucracies!

During his rebellious teen years, when he didn't understand the world, politics, parents or health care, he was selected from his lower-middle class, almost welfare, under the poverty limit but over the assistance limit, home for training as a suicide bomber. With dreams of nubile virgins clouding reason from his brain, his training progressed satisfactorily, from putting on the bomb harness, boarding the bus, and observing crowds for maximum density. However, when lesson four came up, pulling the pin, the virgins disappeared from his mind as the young Ibrihim looked at his handlers and remarked, "Are you out of your freaking minds?" He promptly tore off the harness and threw it on the ground, thereby scattering his instructors, may Allah bless their souls, and creating a six-foot crater.

Ibrihim was not that much smarter than the other students, he just asked the wrong questions. Like, "Where does it say those seventy-two virgins are female?" Ibrihim got smacked a lot by the Imam.

With Ibrihim's miraculous survival, the leadership of his organization had two choices – shoot the uppity little twerp or, in view of his high intelligence (he was the only one of his class of twenty still alive and kicking), they could send him to university in America. The vote was close (five for shooting him, four for college). The maximum leader, who saw potential in the outspoken and extraordinarily lucky Palestinian, called the stalemate. Ibrihim went to America.

Life at an American college quickly changed the young man. He threw himself wholeheartedly into the study of this new country. He learned about girls and cars and girls. He undertook the study of girls and music and delved into special studies in alcohol and girls. Finally he settled on a course of studies in girls.

This lasted until he met the love of his life, Samantha Jones. She was short, nearsighted and pudgy, but Ibrihim loved her. Needless to say, she had no idea he existed. His love was at arms length until one day he brought forth the courage to approach her. He invited her to a college dance. Since the dance had little to do with disco or John Travolta, she declined. There and then Ibrihim declared unmerciful war on the America infidels. Okay, not everybody, just Bubba Kendrick, Samantha's redneck boyfriend, but that is another story.

He threw himself into the study of electrical engineering with side courses in meteorology and ceramic fondue dishes. He eventually graduated with a BS degree and moved on to a prestigious engineering college in Massachusetts to get his Masters. He worked hard and diligently at his studies, his hatred of all things American fueling his concentration and desire to learn. The only things American he cared for were the government, the people, the houses, the land, the food, the freedom, the cars, the dogs, the cats, and the flea markets. Everything else he hated and vowed to destroy.

When he completed his studies and returned to the Middle East, Al Raini broke from his parent organization, changed his name and found backers to fund a new organization called Al Shamute. The name, Al Shamute, meant the fool, which is how he pretty much thought of his old alliance. If they thought they were going to change anything by blowing up old ladies on buses, they should try reading Sun Tzu's "Art of War" or maybe a good Tom Clancy novel.

Turning into a side passage of the tunnel Abu entered his Spartan office. Seating himself in the leather chair behind his teak desk he glanced over at the mahogany wall paneling and rows of first edition books set into oak bookshelves. A fire sputtered softly in the fireplace. "One of these days I really have to get this place fixed up," he muttered as he picked up the telephone.

With long slim fingers he punched in a series of numbers and waited for the ringing to stop.

At the third ring a soft female voice came on the line.

"Welcome to Arab Enterprises," whispered the husky voice. "Thank you for your interest in our business. We appreciate your business and want to serve you in the best manner possible. Calls may be monitored for quality purposes. If you know your parties extension, do not enter it at this time. You will be asked to enter it at an appropriate time later. Please listen to the following menu choices.

"If you are a returning user press one. Press two if you are a new user. Press three if you would like us to send you a full color brochure of our services. Press four to obtain our secret website address. Press five if you do not want to be a user. Press six if you dialed this number in error. Press seven to end this call."

Abu poked his finger on the one button and started drumming his fingers on the desk.

"Press one for Arabic," continued the voice. "Press two for English. Press three for French. Press four for German. Press five for Swahili. Press six for Chinese. Press seven for Spanish. Press eight for Urdu. Press nine if you are totally confused and do not know your own language. An operator will come on the line to assist you. Press nine to repeat this menu or press zero to return to the previous menu."

Abu stabbed the one button.

"Press one to order parts and accessories. Press two for shipments. Press three for passports and documents. Press four for explosives and munitions. Press five for technical services. Press six for executive services. Press seven for cells and moles. Press eight for operator assistance. Press nine to repeat this menu."

With an angry scowl Abu poked the six.

"Press one to order stationary and supplies. Press two for secretaries. Press three for middle managers. Press four for transportation. Press five for senior executives. Press six for travel and accommodations. Press seven for information technology services. Press eight for operator assistance. Press nine to repeat this menu."

Muttering curses in Arabic, Abu rammed his finger at the five.

"Listen carefully to these options. Press one for personnel with names beginning with A through D. Press two for personnel with names beginning with E through H. Press three for names beginning with I through M. Press four for names beginning with N through R. Press five for names beginning with S through U. Press six for names beginning with V through Z. Press seven for operator assistance. Press eight to repeat this menu. Press nine to return to the previous menu."

Abu yanked at his beard and stabbed the five again.

"Listen closely to these options. Press one for names beginning with SA through SP. Press two for names beginning with SQ through SZ. Press three for names beginning with TA through TP. Press four for names beginning TQ through TZ. Press five for names beginning UA through UP. Press six for names beginning with UQ through UZ. Press seven for operator assistance. Press eight to repeat this menu. Press nine to return to the previous menu."

Abu let out a grating sigh and swatted the turban from his head. He rubbed his eyes before he punched the one.

"Listen closely to the following list of code names. Press one for Sarbeh. Press two for Salim. Press three for Serge. Press four for . . ."

Abu preempted the menu and pushed the two.

"I'm sorry," purred the sultry voice. "The menu options have been terminated at the user's request. Press one to return to the first menu. Press two to terminate this call."

Abu slammed the telephone back into the cradle and smacked his head on the desk. At that moment the telephone rang.

Jerking the receiver to his ear he heard, "You must press the two to terminate this call. Canceling the call without pressing the two annoys out robot caller and places you on a do call list that interrupts you seventeen times a day until the two is pressed. Thank you again for your interest in our services."

As Abu jabbed the two and slammed the phone down a second time, Sidi al Down picked that inappropriate moment to step into the office.

Abu stopped rubbing the red spot on his forehead, grabbed the telephone and threw it at Sidi. "You call that crap head Salim and tell him I want a meet here tomorrow," he yelled with rage. "And tell him to get his doofus phone system fixed. That menu crap is horse patootie. Who ever heard of terrorists with menu options? What kind of garbage is that?"

Not realizing that it was a rhetorical question, Sidi said, "As I understand it marketing research has shown that you have fewer problems with customer service, in other words cost, if you annoy the heck out of people by making them go through ten or twelve menus and . . ."

At that point Abu stood up, reached down to grab his turban and yelled, "I don't give a camel fart about customer service! I'm not a customer! I'm the head of Al Shamute and I don't need this aggravation!"

Sidi quickly stepped out of the way as Abu stalked out of the office.

Peeking down the tunnel, Sidi made sure his fearless leader was gone, then walked over and made himself a cup of coffee. Setting the cup on the desk he retrieved the telephone and replaced it on the desk. Grabbing the newspaper he sat down and put his feet on the shiny teak surface.

He took a sip of coffee, flipped the paper open to the comics and folded it neatly. Fully settled in, he picked up the telephone and placed it between his ear and shoulder. Comfortably ensconced, he dialed the number, fully prepared to spend the day going through menus.

CHAPTER TWO

The man leaning against the balustrade of the balcony appeared to be in his mid-thirties with dark hair and a lean muscular look. His face and hands were darkly tanned and glowed with health. The light blue tuxedo and pink shirt with yellow bow tie gave him a shining aura. He looked slightly bored with the cocktail party going on in the room behind him as he gazed out at the city lights.

He took a sip of the martini from the goblet in his hand. He grimaced and looked into the glass. Two flies were perched on the olive while a third appeared to be doing the backstroke in the liquid. He poured the drink into the potted shrub next to the railing and spat a fly out into the air.

A lovely woman in a beautiful black cocktail dress slinked through the glass doors and across the balcony toward the man where she softly laid her hand on his. He turned slightly to look at her. She had elegantly coifed blond hair and a figure that would have done Cher proud, right down to the boobs straining to escape and the slit skirt that ran upward almost to her waist. The pink tennis shoes did nothing to detract from her magnificent appearance.

"The view of Washington from here is wonderful," she remarked with a purr, leaning in close enough for her long eyelashes to tickle his cheek.

"Yes, it is," he answered back, flashing a white toothy smile while absently scratching his cheek. "I particularly like the glow of the lights from the Washington monument, the Reflecting Pool and the distant burning buildings from the protest riots. It gives the city an atmosphere not seen anywhere on Earth except possibly Baghdad or Calcutta or maybe Kabul. Then again . . . ."

The woman pressed the palm of her hand against his lips. "I'm Carla Hooker, and what's your name, handsome?"

"Mflmssmssbnd," he mumbled, then removed her hand from his mouth.

He looked deep into her eyes and said, "I'm Blond, Ames Blond."

She pulled back slightly, her pale blue eyes getting larger. "You're not ..."

He cut her off by saying, "No, I'm not. He's British. I'm American."

She looked slightly confused. "But you're not blond. You have dark hair."

"My name is Blond, not my hair color," he muttered indignantly.

"But that's so confusing," she said taking her hand from his. "Your name should be Brunette."

"My name is not Brunette," he shouted. "My name is Blond! Bloody hell! Why can't you stupid people figure that out?"

"Well, you don't have to get so huffy about it," she exclaimed as she turned and flounced toward the door. Ames fumes as he watched her flounce while trying to figure out how she did that.

At that moment he heard the buzz of his cell phone and jerked it from his pants pocket. The phone caught on the material of the pocket and slipped from his hand. It flipped once, struck the balustrade and bounded out into the air, falling thirty stories to the sidewalk below. Ames looked down to watch its fall. The phone hit the sidewalk and exploded with a loud thump, sending shards of concrete flying through the air. Homeless people yelped with pain and scurried for cover. The doorman walked out onto the sidewalk and peered upward. Ames hurriedly jerked his head backward out of sight.

"Rats," muttered Ames. "R is going to be seriously annoyed about that." He glanced back at the doorway where Carla was no longer visibly flouncing as a telephone rang somewhere inside the ballroom.

A moment later a steward appeared holding a cordless phone. "Excuse me sir," he said. "Are you Mister Blond?"

"Yes I am," answered Ames.

"But you're not ….," the steward said hesitantly.

"No, I'm not blond," Ames cut in with a bite to his voice.

"You're not mister Blond?" asked the steward with confusion.

"Yes, I'm Mister Blond," said Ames angrily. "And no I'm not blond. Just give me the bloody phone!"

Ames grabbed the instrument from the startled steward and held it to his ear.

"Blond here," he said into the mouthpiece.

He listened for a moment. "Yes, sir. First thing in the morning sir." He disconnected the line and handed the phone back to the steward. "Tell Mrs. Jacobs that I had to leave, would you?

"Yes, sir," said the steward gravely. "One thing before you leave, sir. The doorman asked if anyone here knew anything about a somewhat nasty explosion on the street outside the entrance. He is concerned that he might have to contact Homeland Security."

"Tell him not to worry about it too much. It's probably just a difference of opinion over the federal budget. But I have to leave. Please convey my apologies to Mrs. Jacobs for running off. Tell her it was great party, but she should not invite any more of those stupid people like that Hooker in the black dress."

Leaving the steward with a mystified expression on his face, Blond left the balcony and headed across the ballroom floor aiming for the door. He deftly avoided being captured by a number of inebriated conversationalists, two Democrat Senators looking for handouts, two party girls, three elderly matrons with seriously odd looking daughters and the Salvation Army bell ringer at the door.

He closed the door behind himself and stepped back to avoid narrowly colliding with a state governor who was chasing a blond female down the hallway. Ames stopped to watch as the blond skidded around a corner with all the ease of a Porsche at Monte Carlo. The governor had less control and slammed into the wall, knocking over a table and a hotel maid.

Ames was a somewhat secret agent working for the ultra secret Department of Reconnaissance and Knowledge. He had originally trained to be an FBI agent by going through college, taking his degree in accounting, and completing the FBI course at the Marine base in Quantico, Virginia. After graduating he became somewhat disillusioned when he found that he would not be a gun toting accountant, flashing his badge at felonious felons and doing in Frank Nitty. They were going to assign him to the Federal Fraudulent Recipes Division in Bumchuck, Idaho where he would be using his limited computer skills to track fake Betty Crocker recipes into and out of China.

Feeling somewhat miffed at the bureaus lack of appreciation for his skills, Ames looked around the government for some other form of cushy employment with a hefty salary and perky benefits. There were tons of jobs, from lowly clerk to Senatorial appointee. The sheer volume of employment opportunities was mind boggling, but few offered the badge, gun and the use of his newly acquired investigative skills.

There were plenty of agencies that would allow him to play cop like the DEA, NSA, CIA, USFSLEI, TSA, IRS,

ICE, FDP, DIA, BPA, ATF, USSMS, USMS, FTPT, FBP or any of the other 684 federal and state agencies. The number of agencies and acronyms was astounding, but none could guarantee him placement as a field agent. Except for one. The very agency his father had worked for and which he vowed not to.

Swallowing his pride, he had decided to become a DORK to follow in his father's footsteps, working for another classified government bureaucracy. His father, Ashe Blond, had been a scientist at Area 51 where he had spent 30 years studying the remains of the aliens who had crashed at Roswell, New Mexico in the fifties. He had been dedicated to his work until he discovered that the remains were nothing more than bad copies made of silicon, rubber and road kill. The original remains had inadvertently been sent to a landfill near Newark, New Jersey sometime in the early sixties and had caused toxic pollution to the local soil there. The residents blamed the problem on New York City.

The only living alien had been taken into the Witness Protection Program shortly after that and was now residing in Oakland, California where it lived under the name of "Candy" and operated a pornographic website.

His father had become disillusioned by the whole alien thing. He had resigned from the government, grown a ponytail and now operated a radish farm in Boise, Idaho. He spent his free time writing letters to Congressmen about black helicopters stealing his radishes for immoral purposes. He is still waiting for a reply.

Summer Blond, Ames' mother, had been a special education teacher until she started the practice of showing her school kids that it was easy to take the mood controlling pill, Ritalin. She did this by demonstrating the swallowing process. Unfortunately she was actually swallowing the pills. One day she wandered away from the school and was never found again.

There were rumors that she had been sighted in a Best Buy store in Nashville, Tennessee staring blankly at a television screen, thereby being indistinguishable from the other customers. There were also hints that she was a store dummy in Manhattan, but subsequent tests of the dummy showed that, although the skin was supple and had a healthy glow, there was no brain activity. The family is still looking.

CHAPTER THREE

General "Manystars" Tenstars, otherwise known as N, glowered at the map hanging on the wall of his overly ornate office. The map took up almost one complete wall and showed the world in multi-colored swatches. The other three walls were covered with plaques, trophies and photos of the General with famous and not-famous people. A huge teak desk stood in the center of the room, its surface littered with papers and coffee cups. A number of straight back wooden chairs sat along the wall opposite the map.

The General was resplendent in a blue Army uniform festooned with glittering badges, patches and two medals, one for good conduct and the other for national defense. He was a graduate of the military academy at West Point where he had excelled at basket weaving. His aptitude and brightness made his fellow cadet's feel he was slated for General, or at least Captain or possibly Lieutenant if he graduated, hence his nickname of "Manystars." Or, as rumor would have it, it could have been his habit of walking into posts, walls and other vertical surfaces.

While at the Academy he played a number of sports including football, soccer, baseball, wrestling, basketball, table tennis, ice hockey, darts, ballroom dancing and tiddlywinks. Another Academy rumor had it that his name was displayed on a brass tag connected to the bench where he sat out every game.

Upon graduation from West Point, and distinguishing himself for doing it in less than seven years, he had been slated for a position as a platoon leader in Vietnam. His serving there was curtailed by a tragic accident in Hawaii when he fell down the airplane steps and broke his hip. Two years later, after surgery and physical therapy, his chance for combat disappeared with the end of the war. He was subsequently assigned to military intelligence.

At the outbreak of the Grenada campaign he suffered a concussion during pre-deployment training when he smacked himself in the head with a rifle butt while going through the obstacle course. By the time he left the hospital his second chance was gone.

Other chances slipped by with the same annoyance. Nicaragua, broken leg. Haiti, smashed hand. Lebanon, slipped disc. When Desert Storm loomed, the now Lieutenant Colonel pulled strings to be assigned to the intelligence staff at King Khalid Military City in Saudi Arabia. Being extraordinarily careful, the Colonel set out to meet his destiny. He packed his duffle, grabbed his rifle and jerked the bag to his shoulder. The doctor told the crying officer that he had torn his rotator cuff and would be out of action for at least six months.

Sensing his despair, his fellow officers within the West Point Protective Association pulled together and got him the job at DORK. This came with a promotion to Brigadier General, a car with driver, an office with a secretary and his own personal coffee machine. As the head of DORK he became the infamous N, master spy and all around bureaucrat. The clandestine budget for his office was regularly stripped by Republicans and stuffed by Democrats. Nobody had any real idea where the money went including the General Accounting Office.

A knock on the door broke the General's concentration on the map and he barked "Enter" without turning his head. The door swung open revealing Ames Blond and a sign on the door that read,

Brigadier General Otario Uther Tenstars
HEAD of DORK
Department of Reconnaissance and Knowledge

Ames Blond entered the room and almost saluted as he walked over to the General. "I'm here, sir. What do you need?" he asked, standing at a semblance of attention.

The General noted Ames' disheveled and haggard look. "Have trouble sleeping last night, did you? Still having that dream about falling off that darn cliff?"

"Yes sir," said Ames. "Ever since that mission in Brazil to retrieve the lost nuclear switch I've been dreaming about going off that cliff. It scares the crap out of me every time I think about what would have happened if the glider didn't open. I guess that fuels the dreams."

"Well stop harping about your psychotic problems; I really don't want to hear them. Hire a psychiatrist or one of those psychoanalysts or stick your head in a toaster oven."

"I've thought about it, sir," muttered Blond. "But our medical plan doesn't cover toasters or psychologists"

"So move to Sweden or skip across the border to Canada. Or run for office and get to be a Senator. Take a seat," said the General, pointing at the chairs against the wall.

Blond sat down in one of the straight-backed chairs.

"Look at this map and tell me what you think," said Tenstars.

Ames stood up and walked toward the map.

The General glowered at Ames and said, "I told you to sit down!"

Blond scuttled back to the chair and sat down. He peered across the room at the map and tried to see it around the General's impressive bulk.

"Well?" asked the General. "What do you think of the situation?"

Blond stood up and approached the map, again trying to see what the General was talking about.

The officer gave Blond a discrepant look. "Blast it Blond! Do I have to nail your butt to that chair?"

Blond rushed back to the chair and sat down, gripping the seat with his hands.

"Well," said the General with a rasp to his voice. "What about the situation?"

Blond held the chair with his hands, his bottom glued to the seat and leaning forward, he picked up the chair and inched his way across the carpet until he was beside the General. He set the chair back down and looked up at the map.

The General gave Blond a wilting gaze. "Did you ever consider picking up the chair and bringing it over here before you sat down? It would have been easier than that crab bull you just did. Bloody secret agents always have to do things the hard way." The General stared at Ames for a moment and then turned back toward map, tapping it with his finger.

"We have indications that the terrorist network al Shamute is operating somewhere in the Middle East and plans an attack on Liechtenstein. Not that we give a fig about Liechtenstein, but it could be an indicator of al Shamute's growing power. The head of al Shamute is the dastardly terrorist Abu al Raini. Al Raini is fanatic about destroying the United States, for what reason, we don't know. His organization is being funded by the Non-European Resources and Development Society. These NERDS are into all kinds of technology and computer stuff. You know, like hacking, ripping off banks and creating really stupid video games. We want you to locate al Raini and his network and put a stop to these NERDS before they infect the rest of our global society, not to mention getting those dumb and addictive games off the shelves at Toys R You."

Blond looked closely at the map while the General was speaking. When the General finished, Ames raised his hand. The General ignored him and continued. "Al Raini is supposed to be in the process of completing some sort of machine that could be bad for our economy, and we need to know where that thing is and what it does."

Ames was waving his hand back and forth. The General turned his back on Ames and poked a finger at the map. "The al Shamute ring could be in any of the Middle Eastern countries, or it might be Central or South America. Some of my analysts are guessing Africa or Asia. We are somewhat sure they are not in North America."

By this time Ames was hopping up and down in his chair and frantically waving his hand in the air while tugging on the General's coat.

"Oh, fudge, Ames," said the General with a touch of anger. "The bathroom is down the hall, third room on the right. You should take care of things like that before coming in here."

"N-no, sir," stuttered Ames. "I don't need the bathroom. I just wanted to ask where I should start looking. There isn't a single marker on that map. Heck, it doesn't even have city or country names on it."

"Well, heck," said the General with a grin. "Why didn't you say so? I just got this thing and had it put up. I like the colors. Makes the room look fancy, don't you think? Those black and white words would just screw up the motif. I got a better system."

The General walked over to his desk and opened the top drawer. He reached in and pulled out a large red dart. Facing the map, he closed his eyes and lobbed the dart at the map. Ames ducked as the dart flew toward his head. With a "thunk," the pointy missile imbedded itself into a blue blob on the map.

Ames stood up as he and the General looked at the map. The dart had stuck in the lower part of the Pacific Ocean. "Is there an island there?" asked Tenstars peering at the map.

"No, I don't see anything there. Maybe someone has a submarine parked out there?" Ames asked hopefully.

"Nah," replied the General with a grunt. "I doubt the ragheads could drive one without sinking it. Gim'me that dart."

The General wound up and threw the dart again.

"Where is it now?"

"About 50 miles from Ames, Iowa," said Ames. "Do you think I could take a turn tossing that?"

"This is my dart," admonished the General with a slight whine. "Get your own. In the meantime do you think those farmers are hiding terrorists in their corn cribs?"

With a sigh of disappointment Ames replied, "Maybe they're hiding under the corn fields, you know, like in that Stephen King book?"

"Drat," muttered the General as he grabbed the dart.

This time it struck the clock on the wall.

Another shot hit Argentina, followed by Southern Florida.

An hour later the map and wall were covered with holes and the General was sweating. The minute hand on the clock was missing and the hour hand hung at an odd angle. "Well phooey," he growled going to the desk and picking up a sheaf of papers. "This isn't working. Here take a look at this CIA report."

Ames glanced wistfully at the map and dart and then turned to scan through the Top Secret document. "It says here that there is a guy in Iraq who might know something about al Raini. The CIA thinks this guy is the brother to the second cousin of the barber who cuts the hair of the man who walks the dog for a Private in the Iraqi army who knows the brother of a third cousin who happens to supply turbans for the wholesaler who might have some connection to al Shamute. Sounds like a solid lead to me," said Ames looking up at the General.

"Well," said the General. "Looks like you're starting in Iraq. Get your butt down to Travel and make arrangements to get over there and then stop at Dirty Tricks to pick up your equipment. And tell those people in Travel that I want no more of this first class stuff. You'll fly stand-by just like all the rest of the agents. Got'ta 'a keep the budget in check until the Democrats get back in power.

CHAPTER FOUR

After leaving the Travel Office with a stand-by ticket to Iraq and three brochures for Caribbean cruises, Ames headed for the basement where the Department of Dirty Tricks was located. The DDT was actually known as the Advanced Special Sciences and Hidden Office of Laboratory Studies. The people who worked in ASSHOLS were keen-minded, or at least not quit stupid, scientists and engineers whose job it was to develop new and interesting gadgets for secret agents to play with, and sometimes, to even come up with things that might actually be useful.

The department was headed by the infamous R. Nobody knew his real name, but then again, nobody really cared. R was a graduate of MIT (219 of 220 with a GPA of 1.76) and had a total of 237 useless patents to his credit. He was somewhere around sixty years old and lived with his mother. Rumor had it that she was the actual idea person behind all the inventions, or that she was the probably the cause of the ideas.

Ames walked up to the door to DDT, reached out, twisted the doorknob and pulled the door to open it. The knob came off and Ames slipped backward slamming his head against the opposite wall. He slid to the ground and watched the stars spin around. As his vision began to clear a wizened face topped with a frizz of white hair peered out the door and chuckled. "Did you like that one?" asked R excitedly. "Did you? Did you? I have a patent on that sucker. Just the thing to keep Mom, er, I mean people out of rooms where they shouldn't be." R gave Ames a toothy grin that ended when his upper dentures dropped down and almost fell out of his mouth. "Ahm, gotha get mahr entur crehm," he muttered as he pushed the miscreant molars back into place.

R ducked back in and shut the door as Ames stood up and brushed off the seat of his pants. He checked the back of his head for blood and seeing none, tried to follow R through the door. There was no doorknob.

He glanced around and found the missing piece lying on the floor. He picked it up and carefully inserted it back into the hole in the door. There was an audible click as the knob seated into the mechanism inside the door. With some trepidation the agent rotated the knob and began to pull the door open. With a bang the door slammed Ames backward and he barely missed hitting the opposite wall again. R glanced out the door at the shaky agent. "Stop fooling around with the door and get in here." The elderly inventor ducked back as the door closed again.

Slipping the door knob back into the door Ames tried to pull the door open without turning the knob. It wouldn't budge. The agent moved to the right side of the door and carefully turned the knob with his left hand. The door slammed open, the knob smacking Ames' hand as he tried to let go in time. Except for his stinging fingers Ames was in great shape. With a self-satisfied smile Ames moved through the doorway. The door swung rapidly closed behind him swatting him in the butt and pushing him forward. A small smiley face stuck to the inside of the door grinned at his back.

The room he entered seemed to be huge, crowded and awash with noise and people. There was something going on in every corner of the room. Also in the middle and sides. Ames was agog with all the activity. Shaking his head to remove the gog, Ames looked around to find R standing behind him, almost breathing in his right ear.

R put his arm on Ames' shoulder and said, "Ignore all the noise and people. The annual inventor's conference was thrown out of the Ramada for blowing up the conference room, three suites and the bar. I offered them the use of our facilities and they went ape crazy with all of my toys. Apparently most of them are underfunded and don't have the kinds of gadgets I get to play with. And who knows, they may actually come up with something useful." At that moment there was a puff of smoke and one of the would-be inventors flew into the air and slammed into the ceiling. He fell toward the floor knocking over four or five other people and causing a number of strange devices to flip into the air. Those objects struck other people and more things went flying. This continued until every person and item in the room was either, on the floor, stuck to the wall or in transit from point A to point B. R ducked as a thing-a-mabob flew over his head and struck the door. "Then again, maybe not," he muttered as he pulled Ames into an adjacent room.

This room was a tad tidier, with various items sitting on tables or hung from hooks in open closets. There were bags and boxes, things with arms and some with hoses. One particular piece seemed to have hundreds of wires leading out from it and back in, all without actually going anywhere. As Ames tried to figure out the wired thing, R reached down and selected an item from a table and passed it to Ames. "Here you may need this," he said. Ames saw it was a watch and he grinned as he slid the flex band onto his wrist. "Hey," he said. "This is cool. What does it do?"

R glanced at the watch and looked up at Ames. "It tells time," he said.

"No, no," interjected Ames as he pulled the fob out and pushed it back in. "I mean what cool things does it do? Does it have like this super magnet or a long cable for rappelling or maybe a super saw for cutting through concrete?" He slipped the watch off and tried pulling the back off.

R looked at Ames as if he were an idiot. "No, it just tells time." He grabbed the watch and examined it before handing it back. "You break this thing and you pay for it."

"You mean it doesn't do anything really neat?" asked Ames with sadness as he slipped the watch back on.

In exasperation R said, "Well no. It has a stopwatch function and a snooze alarm, but neither one of those work very well. We get them from China so how much can you expect?"

R turned to another table and picked up a pen. Ames grabbed it and examined it closely. "I know this one," he said with excitement. "This has a poison tip for getting rid of your enemies. How do I make it work?" He started snapping the plunger in and out with his thumb while grinning like a kid with a toy monkey.

R peered at Ames and grabbed the pen. "It's a freaking pen, you dummy. I want you to sign for that watch. We can't be giving them away, you know. The budget sucks. And speaking of which, where's that cell phone with the explosive pack? Don't tell me you screwed that up?"

"Well, uh, you see there was this snag in my pants pocket," Ames stuttered. "And, uh, the phone kind of flipped into the air."

"So where is it?"

"Mostly on L street, but there are some parts on K and M. I think some homeless guy has some of the parts as well."

"What's a homeless guy doing with parts of your cell phone?"

"I think he's learning to breathe through them."

"I'm having accounting deduct that from your pay. Come on you twit. You need to pick up your car," R continued, beckoning Ames forward. They went through another door and entered a large garage. Sitting in the middle of the floor was a sparkling gray Jaguar XJ, its bright work gleaming under a battery of mini-spotlights. A dazzling redhead attired in a skimpy silver bikini lounged against the hood, stroking the windshield softly with a lightly tanned hand. Her smile sparkled as much as the car.

Ames' eyes grew big at the sight of the car. His pants grew big at the sight of the girl. "Wow!" he exclaimed with excitement. "That's some car! What kind of gadgets does it have and where do I sign for it? Does the girl come with it?"

R sighed. "It comes with all kinds of stuff that you don't get to touch. And the girl is my niece, so don't get any ideas or I'll chop your equipment off."

"But that's the car I get, right?" Ames asked hopefully looking wistfully at the Jag. R pulled on his arm and led him toward a corner of the garage.

"No," said R. "That's a TV commercial they're paying us to shoot. I told you the budget was tight. Your cars over here," he said pointing to a tarp-covered object. He pulled the tarp away, raising a cloud of dust to reveal a dull blue 1976 Pinto with rust streaks along the rocker panels. Somewhere along the line someone had hand-lettered "Mini-Goat" on the front fender in ugly purple paint. The left rear window was cracked and the roof had a large dent in it. The rear bumper appeared to be attached with coat hangers and possibly a large wad of bubble gum. The springs sagged and Ames was not exactly sure that the thing had any shock absorbers.

Inside was more of the same. The rear seat had definitely been used for roosting chickens at one time while the front seat was covered with unidentifiable stains. A faded plastic hula girl stood dejectedly in the middle of the dashboard. A semi-crushed Coors can peeked out from under the seat and there was a condom hanging from the ashtray. Gravel, cigarette butts and candy wrappers littered the floor. The air had a dusty smell of age-old vomit, urine, sweat and cigarettes.

"Don't tell me this is the car you plan on giving me?" asked Ames with horror.

R grinned wickedly. "Yep, this is your car. It has all the options - steering wheel, tires and a motor that works sometimes." R starting cackling then pulled himself under control as the cackle reduced to a snorting from his nose. A bubble of snot formed from his left nostril and he pulled a faded yellow hanky from his pocket and wiped at it. "Got'a stop that cackling," he muttered.

"And just how the heck do you expect to get this thing to Iraq?" asked Ames.

"Oh the usual way. We load it and you aboard a C-141 and fly you to Baghdad," said R with suspicion.

Ames reached into his pocket and pulled out the stand by tickets on Economy Air. "And what do I do with these things?" he asked waving the ticket folder in the air.

R grabbed the tickets and stuffed them into his pocket. "No sweat, I'll take care of them. I've been promising my niece a trip to Disneyworld. I can trade these useless things for a pair of first class on Delta."

The agent stared at the elderly inventor for a moment, not sure what to say. Then he shook his head as if he were making a decision. "So, let's see," Ames said holding up a finger for each item. "You need an airplane, the aircraft crew, the ground crews on both ends, and fuel for that great big airplane. You're spending close to twenty thousand dollars to get a four hundred dollar piece of junk and me to Iraq. You could have rented a new Porsche for a month for a tenth of the cost. So much for your budget!"

"Well," grinned R, "You could be the President and have dinner in Paris where you and your entourage of seventy five people, sixteen cars, fifty three reporters and two hundred security troops all travel to Paris from Washington in three 747's and six C-141's protected by a squadron of eight F-15's. And that's not counting the two thousand three hundred and seven French police mobilized to protect them on the ground, or the three hundred and twelve innocent people arrested for trying to get a look at you while you and your wife ate at a restaurant that was cleared of all the patrons before you arrived. All at the lowly cost of seven million, eight hundred and forty four thousand dollars paid for by the U S taxpayers. And that's not counting the tip." R started cackling again. Ames shook his head as the old man's dentures slipped out and landed on the floor.

CHAPTER FIVE

Sidi Al Down slammed the drawer closed and yanked another one open, his hands dipping in to scrabble around. He jerked out a sheet of paper and looked at it, then threw it back in to grab another. With a disgusted sound he tossed the paper back in, slammed that drawer shut and leaned against the cabinet with both hands. His breath came in short spurts and sweat dripped off his forehead. "He's gon'na kill me," Sidi muttered. "He's gon'na kill me. I'm a dead man. I'm gon'na meet Allah and I darn sure ain't ready. He's gon'na strap a bomb to my butt and toss me in front of some Jewish grandmother's car. Ah, crap. This sucks!"

Sidi was the rebellious son of a wealthy Saudi prince who had been sent to Paris for his education. There he had discovered the joys of dissent and the effect beards and ragged clothes had on girls. He happily joined into the demonstrations and coffee house chatter of the Left Bank. Without the worry of earning money he spent freely on his "friends" who were more than glad to have a rich sponsor for their counter culture activities, drugs and video games.

He joined in with the crowds supporting Ayatollah Khomeini and called for the ousting of the Shah. When Iran became a theocracy he partied with the rest of the dissidents, eating hot dogs, drinking gin rickies and playing Mortal Combat into the wee hours of the night. Sidi had a heck of a good time – until daddy cut off his funding.

Angry and destitute the young al Down looked for a means to gain revenge and his next chicken sandwich. He found it in Hammas and the liberation of Palestine. The backers of the rabid militant organization were happy to provide funding for the son of a prestigious Arab who would provide them with a semblance of legitimacy. It also gave them another idiot to blow up if the need arose.

Sidi enjoyed the summer camps in Libya, playing with explosives and firing really cool guns. Then he was selected for a mission to attack an Israeli garrison on the Golan Heights. Amid thundering artillery, ricocheting bullets and blood, Sidi was heard to say, "To heck with this! These idiots are trying to kill me!" A later review of the battlefield determined that he was not dead or missing in action, he had apparently taken off for safer surroundings. A bounty was declared for the return of the treasonous Saudi, but the price was so ridiculously low that no one bothered to claim it.

Casting about for a new sponsor, Sidi met a charismatic man of his own age. Ibrihim Al Rashid was everything that Sidi wanted to be – intelligent, good-looking and not fat. Sidi vowed to follow him to the ends of the Earth, or until dinner, whichever came first.

Now it appeared that he would have to move on again - if he lived through it.

Sidi pushed himself upright and turned to look around the small cave. While the cave was small, it was cluttered. He could hear the gurgle of water somewhere behind the rock wall. Inside the cave there was a large drafting table complete with a drafting machine. Two desktop computer systems sat on desks, one of which had a 52-inch LCD screen attached to it. There was a table with a printer on it and a large vertical plotter for making blueprints hooked up to one of the computers. A dehumidifier chugged away in a corner. A tunnel led from the door off into darkness. And then there was the cabinet that Sidi had been frantically pawing through.

The cabinet was tall, wide and deep with narrow drawers extending the full length of the cabinet front. It was used specifically to hold blueprints and mechanical drawings, or, in a pinch, really thin sandwiches, one of which Sidi munched on as he searched and decried his fate.

Sidi hung his head and shook it from side to side, spattering mayonnaise and causing a thin slice of ham to dribble down his chin. He then noticed a sheet of paper crammed into a small crack in the wall. He slapped his sandwich down on the cabinet and reached into the crack to pull out the waded up paper. He carefully unfolded the creases. It was the paper he was looking for, but as he unfolded it his hands became slimy and slick. Looking closely at his hands and the paper he suddenly yelled, "Ewww, snot. What retard blew his nose on this?" He hurriedly re-crumpled the paper, wiping his hands with it in an effort to get the sloppy mess off. He shoved the paper back into the crack far enough that it could not be seen and started wiping his hands on his robe, smearing the nose sweat in with the mayo and mustard already staining the cloth.

Inside the wall the paper dropped into a rift in the rock and fluttered downward. Eventually it dropped into an underground stream and was swept away.

Only after the paper was out of sight did Sidi realize what he had just done. "Oh no," he groaned, his hands scrabbling at the rock trying to find the now gone paper.

Giving up in despair, and because his fingers were getting sore, Sidi leaned his head against the wall and began to sob. He had just destroyed the set of plans that Al Raini had sent him to get.

He stood there a moment and let his guilt and fear wash over him. Then he straightened and rubbed his eyes dry. He again wiped his sweaty, snotty hands on his robe and hung his head as he walked slowly out of the cave through the short tunnel. He was muttering, "I am a dead man. I am a dead man," over and over. Then he suddenly stopped and a sly grin crossed his face. He picked up his pace as he straightened and almost ran through the tunnel toward the main cave.

Abu Al Raini was in the midst of a conversation when Sidi rushed up to him. Breathlessly Sidi said, "Master I have terrible news."

Al Raini shushed him with a wave of his hand. "Quiet Sidi! I am in the middle of very careful negotiations. Go stand by the entrance until I call for you." Abu turned back to his guest, a well-dressed man of European origin. The guest glanced at Sidi and back to Abu who resumed speaking. "I believe we can install the new components within a week. We should be ready for the initial tests by then."

He was interrupted by Sidi who grabbed Abu's arm, "But master, something terrible has happened!"

Abu gave Sidi a baleful look and said, "Go stand by the door. I am not ready for you yet! And take your hand off me you miserable cur!" Abu turned back to the stranger.

Sidi got a strange look in his eyes, reached over and slapped Abu in the head knocking his turban to the floor. "Listen up, you overbearing stuffed robe!" he yelled. "The plans for the Hydrogen Ovulator are missing and it looks like we may have a spy in our midst. This bull with your buddy can wait!" He suddenly stopped and put his hands to his mouth and took a step back as he realized what he had done.

Al Raini looked startled and cringed slightly as Sidi raised his hands. He then regained his composure and shot Sidi a hateful look. Grabbing his turban from the floor he stuffed it back onto his head. A tail of the rag had come loose and trailed down his back.

Abu glanced at the startled stranger and turned and pushed Sidi across the cave to the wall. "What the heck is the matter with you?" he hissed. " I'm trying to arrange extra financing to get the components we need and you run in yelling about how screwed up we are! Are you out of your freaking mind?" Abu raised his hand to strike his fellow Arab.

Sidi cringed against the wall and started to sob. "But I thought you should know right away. I've always been your loyal servant. I've always been there to help you. Why when there was that thing with girl, the ham and the cat in Buffalo I . . . ."

Abu slapped his hand across Sidi's mouth. "Never speak of that," he hissed again. "What about the plans? You said they were missing?"

Sidi stopped crying, his hands brushed at his eyes. "I went to get the plans like you said. They weren't in the drawer and I looked all over. They were just gone! Somebody must have taken them!" He sucked in a breath and gave out a long ragged breath. "We must have a traitor in our midst. Maybe an American infidel dog, or one of those Israeli scum, or maybe one of those sneaky Russians or it could be a Chinese. I never liked them with their slanty eyes and funny talk. Why the other day on the History Channel, they said . . . ."

Abu put his hand over Sidi's mouth. "If we have a traitor, we will ferret him out," Abu said. "In the meantime, pull yourself together. Crying! Cringing! How can you represent the great Arab race? Muhammad, bless his name, would spit on you if he saw you. Get back in there and check the computer files. See what else is missing. And, if it hasn't been destroyed, print off a copy of the ovulator file for me to give to Samir."

Sidi gave Abu an odd look. "Samir? That guy looks like a Harold or a George. No way is a he a brother of the sand."

"Sand, schmand," replied Abu. "The closest you've been to the desert is a sandbox. Never mind who I'm talking to and go get that file."

Sidi looked indignant as he whined, "I have too been to the desert. Why, I've even made the Haj to Mecca and walked around the kabala." His chest swelled with pride at these words.

Abu giggled, "Sure you made the Haj, but I don't think anyone else had seven hundred and three strangers walk over them when they fell down making the first circuit of the holy stone. Cut the bull and go get those plans!"

Sidi looked abash and rushed out of the room while Abu returned to Samir. "Sorry about that," he explained in English. "Sidi tends to get flustered sometimes."

Samir waved his hand in dismissal. "Don't worry about it. I have the same problem. Good help is hard to get. Why just yesterday my secretary told me some lunatic had called on my private line muttering something about our menu system. Why, that's the very thing the menus are supposed to stop. I had our IT guys add three more menus to make it even more difficult for those nut cases to get through."

Abu cringed at the thought of using the telephone. "Well, enough of that. What about the three million we need to complete the project?"

Samir gave Abu a thoughtful look. "You know, these are hard times. Our investors are looking for short-term profits. It's getting very difficult to get them to focus on long-term gains. And, while your project has merit, you'll have to admit the final goal may be years away and we can't always expect the Americans to stimulate us."

"Not so," said Abu, shaking his head. The turban started to topple off and he grabbed it with both hands, pulling it more tightly down around his scraggly hair. "With the new components we can have the system operational within the week and start initial testing, as I said before. The testing phase should take no more than thirty to sixty days. After that the sky's the limit." He chuckled at his own pun.

"Okay, show me where you're at," said Samir waving his hand around the cave.

Abu led the executive around the cave as he pointed out the sights. The cave was huge, measuring over three hundred feet in rough diameter and had a sloping roof that rose over two hundred feet from the floor. The area was cluttered with various large pieces of machinery. There were wires and pipes running every which way without any seeming order or sense. A large cylindrical thing, with lights and high voltage insulators poking up here and there, dominated the center of the cave. The top of the cylinder had a massive parabolic dish attached by a multi-legged metal framework. Tubes, wires, sticks and stones led to the massive dish.

Pointing upward, Abu explained. "When we are ready to begin testing, the roof of the cave has a door that slides open along tracks. The dish is moved upward into position and focuses the charge. Our problem right now is the Hydrogen Ovulator. It seems to be producing nitrogen instead of hydrogen. I think it has something to do with the valence rings, or maybe I just screwed it up. Whatever. It'll be running in time for the tests, if we get the funding." He looked at Samir for approval.

Samir was staring at the red light flashing on the top of the big cylinder. As he stared his face grew slack and drool started dripping from his mouth. Abu waved his hand in front of Samir's face without any reaction. He clapped his hands close to the face, again, without reaction.

"Well bugger," he muttered and slapped Samir hard with his open hand. Samir's head rocked back and forth but he continued to stare.

"Well this is a hoot," said Abu as he grinned and slapped Samir again. "That'll teach you to screw around with those darn menus." He slapped the man a third time.

At that moment Sidi walked up to them and pressed a switch. The red light went off. Samir shook his head and looked around.

"Sorry," he said. "You were saying something about a dish?"

"Never mind," Abu said, giving Sidi a dirty look. "Are we going to get the money?"

"Uh, yeah, no problem," stuttered Samir. "Say did something happen here? My face is burning like I have a rash or something." He touched his hand to his reddened cheeks.

Abu pretended to look closely at the occidental. "Yeah as a matter of fact your face is kind of red. You might be allergic to something here in the cave. We've had some problems with black mold. You might want to have that looked at."

Sidi glanced around, "We have a problem with mold? Jeez and nobody said anything! My gosh, we could all get like rabies or toe fungus or something. I'd better call the exterminator; we can't have those mold thingies running all over the cave biting people or whatever they do!" He rushed from the cave.

Samir looked at Abu. "Is that man a complete idiot or is it some special training you use?"

Abu shook his head with a sad expression, "Sidi used to be highly intelligent until one day he fell on his head. He's been a moron every since. I've got an old Compaq computer that's smarter than he is now."

"So why do you keep him around?" asked Samir.

Abu shrugged, "I've had him for a long time, he's house broken, most of the time and he's good for a laugh now and then."

CHAPTER SIX

Baghdad sat in the desert heat pretending to be Paris on the Tigris. The new city sparkled like a diamond, the old city shone like granite. The whole smelled like smog and camel dung. Collapsed and bombed out buildings provided a contrast to new construction sprouting up like weeds.

Ames Blond sat in the aged Pinto desperately trying to get the air conditioner to work. He poked buttons, flipped the heat lever back and forth, adjusted the vents. He even tried turning on the engine. His efforts resulted in a wash of hot air that smelled like old sweat socks. He gave up, shut off the car and swabbed his head with a handkerchief that was already too sodden to accept more. Droplets of sweat rained down onto his suit jacket creating dark spots against the cashmere.

His plane had landed at Saddam International airport just outside of Baghdad, on the military side of the airfield. While the ground crew spent thirty minutes trying to get his junk heap started and off the plane, Ames had contacted the American Embassy by phone to see if there had been any new contacts. The secretary he had spoken with had refused to let him speak to anyone except the passport officer who was pretty much useless. No one admitted to being CIA or any other kind of intelligence. Ames was sure there was none in the building to begin with.

Returning to the plane the agent found six Marines slipping metal poles under the dead car. With an "oo-rah" the Jarheads lifted the hulk into the air and carried it off the plane. Once on the tarmac the Marines stopped and, as one, let go of the poles and stepped away. The car dropped and hit the concrete, blowing a tire and creating a dust cloud of dirt, feathers and chicken remnants. The thing looked like an escapee from a demolition derby. The Marines walked off shaking their heads and looking back at the crap on the runway.

After changing the tire, Ames spent twenty minutes thumping on the gas pedal and twisting the key. After watching the agent sweat, cuss and yell at the thing, a grizzled Air Force Master Sergeant who was about 22 years old, wandered out of an aircraft hanger and over to the car where he popped the hood, looked briefly at the engine and reconnected the throttle rod to the carburetor. He dropped the hood and walked back to the hanger. Ames stared at the man's receding back while muttering unfriendly words. The car started immediately.

With the car running, and a set of international tags attached, Ames drove down Saddam Road to Saddam Boulevard in the city. He had turned off onto Saddam Street and checked into the Saddam Hotel.

While Baghdad is a cosmopolitan city boasting many fine hotels such as the Hilton, Sheraton and the Holiday Inn, the agency had reserved him a room at the Saddam, voicing budget cutbacks for the inconvenience.

The proprietor of the Saddam, a scruffy little man in a dirty robe and even dirtier turban apologized to Ames about the hotels name. There were plans to change the name to the Bush-Cheney Plaza Ritz Hotel, but the sign company had more important contracts for the near future, such as the two big Halliburton signs on the highway entering the city. Not that the name mattered. The Saddam Hotel would have made a New York fleabag look good. The lobby had one ancient chair that had a list to port. The stairs were dark and rubbery. In his room were a saggy bed with a flea-infested mattress, a dresser with only one drawer and a chair with three legs. Bedbugs had built their own hotel in the corner and business was thriving. The bathroom, called the Obama defecation point, was down the hall, out the door, down the stairs and two blocks to the left. The view from the window pictured the glorious sight of a camel parking lot and three bombed out buildings.

He had decided against putting his things into the dresser and left his luggage in the car. His fervent hope was that he would be on a plane out before nightfall.

Ames was now sitting in the steaming hot car, waiting for his contact to appear, outside the Blue Mosque, which should not be confused with the Blue Mosque Canteen in Amarillo. The Blue Mosque, in Baghdad, was two blocks from the Green Mosque and eight blocks from the Red

Mosque that was four blocks from Wal-Mart. The Muzeen had sung the afternoon call to prayer an hour ago, so the worshippers should be getting out soon. Ames kept his eye on the main door to the mosque looking for a heavy set Arab with a beard and blue turban. The trouble was, there were a lot of heavy-set Arabs with beards and blue turbans.

Suddenly the car dipped to the right and Ames' eyes darted to the passenger window. A large face with a heavy black beard jutted into the window. There was a dirty blue turban on the head and light brown eyes stared out at Ames.

"You must be the American spy?" said the face.

"What?" Ames replied wittily.

"Only an American spy would drive such a crappy car," said the face that was attached to a hand that reached down and yanked the door open.

Ames reached for his gun as the large Arab slid into the passenger seat, further dragging the car down to the right.

Ames yanked the gun out of his shoulder holster and yelped as he caught his finger in the trigger. He tugged at the barrel and started shaking it to get it off. The gun flew loose and smacked into the dashboard. It then fell into the Arab's lap. Ames put his hands up and leaned against the door as the Arab picked up the gun.

"Also a piece of crap gun," said the Arab handing the weapon to Ames. "Nobody uses these wimpy nine millimeters anymore. The ten-millimeter has better stopping power. I could get you a nice Tokarov in the bazaar if you want. There are a lot of them around now and I can get a very good price. My brother-in-law owns the stall."

Shaking his head Blond carefully took the pistol and slid it back into his shoulder holster. He was examining the purple welt on his finger when the Arab stuck out a meaty hand, "I am Hassim Abdul-Aziz ibn Najid al Mustafah, purveyor of olives, donkey doo and really crappy tin jewelry. Also a gee ess fifteen with the CIA."

Ames took the hand and said, "I'm Blond. Ames Blond."

Hassim looked confused as he asked, "But you're not...."

Ames cut him off. "Don't start! We did that bit twenty pages ago."

Hassim shrugged. "Just getting into the swing of things."

The agent scowled at the Arab, "How come you're a gee ess fifteen? They only gave me a twelve."

"There are not many men who can do what I do," smiled Hassim. "Also I have a PhD in political science from UC Cal and a Masters in language from Harvard."

Ames looked agog at the fat, dirty Arab with the dribbles of rice and unknown substances in his beard. A large bulbous nose rose from the mustache and small brown eyes peered out from under seriously shaggy eyebrows.

"I suppose you're here to follow up on the information on Al Raini?" asked Hassim.

Ames nodded.

"Well we're somewhat out of luck. The Private's dog died, so that avenue of information is cut off for now. I understand the dog made a fine stew. However, before his family finished off the dog burgers I did find out that Al Raini is in a cave working on some kind of mystery weapon."

"Is that all you've got?" asked Ames.

"That seems to be it for now," said Hassim.

"I fly seven thousand miles with this piece of junk car for you to tell me that you had Rover for lunch? I knew most of that before I left! You could have put the remainder in an email and saved the taxpayers twenty thousand dollars!"

"Hey, it's not my fault! The budget is tight. There's no money for computers."

"So you have nothing for me?" asked Ames glumly.

"No, I did not say that," replied Hassim with an evil smile. "I said the dog died. I have it on reliable authority that Al Raini will have his mystery machine up and running within two weeks. My source also says that the machine is in the mountains in Afghanistan or maybe Iraq. He's not sure. It could be in Colorado or maybe in France. He wasn't quite as specific as I wanted but it was hard to understand him while he was chewing on a Scooby Doo sandwich."

With an annoyed look Ames interjected, "But you still could have sent this by email. Give me one good reason for coming to this hot dirty country."

Hassim gave Ames a baleful look. "Oh, come on. I didn't say anything bad about your country. Why do you have to pick on mine?" He crossed his arms and looked out the passenger window.

"Okay, okay! It's a beautiful country. The people are fine intelligent examples of humanity. Your camels smell like roses. Your rebels are kind and caring human beings and your rugs are better than Persian. Now tell me why the heck I'm here!" Ames ended up shouting.

Hassim brought back the evil smile. "Thank you. Not that I give a rat's banana about this hole. I'm from New Jersey." He reached into his robe. "Here. This might interest you. It was found floating in the Tigris. I'm not real sure how it ended up in Baghdad or what it means but you can have it."

Ames took the paper from Hassim and carefully unfolded the waded sheet. It was covered with dark lines and Arabic writing with lots of numbers. In bold English lettering in the corner were the words "Hydrogen Ovulator."

"What the heck is a hydrogen ovulator?" asked Ames, while turning the paper this way and that trying to make some sense out of it.

"I don't know," answered Hassim. "But it sounds kind of kinky to me."

Ames edged toward the car door, putting more space between him and Hassim. "Okay, I'll take it back and have R take a look at it. Maybe he can make some sense out of it."

Hassim shook hands and climbed out of the car. Ames spent a half hour trying to start the car before getting out and reconnecting the throttle rod while making rude comments about Air Force Master Sergeants.. He then drove off down Saddam Street headed for the US Embassy. He had gone just over a block when a truck came out of an alley and cut him off. With a squeal of the worn brakes, the Pinto crashed to a halt.

Ames jammed the transmission into reverse and stomped on the gas. The engine died with a loud thump.

Frantically Ames twisted the key, trying to restart the car as men carrying clubs and Kalashnikov rifles streamed out of buildings on both sides of the road. Ames gave up on the key and hurriedly rolled up the driver's window and snapped the door lock.

One of the Arabs grabbed the door handle and gave it a yank. Ames gave him the finger. Another Arab reached in through the open passenger window and grabbed Ames by the collar jerking him part way out of the car. Another Arab joined in and with a tug hauled Ames out of the car through the window.

They let go of the agent and he flopped onto the dusty street letting out a "whoof" as he landed on his back. As he was lifting himself to his feet a large man pushed his way to the front of the crowd. He wore a faded blue and yellow striped robe with a pink turban. His black and gray beard hung almost to his chest. In his hand he held a huge sword with a wide curved blade.

"Give us what belongs to us," roared the big man, poking Ames in the chest with the tip of the sword. The agent put his hands in the air and stepped back until he bumped into one of the Arabs that made up the circle around him. The Arab behind him pushed him forward again.

Ames looked at the thirty or forty men surrounding him and calculated the odds of making a get-away. With a sudden movement he twisted his body and lashed his foot at the big Arab in the pink turban.

The Arab leaned backward and Ames spun around and flopped back down onto the ground. He let out another "whoof."

The big Arab looked down at him and said in remarkably good English, "What the heck was all that about?"

"Ballet," muttered Ames. "I'm taking classes and needed the practice."

"Pansy dancing," said the Arab with derision. "Give us what is ours and you may live."

Slowly Ames climbed to his feet and reluctantly pulled the Tigris drawing from his pocket. With downcast eyes he handed the paper to the Arab.

The man unfolded the paper and examined it. "What is this?" he asked looking from the paper to Ames.

"That's what you want, isn't it?" asked Ames with some confusion.

"What do I need with a blurry water soaked piece of paper?" asked the Arab. "Give me the pink slip to that beautiful car," he demanded. "Also the car keys."

Ames turned astonished eyes to look at the car. The blue paint looked splotchy and dull in the bright sunlight and the car seemed to have gained a list to the right from a broken shock absorber. The hula girl looked more dejected than ever. A look of cunning lit his eyes.

A half hour later the blue Pinto deposited Ames at the gates of the American embassy. The car's chassis was dragging the ground from the ten people stuffed into it and the eight sitting on the roof and hanging from the sides. The remainder of the horde trailed along behind at a slow walk.

Ames exited the car and shouldered four of the AK-47s while waving to the bearded men. The men waved back and the car took off in a screech of dust and sparks as the chassis ground against the roadway. The multitude trailed after it like a gaggle of geese.

Ames walked up to the embassy gate and looked at the two nattily dressed Marines standing guard. "Hi, I'm Ames Blond and I need to see the ambassador."

Both Marines looked at Ames and one said, "Yeah, right and I'm Madonna. Which one are you supposed to be, Sean Connery or Pierce Brosnan?"

"I'm not that guy," said Ames indignantly. "The name is Blond and I work for DORK out of Washington. Just tell the ambassador I'm here!"

The Marine had a skeptical look on his face as he lifted a telephone from the wall beside the gate. "Lieutenant," he said into the instrument, "I've got a guy out here claiming to be a British spy and wanting to talk to the ambassador. No, sir, he said Blond. Yes, sir. Tall, dark hair. He was getting out of a really ugly Pinto driven by some insurgents. Yes, sir. Are you sure about that, sir? Yes, sir." He hung up the phone.

He walked over and unlatched the gate. "Well, I guess it's your lucky day, but you have to leave those rifles here and we'll need to see your driver's license, two ID's, your Social Security card, passport, birth certificate and a note from your mother. We have to make sure you're an American citizen before you can cross the border."

With a puzzled look Ames asked, "Why all the identity requirements, I'm not looking to be president of the United States?"

"The Marine chuckled, "If you were trying to be President you wouldn't need all that ID, but you do need them to get into this embassy compound."

Fortunately Ames was carrying all the right documentation and was granted immediate entry. After negotiating past the gate and the two irate Marines with M-4s, who relieved him of the assault rifles, Ames wandered around the embassy for an hour before he finally found himself in the office of the Ambassador.

A secretary had just handed him a cup of coffee and a donut when the Ambassador entered the room. "You must be the DORK who came in on that C-141," he said extending his hand. "I'm Harold Hardiman, the Ambassador to Iraq."

"Blond. Ames Blond," said Ames as he shook the hand.

The ambassador looked startled. "I thought you were British? Their embassy is two blocks over. Hang on, I'll get one of the Marines to guide you there."

"No, no," said Ames. "That's the other guy. I'm an American, not English. And don't even think about the hair."

Hardiman gave Ames a strange look and sat down behind a massive teak and balsa wood desk. "What can I do for you Mr. Blond?" he asked.

Ames leaned back in his chair and took a sip of coffee. "I need to arrange transportation back to Washington. Apparently there's been a slight mix-up. My travel voucher to here was one-way. I have vital information that the head DORK in Washington has to have."

"Gee, I'm sorry," said the ambassador. "The C-141 you came in on has already left. The best I can do on short notice is a commuter flight on Iraqi Air. They bounce from small airfield to small airfield all over Iraq, but the plane will eventually land at George Bush Senior International Airport and Rug Bazaar in Kuwait. You can catch a flight to Washington from there. I'm not sure what to do with your car."

Ames smiled. "I already took care of the car problem. When can I catch the flight?"

"You have time yet. I think the flight leaves Saddam International in about two hours. I'll have my secretary set it up. In the meantime can I ask you a question?"

Ames nodded.

"Do you have like a secret agent number or something? You know like that other guy?"

"Sure. Mine is three four seven six five three four nine eight eight two one three four," he said with pride. "It's the lowest number in the department."

The ambassador looked dubious. "But do you have a license to kill?"

"Well, no." said Ames with a little shame. Then he brightened. "But I do have a learners permit and I take the road test next month!"

The ambassador gave him another strange look and said, "Well, I'll have the duty driver run you out to the airfield and I'll have my secretary call ahead and arrange for your ticket. I hope you have a Visa card, Saddam International doesn't take American Express."

Ames stood up to leave, his coat making a clanking noise. He walked to the ambassador and held out his hand. "I want to thank you for your help. It's really important that I get my information back to the General Tenstars for analysis as soon as possible."

The ambassador took Ames' hand and asked, "This may be out of line, but what do you have stuffed in your pockets?"

"Oh, that's how I took care of the car. Some Arabs led by a guy named Ali Baba were going to steal it, but I traded them the car for four AK-47s and a couple of pounds of silver jewelry. Pretty good deal, huh?"

The ambassador chuckled. "Not really. There's about ten million of those Russian knock-offs floating around the country so they have almost no value at all. And the silver jewelry is probably tin. There's some crook named Hassim Mustafah who is selling aluminum junk all over Baghdad telling the soldiers, oil workers and tourists that it's silver. Between that and selling camel crap pies, he's got a heck of a scam going. I hear he's even telling people he's from New Jersey and in the CIA. And your friend Ali Baba is the biggest thief in the area. He's been making a killing in olive oil. It's reputed that he has a huge cache of gold and confederate money stashed somewhere in the mountains."

Ames gave the ambassador a blank look and then stared at the floor. Then a startled look crossed his face and he looked up at the ambassador. "Drat, I left my luggage in that blasted car!"

The ambassador laughed. "Looks like Ali is going to add some pants and shirts to his stash."

CHAPTER SEVEN

The ride to the airport had been pleasant enough. The car was an almost new silver Lexus with a Marine Lance Corporal as the driver. The driver looked like a sixteen year old body builder with short-cropped blond hair and a really weird black and gray uniform that looked like a crossword puzzle and was difficult to look at. There was an M-4 clipped to the dashboard and the Corporal wore body armor made of tin cans and cardboard. Ames felt a little miffed that no one had offered him any armor, even if it said Campbell's in one spot and Pureed Tomatoes in another.

The car rolled along in silence for ten minutes before the Corporal looked in the rearview mirror and said, "Pardon me sir, but might I ask what you do? The ambassador seems to think you're pretty important."

Ames thought about it for a moment and then said, "I'm a secret agent. My name is Ames Blond."

Now it was the Corporal's turn to look miffed. "Well if you don't want to tell me, that's okay. I'm just a dumb Marine, but even I know that guy is just somebody from a movie."

"Sorry if you got offended Corporal," said Ames with a smile. "But I really am an agent and my name really is Ames Blond."

"But I thought you were supposed to be English? The ambassador said you were an American. How come you're not driving a neat car like you do in the movies?"

"Pay attention, kid," Ames replied. "The name is Blond with an L. I work with DORK in Washington and sometimes with ASSHOLS."

The Marine glanced in the mirror again. "Okay I think I understand. But my momma said that you should not talk bad about people even if you don't like them. And lay off the kid stuff."

"Sorry, no offense intended and what do you mean your momma said?" asked Ames staring at the Marines eyes in the mirror.

"Well, calling your coworkers dorks and assholes. You shouldn't do that."

"Hold on, I'm not a dork. I work for DORK. It's an acronym that stands for the Department of Research and Knowledge."

"Oh, I get it. Sort of like USMC stands for United States Marine Corps or as some of the guys say, Uncle Sam's Misguided Children!"

"That's right, and ASSHOLS is the Advanced Special Sciences and Hidden Office of Laboratory Studies."

"So you're telling me you're a dork who's an asshole?" the Corporal asked dubiously.

Ames grimaced. "No, I'm telling you I'm a DORK. I work with ASSHOLS."

"Now let me get this straight. Some DORKs are ASSHOLS, but not all ASSHOLS are DORKs."

"No, you have it almost right. Its, some DORKs are ASSHOLS but all ASSHOLS are DORKs."

"Son of a bitch, but that's hard to understand," said the Corporal scratching his head.

"No, actually the son of the head of the British Intelligence, Technology and Communications Heralding has nothing to do with this, although he did show up for our annual Chrisukaza party last year. If I remember right he had on this really nifty uniform with lots of gold braid and medals and stuff. The last time I saw him, Sally from accounting was dragging him into the stockroom."

"What?" the driver asked in confusion.

"The Chrisukaza party and the son of BITCH. Now, mind you, I like Sally but she really needs to go on a diet. That kid from BITCH couldn't have weighed a hundred pounds soaking wet. It's a real scary thought thinking of her sitting on that skinny kid."

"Jesus Christ, now what are you talking about?"

"Well the people from the Jet Engine Special Usage Section and those guys from Communication Handling Reporting, Information Specialization and Training did show up for the party, but they had to leave early. They always get real drunk and start spouting religious stuff."

"Damn, you got stuff to say about everything?" the Marine muttered.

"No the Defense Ammunition Maintenance and Nomenclature section didn't come. Apparently they were short on names and had to work late. You know, I'm surprised you know about some of these departments. Most of them are real small and a lot of people have never heard of them."

"God!" The Corporal was shaking his head.

"Yeah, he was there. The General of Defense always shows up and acts real important, although he's really a pain in the butt."

"Okay that's about enough of this shit. I have no idea what you're talking about! You're giving me a pain in my head."

"Well truthfully the people from Special Habits Intelligence Training are real pains. They always show up and start causing hate and discontent. Sort of throwing crap into the fire as it were."

The Corporal stomped on the brake in front of the terminal, making the car rock back and forth. "Sir, no offense intended, but could you just take you're weird stuff and get the heck out of the car?"

Ames barely made it out of the vehicle before the Corporal stomped on the gas and took off. Ames shook his head at the eccentricity of youth.

The terminal building was a collection of modern looking boxes constructed of sand colored concrete. Ames stood on the sidewalk and watched the Lexus drive off, then, after skirting a Bradley Fighting Vehicle, entered the building. Inside he found a western looking waiting area with light green carpeting, dark and light gray benches nested into convenient conversation groups all surmounted by a fairyland ceiling that had delicate metal archways with spider web detailing. Looking around the ornate concourse he saw kiosks for various companies, such as Air France, United Airlines and Deutch Aero, but though he walked the concourse twice, he could not find Iraqi Airlines. Finally he overcame his natural male tendency and stopped at the United Airlines counter to ask.

A pleasant looking Iraqi girl in a white blouse and blue tie looked up from her computer.

"Can I help you, sir?" she asked with a smile.

Ames smiled back. "Yes, ma'am. Can you tell me where I can find Iraqi Airlines? There doesn't seem to be a booth for them."

Her smile faded. "Are you sure you want them? We have some nice flights and terrific service to Paris, London, New York and Washington."

"I'm afraid I'm already booked on a flight with Iraqi Air."

"If you're going to Mosul or Kabul, or possibly on to Kuwait City you might try Air France." She looked down and started pecking the keys on her computer. "I'm sure they could find room for you."

"No thank you," Ames replied just a little nervously. "I just need to find Iraqi Air."

"Are you absolutely sure, sir?" she asked looking up and attempting to smile again. "I think ElAl could fit you into a flight to Haifa or even Jerusalem."

"Look miss," said Ames in exasperation. "I don't mean to be rude, but is there some reason you won't tell me where I can find Iraqi Air?"

With a sigh she pointed to the right. "Go toward the end of the concourse and you'll see a tan door on the right. Go through there and down the stairs. Turn right and follow the hallway to a brown door on the left. Go in there and down the stairs. Turn left and Iraqi Air will be right in front of you." She gave Ames a pleading look. "Are you sure you don't want United or Air France?"

Ames gave her a quick smile. "Thank you, no. I'll be fine."

Ames followed the girl's directions and only got lost twice trying to find the brown door, but eventually he pulled it open and headed down the last flight of stairs. At the bottom he stopped.

He was in a dark, cavernous room with dimly glowing light bulbs spaced far apart. In front of him there was a huge boiler with a myriad of pipes and heating ducts. Looking to the left he saw a stack of crates with some planking on top.

As he neared the crates he saw there was a fat scruffy looking Iraqi in a T-shirt imprinted with a half-naked Madonna on it lounging in an old overstuffed chair behind the makeshift counter. A well-worn copy of "Playboy" magazine was perched in his lap and an old black and white television played in the background. There was a cigarette drooping from his lip that threatening to catch his beard on fire. Smoke curled up toward the dark unseen ceiling. He glanced up as Ames strode up to the counter.

The Arab muttered something in Arabic as he swatted at a fly with the magazine.

"Please tell me this isn't Iraqi Airlines," Ames said as he put his hands on the counter. His hand felt something wet and he glanced briefly at it before wiping it on his pants. There was a round spot where something had recently been.

"Okay, dis is not Iraqi Airline," the man said in bad English. He looked back down at the magazine.

"That's a relief," Ames continued. "Can you tell me where I can find it? The girl upstairs said it was down here someplace, even if it seems a little odd to have an airline reservation desk in the basement. I'm sure she made an error."

Heaving himself out of the chair with a grunt the Arab waddled down to the end of the counter. "Come here plis," he said waving Ames over.

With a hint of suspicion Ames moved down the counter.

The Iraqi smiled. "Dis is Iraqi Airline. You want ticket?"

"I thought you said this wasn't Iraqi Airline?" the agent asked looking toward the other end of the counter. The wood was scarred with marks from heavy objects and stained with coffee cup rings. Faded red letters on the planking read "FRAGILE DO NOT." Whatever was NOT did not carry over to the next board.

"No, up der not Iraqi Airline. Dat is sanidation engineering for building. Dis here is Iraqi Airline. I do bote." The Arab chuckled at his own joke causing the ash from his cigarette to fall onto his ample stomach. He ignored it.

With a sigh, Ames said, "I'm supposed to pick up a ticket here for Kuwait City."

"Oh, yes. You are de American." He pulled a pad of pink Post It notes from under the counter. "We don get many American here. What you name?"

"I'm Blond. Ames Blond."

The Iraqi looked surprised. "Hey, you de guy in da movie. I remember I see you. You shoot em up and get da girl. I taut you England man?"

Ames sighed again. "Yeah, that's me. Shoot em up and get da girl. No, I'm American. Do you have a ticket for me?"

"Sure ting, mister secret agent! I got ticket for you." He proceeded to write on the Post It note and handed it to Ames. "Der you go. Dat be two hunert dollars American."

Looking at the Post It, Ames saw it had a bunch of Arabic squiggles on it. "What the heck is this?" he asked looking up.

"Dat you ticket. Don loose it. You not get good seat on plane you loose it. Dat be two hunert dollars American."

Another sigh escaped from Ames. "Phooey, I just knew that girl upstairs was trying to tell me something. The fare is already paid by my agency."

"Dey mus hab forget to send money. You wait, I look." Mister congeniality bent over and started rustling papers under the counter. Ames could hear things dropping on the floor. With a loud SNAP the Arab yanked his hand out with a mouse trap latched to the first two fingers. With a howl the big guy flipped his hand in the air. The trap slipped off narrowly missing hitting Ames in the head.

With his fingers in his mouth the ticket agent muttered, "Der bef na pau tekt."

"What?" asked Ames.

"Der na tekt," replied the fat guy, slobber dripping down his hand as he sucked on his damaged digits.

I have no idea what you're saying," aid Ames. "Take your fingers out of your mouth, could you?"

The ticket guy pulled his soggy fingers out and said, "Der be no paid ticket ionforbation for you. You need to pay two hunnert dollars American."

With a sigh and a muttered comment about the reservations people at DORK Ames asked, "Do you take credit cards?"

Shaking his head the Arab said, "No, not take credit. Cash only. You got cash? If no you give back ticket."

Ames pulled out his wallet and looked inside. "I've only got a hundred and ten. How far will that get me?"

The Arab stroked his beard for a moment and then reached out and pulled on Ames' hand. "Dat nice watch. I maybe give you ticket for watch and money. Okay?"

"I knew this was going to be a bad day when I met Hassim," Ames muttered as he passed over the watch and money. "What time does the flight leave?"

The attendant took the watch and money and stuffed them into his pocket. "Plane leave when get 'nough people. You go to airplane now."

"And where do I find this airplane?"

The Arab pointed up. "Go upstairs. Go to end of concourse. Go out door. Get on plane. You see plane there. Thank you, have good flight." He dismissed Ames and waddled back to the chair. As Ames turned to leave the attendant pulled out the watch and began to inspect it.

With trepidation Ames made his way back upstairs to the main concourse. When he walked by, the girl at the United counter glanced up and spotted him. She gave him a weary smile and a wave. Ames gave her a half-hearted wave back.

The plane was an ancient looking Russian AN-24 Anatov with four engines and propellers, formerly produced by the Soviet Union. When new it was used as a people and cargo transport capable of carrying up to 44 passengers. The thing in front of Ames looked like it would have trouble getting its own weight in the air.

The tires were almost flat and the wings sagged as if the plane felt its age. On the side of the plane the words Iraqi Air in both English and, presumably, Arabic had been hastily spray-painted in day-glow orange. Small rivulets of paint went from the words toward the planes belly providing a contrast to the faded gray-green color of the aircraft. Here and there were patches of light gray and deep green duct tape. The tail rudder was wrapped in the tape where it met the fuselage and Ames wondered if that was all that was holding it on. Two of the windows were covered with cardboard.

A line of passengers, most with bags and boxes and a few with chickens and someone with a goat, waited on the tarmac. The man at the head of the line held the leash for a camel and was arguing with the pilot about boarding the animal. The argument was very heated with the airman and camel-man yelling and waving their arms. Finally camel-man threw some money at the pilot and both of them proceeded to push the camel through the small passenger door.

Ames groaned as he watched as the camel's butt disappeared into the plane.

With the camel semi-safely out of the way the line moved a bit more quickly until it was finally Ames' turn to board. He stepped through the passenger door and skirted the camel that was tucked into the cargo space behind the last row of seats. It was lying down with its feet under it and its rear end stuck out into the aisle. The agent flopped into a seat in the second row from the rear on the opposite side from the ruminant.

The plane quickly filled with passengers and caged and un-caged animals. The goat stood in the aisle next to Ames and began chewing on his coat sleeve. Ames jerked his arm away and brushed at the goat spit. "This thing is like a Mexican bus," he muttered. "I'm surprised they don't strap people on the roof."

Finally there was a dull thump as the engines fired up and the propellers began turning. The sound quickly rose to heavy thrum and the goat gave out a bleat of despair. The camel looked around as if unsure about the whole concept of flight.

There was no stewardess and no announcement of safety or destination that one usually expected on an aircraft. Without a word there was a jerk and the plane started moving down the runway. The movement continued for about three minutes and then the plane stopped. Ames could hear a slight bit of radio static over the noise in the passenger area.

After another five minutes there was another jerk and the plane began moving again. By this time the air inside the plane was getting a tad humid and hot. Ames could feel the sweat building up under his arms and drops of perspiration were forming on his forehead. The smell of the goat, camel, chickens and unwashed human bodies made the air stale and close. The American began to feel sick to his stomach and he started to wish that he had kept the Pinto and drove it to Kuwait, or maybe listened to the girl at United. To make matters even better the fake jewelry in his pocket was cutting gouges into his leg.

The plane gathered speed as it ran down the runway. With a lurch it took to the air and then dropped back down, hitting the concrete with a thump. A second later it bounded back into the air and Ames felt his stomach jump into his throat.

Apparently the camel felt the same way. It let out a roar and expelled gas from its rear. The goat gave a loud bleat and butted his head into Ames' arm. A green cloud settled over the inside of the plane. Some of the other passengers giggled and laughed. There was loud conversation in Arabic.

Ames yanked his handkerchief from his pocket and covered his nose. With a sinking feeling he knew this was going to be a long flight. Holding the handkerchief in place he leaned his head against the back of the seat and closed his eyes.

CHAPTER EIGHT

Abu pushed his face against the glass, flattening his nose and lips, making his face look like a skunk that had lost a fight with an 18-wheeler. Pulling back he glared at Sidi, who was holding a windowpane in front of Abu's face. "Get that darn thing out of my way and put it back in the window of the control room where it belongs! This is not the time to be playing practical jokes!"

As Sidi meekly slid the glass back into its metal sash, Abu turned back to the circuit board he had been peering at and poked at it with a voltage probe. The meter attached to the probed registered a solid zero. "Rat crap," muttered Abu as he dropped the probe. He turned back to Sidi while waving the board in the air. "This sucker is fried. Somewhere we're getting a voltage spike that is taking out the condenser control chip. Tell that screwy Lebanese engineer to recheck the circuit and find that spike!"

He tossed the board down on the table, stood up rubbing his head and knocked his turban off. Scooping up the discolored pink rag he stuffed it back on his head and walked over to the control booth. He stopped and stared at the wall outside the door. Someone had taped up a sign with a red bull's eye on it. The caption under the bull's eye read, "When stressed out, hit head here." Abu glared at the sign for a moment trying to decide whom to chew out for placing the not-so-humorous message on the wall. He then shrugged his shoulders and began smacking his head against the metal wall. The cave resounded with a series of hollow clunks.

After a minute of this Abu reeled and fell backward onto the ground landing on his tailbone. Holding his head he muttered, "Whoa, that feels better." His turban had fallen off again. He shook his head a couple of times and rubbed the red spot on his forehead. As he rose shakily to his feet he grabbed his pink headgear.

Holding the turban up he looked at the sweat-stained pale pink pile of cloth for moment then muttered, "What moron thought up these doofus things? Why can't we have cool berets like the French or even sensible ball caps like the Americans? Blast it all!" He jammed the thing back onto his head scrunching his ears down.

Sidi looked at Abu and said, "The turban is the product of Arab culture wherein the nomadic life of the Arab in the desert required some form of protection for the head from the heat of the sun. A beret or ball cap would not provide the necessary insulation from . . . ."

Abu grabbed Sidi by the arm with one hand, slapping a hand over his mouth with the other. "It was a rhetorical question, doofus. I really don't care about the history of turbans, Arabs, the History channel or the migration of the spotted owl. If you people don't get your thing together we are going to miss the deadline and those people are going to put their money into more promising projects. We start primary testing tomorrow and the process won't stay on line for more than two hours. Get that Lebanese twit, find that spike and fix it!"

He grabbed Sidi's nose with two fingers and pull his face down. "You tell those scum that the next thing that goes wrong, I start adding people to the crap detail. They can join Jamul in carrying buckets of slop out of the cave." He let go of the nose, looked up at the cave roof and put his hands together. "Allah, blessed be your name, please send me one decent Japanese engineer or a semi-competent American. I'll even take a half-trained conceited French one!" He stood for a moment and lowered his head He then quickly looked up again. "And, Allah, while you're at it, send some indoor plumbing."

Sidi rubbed his nose and took a step back from his glorious leader. "Master, you should not get so upset with your people. You're getting a dent in your forehead. Also, these are good people you have here. They are very devout and dedicated to you and Allah, blessed be his name. It is not their fault that they must work in such bad conditions.

"The roof leaks, the toilets make it smell bad," he continued, "It is very humid and the electronics do not like it here very much. It might be a good idea to pen up the camels outside instead of letting them wander all over the place in here. In addition to their making it difficult to walk stalactites keep falling on things. Or maybe they're stalagmites? Whatever. We should have set up in

73

Saddam's old palace like we had planned from the beginning."

"Yes Sidi," said Abu lowering his face to look at his fellow Arab, "I know this place sucks, but we could not use the palace. The Americans, the Germans, the Japanese, the Sudanese and all the rest would have stolen our design and stopped us from fulfilling the plan. No, we must stay hidden until we are ready to strike. Also we would lose out on the royalties. Al Shamute must go forward! We must show the world that we are more than camel jockeys and ragheads! The world must fear our power! They must fall to their knees and bow to us!" Abu was shouting now. "They must feel the power of the Arab mind and hear our shout to the heavens! We will succeed! Allah has shown me the way!" Abu yelled at the roof.

Sidi pushed Abu toward the control room wall. "You are getting stressed out again, go bang your head a couple of more times."

* * * * * * * * *

The flight was indeed a long one. From Baghdad the plane went west to Hadithah, then east to Tikrit and south to Hillah. Each time the plane took off the camel felt the need to voice its opinion of the pilot. Ames' nose had long since ceased functioning. At Ar Rutbah, Allah blessed Ames by removing the camel. However, he left the goat. The horned devil had backed into Ames and left a green-brown stain on Ames' trouser leg. It smelled vaguely of used fertilizer.

The plane departed Ar Rutbah and headed north to Mosul. Here Ames hoped to change planes to something a little more conventional that would take him to either Turkey or Kuwait. The agent felt that time was slipping away from him and he needed desperately to get to Washington.

Finally the city of Mosul appeared in the plane windows and Ames was glad to see it. The flight from Ar Rutbah had been long and the goat had not been great company. Whenever Ames tried to start a conversation the goat would bleat and turn its back. At last the plane descended to the runway and the tires screeched on the concrete, bounced into the air and then settled to the ground to bump along on what felt like flat tires.

Ames watched as the terminal building flashed by at a slow crawl until the pilot parked the crusty Russian aircraft a good half-mile from the main terminal. As Ames departed the plane to stretch his legs and clear his head, he gazed longingly toward the big 727's that were parked near the modern terminal building. He then looked over at the Iraqi Air terminal, a brown sun-baked shed with a bold sign in Arabic and English, "Restrooms This Way," with an arrow pointing vaguely behind the building across an open field and to what looked like a large open hole in the ground.

Hoping against hope, the man from DORK entered the small terminal to see if he could arrange passage on another carrier. Inside he found a snack bar serving stale chicken sandwiches and seriously strong coffee at outrageous prices. An Imam sat at a small table telling fortunes and passing out Koranic tracts. There was no one behind the makeshift counter.

Not feeling the need for a chicken sandwich or having his fortune told, Blond left the building and headed toward the main terminal. As he walked he glanced around for a bus or taxi, but neither was in evidence. He had gone no more than a hundred feet when he heard a sign-song voice behind him. Looking back he spotted his fellow travelers hustling to board the plane. With a sigh he turned and hustled back with them.

Minutes later the ancient Anatov took off for Irbil with Ames stuck in a seat beside a fat Arab woman. While she was covered in a chador and there was no way to determine her age or looks, the man in the seat across the aisle, who was may have been her husband but could have been her father, uncle, brother or boy friend, kept giving Ames extremely dirty looks. He had a large bushy black beard with red pouty lips set into a scowl and coal black eyes. Ames leaned to the far side of the seat to keep from touching the woman and smiled at the man. The man responded by pulling out a long curved knife and began stropping it on his bare foot.

To round out a pleasant flight Ames turned away from the couple and glanced out the window to see black smoke drifting from the port inboard engine. He pointed out the window and the woman's male companion glanced that way. He shouted something in Arabic and the rest of the passengers, including the chickens and the goat, began yelling at each other, pointing and, in some cases, making lewd gestures.

The co-pilot came into the back and leaned across Ames to look out the window. This required that he get close enough to lean over the fat woman. Before he knew it, Ames was in the middle of an argument between the husband and the pilot. This included brandishing fists, the knife and a chicken. Ames ducked as the chicken flew over his head, wings flapping, its feet held firmly by the co-pilot.

The chicken retaliated by spraying white droppings around the cabin and squawking as loud as possible. A number of others, chickens and humans, joined in the squawking and it was few moments before Ames realized that the air in the plane was getting dark and smoky.

The floor began to tilt downward and the goat went sliding toward the cockpit. The husband lost his footing, grabbed the co-pilot by the arm and they both followed the goat. Those passengers who were not strapped in, and that included most of them since there was a shortage of seat belts, fell, slid or flew in the direction of the goat. Within minutes there was a jumble of humanity stacked against the cockpit door, all flailing arms and legs and cursing in Arabic. Chickens squawked and tried to fly around the cabin leaving a trail of feathers and white spots. The goat could be heard bleating from the bottom of the pile.

Ames barely missed joining the mass by gripping the arms of his seat. He was further assisted by the fat woman who insisted on holding his head in a vice like grip. Ames lost track of things as his face was mashed into a triple G bosom and what felt like an army tent of black cloth.

His world was turning gray from lack of oxygen when there was a thump and a bounce, followed by another thump. Ames could feel a steady vibration in his feet followed by a swaying from side to side. With a mighty heave he pulled his head loose and stood up. As he gasped for air the woman grabbed his leg around the thigh. Ames lost his balance and fell forward out of the seat into the aisle, his legs lying across the woman's lap. He kicked his legs back and forth knocking the woman's veil off and mashing her nose. Finally he was able to pull himself loose and stand up. As he was gasping for breath he glanced out the window and could see trees and bushes rushing by. Somehow the pilot had brought the plane into a touchdown on a road, somewhere.

His breathing had not improved as the plane came to a halt. He was drawing in great quantities of smoke laden air and he began to cough. His head felt dizzy as he staggered toward the door. With a grunt he yanked the handle upward and fell forward as the door released, dropped downward and the service stairs fell into place. The agent fell out and thumped down the three small steps and landed in a pile on the ground.

With effort he pulled himself to his hands and knees only to be knocked over again as the fat woman stumbled out the door and tripped over him. She dropped and rolled several feet away and Ames went back to gasping for breath. It felt like a truck had hit him.

Again Ames pushed himself to his hands and feet and had just started to force himself upright when the goat emerged from the door. Dazed, confused and angry the goat saw the perfect target for its wrath. Launching itself from the stairs it struck Ames squarely in the buttocks. The goat staggered backward and Ames went flying forward. His head went down and he began rolling away from the plane to land behind a bush some distance away.

Ames opened dazed eyes and looked around. He had a fleeting glimpse of people rushing from the plane with rolls of duct tape when the world started spinning and then went black.

CHAPTER NINE

Ames awoke to a pair of beautiful brown eyes. The eyes sparkled behind long black lashes, the whole above a pert nose and bright white teeth behind pouty red lips that produced a gorgeous smile. Long dark hair with Farrah Fawcett curls framed the rosy brown face.

"You are awake," said the face, the beautiful lips moving to show those bright white teeth with a bit of green something hanging between the two in the front. "You took a rather nasty tumble I'm afraid."

Ames moved his hand to his head, rubbing his front teeth and pointing casually at the girls face. "Not to belabor a couple of clichés, but where am I and who are you?" The agent vaguely wondered how it was that he understood Farsi, Arabic, Kurdish or whatever it was she was speaking.

The girl totally missed the gesture. "You are in the village of As'al Quarba and I am Fatima the head mans daughter," she said with a breathy soft musical voice. "You fell out of an airplane and we found you on the road." Her breathing made the green thingy flutter in the breeze.

"What happened to the plane?" asked Ames as he struggled to sit up. He surreptitiously pointed at his teeth and back at hers again.

He glanced at his finger with a scowl. "The plane is gone. It left without you."

Ames managed to sit up with his legs hanging over the side of the wooden frame bed. The girl was slender and wore a bright red skirt with yellow flowers. Her blouse was white with long sleeves and buttoned to her throat. And it was a lovely throat, slim and long and elegant. She looked about eighteen but could have been older or younger. She started to blush under his direct gaze. It was a nice blush.

She had been kneeling beside the bed, but now stood and moved across the room to a washbasin. She picked up a stone pitcher and poured water into a glass. When she turned and handed it to him she was no longer red.

"Here. You must drink something and then you must go and meet my father and the other men of the village."

Ames took the glass from her hand, feeling the softness of her skin as their fingers touched. She started to blush again.

To break the moment Ames glanced around the room. It was very simple and austere and was made of plaster with tan walls. Besides the bed there was a small washstand with a white, flowered ewer and a bowl. Some towels lay beside the bowl. On the walls there were some pictures of fierce looking men in turbans and a couple of crewel works with Arabic writing. A door led into another room.

She smiled at him and asked, "What is your name, oh handsome one?"

Ames smiled back at her. "I'm Blond, Ames Blond."

A look of confusion crossed her pretty face and her tongue licked his lips and teeth, almost but not quit disturbing the green thing. "But I though blond was a light color. Your hair is dark."

"Oh Christ," he muttered. "Not you too!"

"Why do you pray to the Christian prophet? Did I say something wrong?" She asked.

"No, no. My name is Blond, not my hair color. Some people confuse the two."

"Oh, I see," she said smiling brightly. "You are a blond who is dark." The green thingy winked at Ames.

"Close enough," he said smiling back. "What happened to the airplane that I was on?" He scratched at his front teeth with a fingernail.

"It is gone. The airplanes around here are used to catching bullets from the ground. They pass out duct tape to the passengers and when the plane crashes, everyone jumps out and tapes up the damage. Then they all jump back on board and the plane leaves again."

"I didn't get any duct tape," said Ames.

"Oh, well you are not a frequent flier," she explained patiently. "You must accumulate frequent flier miles to get duct tape."

Ames nodded his head as if he understood. The, unable to bear it anymore he pointed at her mouth and said, "You got a bit of something stuck between your teeth."

She looked startled and quickly turned around. She poked and prodded at her mouth with a finger and then turned back to Ames. "Is it okay now?" She asked.

The green thing revealed itself to be a bit of lettuce and now dangled from her lower lip. "Sorry, but it's on your lip now."

She rapidly ran her sleeve over her mouth the looked at him with wide, questioning eyes. The thing was on her left sleeve. Ames decided to let it go. "Fine and dandy now."

Taking his hand the girl helped Ames to his feet. "We must go and see my father now," she said as she pulled a scarf over her hair

She led him out of the room, through another room that seemed to be a meeting room with small carpets and cushions scattered about. They went through a second door and Ames found himself outside looking at high craggy mountains. These mountains were rough looking rock and appeared very rugged. He suspected crossing them would be difficult.

The ground around the house was of packed dirt and a number of the plaster homes in various colors from earth brown to bright red were scattered about the village area. Men in turbans and women in chador stopped to look at him as the girl led him along a path through the village. He followed her to a small gathering of men who were sitting on a bench outside a small mosque tower. One of them held a book and they appeared to be arguing about something in it. One of the men, who wore a white turban, stood up as they approached.

Ames stopped a few feet short of the group and noticed that the people they had passed had followed them and there was now a large gathering behind him. It was a good bet that everyone in the village had shown up to meet the stranger.

The man with the white turban said something in Arabic to the girl. She answered him back and he looked confused. The girl spoke again and the look of confusion gave way to a look of enlightenment. Now Ames was confused as he tried to figure out why he could not now understand the Farsi or Arabic the people were speaking.

She turned to Ames and said, "He asked your name and I told him. It also confused him that your name does not match your look."

The white turbaned man identified himself as Shaykh Muhammad al Quddus, the political and spiritual ruler of the village. He was an older man with a white beard and a gentle face hardened by years in the sun. He placed his hand on Ames' shoulder and spoke to the girl.

"He wishes you to know that you are welcome here," she translated. "He says that although you are not of the faith, you are welcome as a stranger and a guest. He will do what he can to help you get to Irbil and find your way back to Baghdad."

As a conversation opener Ames pointed at the book and asked, "What were you and your friends arguing about in that book, some obscure point of Koranic law?"

After the translation the old man smiled and said, "Not hardly. We were discussing whether the spider in Stephen

King's "IT" represented pure evil, Shatan or just some hokey literary allusion to the errors of man."

Ames smiled at the cleric and, dredging his memory for information from his college days. Finding what he was after, the agent said, "Telhasi teezi, sadikie. Charra Alaik." He smiled proudly at the girl and added, "I had a roommate in college who taught me a few phrases in Arabic."

He then noticed the look of shock on the girls face. He turned and looked at the Shaykh. He too looked shocked and then the old man's face darkened and he started yelling at the others in the crowd. Hands reached out to grab Ames. Fists flew at his face and body. He dropped to the ground from a left upper cut and curled into a fetal position. Women pulled his hair and hands beat at him.

After what seemed like minutes some of the men grabbed him and pulled him to his feet. The girl stammered, "How could you say such a thing after we offered you such help?"

In bewilderment Ames was led off while being kicked and punched by the crowd. His captors pushed at the crowd as they dragged him to a building and threw him inside. He landed on the dirt floor, his face bloody and his body a mass of bruises. He heard the door slam shut behind him and a rattle as the door was locked.

People stood at the windows and yelled and threw things at him. Rocks, vegetables and dog and camel excrement found their way into the room. He curled himself into a ball again and wondered just what the hell had just happened.

Hours later, as the room grew dim with the setting sun he heard whispered voices outside the door. He had been leaning against the wall, half asleep, feeling the aches from his bruises. Now he rose painfully to his feet and shuffled to the side of the door. If the villagers were going to come in and get him he was going to be ready to fight back.

Looking around in the gloom he spotted a loose brick in the wall near his leg. He grabbed it and pulled it loose. Three or four more bricks came loose and fell to the floor. Ames bent over and looked at the hole in the wall. A bearded face stared back at him and began yelling in Arabic. Suddenly there was a soft thump and the face fell on the ground with the eyes closed.

Ames turned toward the door just in time for it to bang open and smack into his head. He fell to the ground almost as fast as the guard outside had. Ames groaned as he opened his eyes and again looked up into an angelic face.

Fatima looked closely at Ames' eyes. "Are you alright," she asked. "One of your eyes goes up and the other goes to the side. Are they supposed to do that?"

Ames pushed himself up to a sitting position and rubbed his eyes settling them back into their proper places. Satisfied he was seeing a single image again he said, "Yeah, I'm fine considering people keep hitting me." He looked up at her. "Just what the heck was that all about?"

"You should never have said such things," said the girl as she stood up. "It was very disrespectful to our Imam."

"What are you talking about?" Asked Ames as he pushed himself up from the floor and leaned against the wall. "I called him my friend and wished God's blessing on him."

"Where did you learn our language?" She asked with surprise. "You told my father to kiss your butt and to eat crap. That is not respectful."

Ames stared at her for a moment and then shook his head. "Blast that Ali, the retarded Arab set me up."

"Who is Ali and why would he set you up. Were you falling down?"

"Ali is a Saudi guy I went to college with," said Ames. "He taught me a few phrases in Arabic. He would get me to say them over and over so I would remember them. He always laughed when I said them and said that he was laughing at my accent. The dip was laughing because he was teaching me to say bad things."

The girl started laughing. "You are such a fool! You use words you do not know the meaning of and you trust a Saudi! "

Ames hung his head and kicked at a pebble with his toe. "So I made a mistake," he cried. "Anybody can make a mistake. How was I to know that sucker was lying to me? Tell me that! How was I to know? Besides, if I didn't know what it meant the Imam should not have gotten so mad."

"But you insulted him!" cried the girl.

"Did not," said Ames with a pout. "He just took it the wrong way."

"You did so insult him."

"Did not."

"Did so."

"Did not."

"Did so."

"Did not."

"Whatever," she said in exasperation. "You must apologize to him and the rest of the council and show them you really mean them well."

Ames thought for a minute and glanced around the room. His eyes lit on his suit jacket. It had been thrown into the room and now lay in the corner, wadded up and dirty. His eyes brightened. "I know just the thing," he exclaimed. "Take me to your leader."

CHAPTER TEN

Ames and Fatima were escorted into the council building by the disheveled guard from outside the prison hut. The guard's turban was askew and he had a definite lump on his forehead. He occasionally raised his hand to his head and had a tendency to weave back and forth. His eyes looked a bit odd.

As they entered the room, which was crowded with men, Fatima's father looked up at them and yelled at her in Arabic. "What is the meaning of bringing this infidel dog into my presence? He is a slimy low-life pig with no manners and no respect. Take him away so we can continue planning for tomorrow's festivities." He waved his hand at the guard who stepped forward to grab Ames.

Fatima pushed the man back out of the way. He stumbled backward and bounced off a wall, banging his head in the process. He looked slightly confused and then fell into a heap on the floor. His turban rolled to Ames' feet. The agent picked it up and tossed it to the fallen man who grabbed it and glared at Ames with those odd looking eyes. His eyes now looked different ways, one facing up and the other to the side. The guard shook his head to get them back to proper alignment. He continued to glare.

Fatima looked defiantly at her father. "The infidel has come to apologize. He used words he did not know the meaning of and, like a trained monkey, simply repeated them without thought." She glared at her father, who was getting a headache from the glares, with flashing eyes and her arms crossed her bosom. Then her eyes softened and she dropped her hands. "What festivities?" she asked. "I did not know there was a holiday scheduled."

"Oh, well," her father responded, "we are planning on making a day of it. First thing in the morning we would have a person pull through the village, dragging the infidel behind a camel. That would be followed by a mock trial and a general slap session. Then lunch. After that we could have either a public beheading or maybe a nice burning. My personal choice is a burning. It takes longer and the kids get to do marshmallows. We were even thinking of balloons and maybe covered dishes for lunch."

The girl clapped her hands in delight and she hopped up and down, drawing the attention of every male in the room, their eyes bouncing up and down as fast as she was. "Oh, can we do the snake thing? I always liked the snake thing!"

Her father waved his hand in the air. "Of course all that is now scrapped since this person had the effrontery to apologize. Now I have to tell everyone that its back to business as usual and there will be no paid holiday. That's going to annoy a few people, although I suppose we could still keep the slapping to make him show respect. "

Through this exchange Ames had looked back and forth from the father to the daughter as though it were a tennis match. He stopped long enough to watch her bounce, resuming the tennis match when she stood still. Finally he interjected, "Please tell your father I meant no disrespect and I apologize. I did not know the meaning of the words I used. If it were possible I would take them back."

Fatima translated as he talked, her father watching Ames' face.

"Well I guess that cancels the slapping too, darn it," muttered the Imam.

"Tell him that I would like to show my sincerity by giving him a gift." The agent reached into his coat pocket and pulled out the handful of the faux silver jewelry he had obtained in Baghdad. "Please let me present this fine jewelry to him as a token of my respect."

The Imam's eyes brightened at the sight of the metal ornaments and he reached out to accept them. As he looked closely at the assortment his face fell. "Oh," he said, "Some of Hassim's junk. I think this stuff is all over the Middle East, rather like camel dung."

He looked up at Ames as Fatima translated her father's words. The agent's eyes fell at the mention of Hassim's name.

"Ah well," said the father with a shrug. "It's the thought that counts. I can give this junk to my wives. They will be more than happy with anything as long as it is a gift, and roses are so darned hard to get." Then he had a thought. "I might even get lucky tonight," he said with an evil leer.

Al Quddus waved a hand at the pillows beside him. "Please have him sit and join us for dinner. We would hear of his travels and his country."

Ames happily dropped onto the carpet and assumed a sitting position with his feet stretched toward the Imam. Suddenly the cleric's face darkened and he started to wave at the guards. Two of them moved toward Ames as the girl hurriedly bent and pushed on his legs. "Quickly," she said. "Sit like everyone else. To show the bottoms of one's feet is a sign of disrespect."

Ames rapidly pulled in his legs and crossed them. "Drat it, here we go again," he muttered and ducked as the first fist struck him. The imam quickly shouted and waved the people away.

In a loud voice he said to the gathered people, "Please ignore him and don't hit him again until I tell you to. He is an idiot from another country. Apparently his mother did not teach him respect or how to act in polite company." He smiled at Ames.

The Imam turned and clapped his hands. The men seated themselves in a circle around the cleric and his guest. Women began bringing in dishes of food. There were meats such as lamb and goat, each cooked in exotic eastern spices. There was a Cesar salad with ranch dressing for each of them and a nice rice pilaf with chicken. For dessert there was apple pie with ice cream.

The men started digging in with their hands, picking up tidbits from the communal bowls and popping them into their mouths. With some hesitancy Ames tentatively reached out with his left hand and snagged a piece of goat.

This earned him a disapproving look from the Imam and the rest of the men. He quickly dropped the portion and looked at Fatima.

She sighed and said, "You have much to learn. You do not use your left hand for food, only your right."

"Why's that?" he asked in perplexity.

"Because," she explained, "The left hand is used to wipe your bottom. You don't touch food with the hand you wipe with."

Dumbfounded, Ames blurted, "Have you ever heard of washing your hands afterward? Or possibly using toilet paper? And what's the deal with the feet?"

Poking at her salad with her finger, Fatima said, "If you have noticed, there are many camels, goats and sheep in the village. When you walk, it is almost impossible to keep from stepping in animal droppings. Who wants to sit talking to someone while looking at their crappy feet?"

Ames turned slightly green at the thought. "I still think washing might be a solution, or maybe wearing shoes."

Shaking her head, Fatima said, "Not really. Shoes can be expensive for a poor village like ours and, unless you have not noticed, water can sometimes be scarce in this part of the world."

She turned to her father and explained the conversation. The Imam started laughing and told the other men. The meal was interrupted when everyone began laughing hysterically with some rolling uncontrollably around on the carpets. Ames looked down at his plate and muttered, "I'm glad everyone is having such a good time."

Then a thought occurred to him. "Fatima, have you seen any strange people in the area or seen any strange things?"

She thought for a moment and answered, "There are always some strange men around. There are bandits and insurgents in the hills and smugglers use the passes from Iran and Turkey. A few months ago one of the men said he had seen some trucks in the mountains, but they did not come near here. They were closer to the border with Iran and came from the direction of Turkey. There have been some helicopters, but we assumed they were Americans looking for Osama Bin Laden."

"You know where Osama is?" asked Ames excitedly, taking her hand and squeezing it, smushing the tomato slice she had just picked up.

She pulled her hand away and shook off the remnants of the tomato. "Of course," she said, wiping her hand on a cloth. "Everyone knows where the master is."

"So where is he?" Ames asked looking into her eyes.

"Everyone knows he is a rug merchant in Pittsburgh in the US of A."

"What," exclaimed Ames in disbelief. "Pittsburgh? Rug merchant?"

"Certainly," she said tossing her head. "He has videos made using a back drop that looks like the mountains of

Afghanistan. I have heard that he has a Beemer, whatever that is, and spends the winter in Miami Beach. They say he enjoys the night clubs and has even learned the game called golf."

"But I thought the sucker was dead, killed by American Special Forces!"

"That did not happen. They got the double he uses for commercials for those special Al Queda turbans and promotional rings. You have probably seen the spots on Al Jazeera."

Her father spoke to her and she responded. The father said something else while pointing at Ames.

"My father said I should not be telling you about Osama. He said I should tell you he is living in a cave in Pakistan or dead with his body floating in the ocean for shark food. I am not to tell you about the split level ranch or the motor home."

"Well tell your father I believe him about Pakistan," said Ames with a smile and a wink. "And the name of Pittsburgh will never pass my lips. What about a man named Abu Al Raini? Has anyone heard of him?"

The girl spoke to her father in a long drawn out conversation. After a bit Ames' mind started to wander as he assumed she had not heard him or was ignoring the question. The bowls on the floor were nearing empty and many of the men had gone. There were only a few of them left and they were talking quietly among themselves and ignoring the small party around the Imam.

Ames picked at the remnants in the bowl of lamb, poking a small bit of the meat into his mouth and chewing absentmindedly. The room itself was a rather stark area of whitewashed stone with a single picture of some stern looking Shaykh or other on the wall. There was one small window in each of the outer walls and the floor was covered with rugs of various designs and colors. The rug was littered with many varied colored pillows that the men had used to sit on. Four bare light bulbs lit the room, glaring off the walls. A single archway led to the back of the building and a double doorway, through which Ames and the girl had entered, led outside.

Suddenly the girl turned her head and spoke to Ames. "My father said he has heard of Al Raini. He says that Al Raini has had his agents in the village in the past, going from door to door with little cans asking for money. Sometimes those agents have used children in costumes to collect the money for him. The children come to the door and say, 'Trick or beat.' If you do not give a very large man beats you up. He says that the children think they are collecting the money to buy food for other children, but my father thinks Al Raini is using the money for evil purposes. He has not allowed the collections in many months."

"Do you or your father have any idea where he is?"

"No, there has been no word from him for months. Not since his collectors have been banned from the village. But my father said to tell you that the mountain has been sick lately. It has been making strange noises and sometimes there are funny lights up near the top. He thinks Al Raini has something to do with it."

"Which mountain? I don't remember seeing any particular mountain, but then I didn't see much when I came in anyway." Ames glanced toward the window.

"It is the big mountain northeast from here," she said pointing toward the back of the building. "Its name is Ghunda Zhar. Before Allah came people used to believe that gods lived up there."

"Maybe you could point it out to me when we go out tonight."

"I do not think so," she said turning her face down. "It will be very dark and my father will not allow me to walk with you alone."

"I thought you were liberated?" he asked with a smile.

"Not that liberated. It would be unseemly and would give my father bad face." She turned to look at her father when he started speaking. She listened for a moment and then looked back at Ames.

"My father said it is time for me to go home and for you to go to bed. You have a long trip tomorrow and you should sleep."

Ames, the girl and her father all stood up. One of the other men stood and moved closer to the group. Fatima spoke briefly to her father, then nodded at Ames and walked out through the archway. Her father put out his hand and Ames took it. "Shalom aleikum," said the Imam.

Ames shook his hand and then followed when the other man took his arm. He was led outside and back along the path toward the small building he had been locked in before. He turned his head as he walked and tried to see the mountain the girl had been talking about, but it was too dark. The village had few outside lights and there was no moon.

Ames had a moment of panic when the guard pointed for him to enter the small building, but when he went in he saw that a light was on and the floor had been covered with rugs. A number of pillows and some blankets were strewn on the floor. A table had been added and a water pitcher and cup sat on it.

The guard spoke in Arabic while pointing at the string hanging from the light. Ames remembered one of the words he had learned at college, a word he was sure he knew the meaning of. "Shukran," he said to the guard who nodded and left, closing the door behind him.

The agent pulled some of the pillows together and slipped off his shirt, shoes and socks. He turned pulled on the string to turn off the light and lay down on the rug, pulling some of the blankets over himself.

It was only after he closed his eyes that he noticed that the room had a somewhat strange smell. It was slightly rancid and sweet at the same time. He pushed back the blankets and followed the scent to one corner of the room. Brushing back some dirt he found a number of boards set flush with the ground. He tried to lift one away, but it was nailed down. The odor seemed to come from under the boards. Giving up he went back and lay down.

For a while he lay in the dark thinking about mountains, Arabs and one pretty girl with gorgeous eyes.

CHAPTER ELEVEN

The following morning someone started banging on the door, waking Ames from a disturbed sleep. They kept on banging until he had blearily opened the door. He had not slept well. The odor in the room had disturbed him and the ground under the rugs was littered with stones and, while the rugs helped somewhat, each small lump dug deeply into him. By morning the stones had become very large and jagged rocks. He felt a lot like the princess who had pea problems.

An older woman dressed in a dark robe and a red and yellow colored headscarf handed him a cup and a plate covered with a cloth. She gave the door one more bang and left without a word. Ames closed the door and put plate and cup down on the small table. He pulled off the cloth covering to find food and drink.

Ames was finishing his breakfast of cold goat, goat's milk and feta cheese when the door came open and a fierce looking man with a long dark beard and a sweaty green turban stalked in. He gestured for Ames to get up and follow him.

After they had walked out the door Ames tapped the guard on the shoulder and tried to ask about a bathroom. The guard looked at him strangely and gestured for Ames to follow. The agent stood still and pantomimed holding his pecker and pissing. The guard's eyes grew wide and he winked at Ames. With a wide smile he patted Ames on the shoulder and pointed back into the small building with another wink, then shrugged and waved for Ames to follow him. Unsure what had just happened Ames followed the guard.

The pair followed the path back through the village to the council hall. Inside they found Al Quddas seated on the carpet with his council of nine men around him. There was no sign of Fatima.

The Imam gestured for Ames to be seated and the agent lowered himself to the carpet, being very careful to tuck his feet under himself. The cleric began speaking and a young man on Al Quddas' left translated. "First my father asks if you enjoyed your breakfast?"

"Not really," said Ames. "I mean, goat this, goat that, goat meat, goat cheese, goat milk. Don't' you people ever get tired of eating goat?"

The young man looked surprised. "Why, yes," he answered. "I personally like a good thick steak smothered in onions and mushrooms with mashed potatoes or rice pilaf and a side of asparagus tips. We only haul out that goat stuff for you tourists. For some reason you seem to expect it."

He turned and spoke to his father for a moment and then turned back to Ames.

"Mister Blond, my father has decided to assist you in leaving our village and helping you to get to Irbil. His third son Abdel, that's me, will lead you through the mountains to Irbil and the American Marine garrison there."

The father quit speaking, but Abdel continued. "Our truck is not working, so we will have to walk. It is about sixty kilometers. I will place you with the Marines and I will obtain a part for our truck. If I am lucky, and the Marines are pleased with me bringing them such an important American, they will give me a ride home. You are an important American are you not?"

Without a seconds thought, Ames said, "Oh, yeah. I'm real important. Oh yes, right below the president. Yup, I'm right up there. Really need to get back and take care of the country. Yup, that's me, mister important. When do we leave?"

Abdel looked at Ames for a moment, then turned and spoke to his father. The old man said something back and Abdel said to Ames, "If you are such an important man, possibly we will keep you and trade you for foreign aid."

Ames was stunned that these men would hold him hostage. Hurriedly he said, "Well I'm not that important. I mean I'm just a small cog in a great big machine, you know. The country is bigger than all of us. Without me the government will go on. I have no value. Well, maybe a little, a couple of buck's worth. Or not. Maybe I'll stay here. I can always get a job as a goat herder or something. Your sister might help me get a job. By the way where is she?"

The Imam looked startled at the mention of Fatima and rattled off some Arabic at Abdel.

"My father has decided that you should go to Irbil. The hostage thing was just a passing idea. He would like us to start immediately."

Ames looked at the cleric with a puzzled expression. "But where is Fatima? I thought she was your interpreter?" The Imam waved his hand in a dismissive gesture.

"My sister has gone to her aunt's home in another village," said Abdel. "She is promised in marriage to her second cousin and it is not seemly for her to be seen with a foreign infidel."

Ames looked bemused at the idea and said, "Then your cousin is a very lucky man. I wish them all the happiness in the world. Although I suspect he has his work cut out for him."

Abdel bowed to Ames and spoke to the father. Dad also bowed and then spoke to Abdel.

"My father thanks you for the blessing and says that we must get you on with your journey." With that Abdel rose and gestured for Ames to follow him. Ames stood and bowed to the Imam then followed Abdel.

Outside they found a donkey loaded with bundles waiting for them. Abdel said, "This is Kong the donkey. We will take him and follow the trail through the mountains. It is about 60 kilometers to Irbil and will take us about three days. Come we leave now."

"Wait a minute," said Ames. "Where can I take a leak? I tried to ask the guard but he got real strange so I gave up."

Abdel also gave Ames a strange look. "I thought you knew. The building you slept in is the outhouse. There is no other place available to keep prisoners so we covered up the hole and stuck you in there. If you needed to piss you could have just pulled up the boards in the corner."

"Well that really sucks," said Ames indignantly. "You stuck me in the crapper! A blasted outhouse! And you got on my case about my freaking feet!"

"Please do not get all bent," said Abdel holding up his hands. "And do not take the Lord's name in vain. It was not meant as disrespect. We had nowhere else to put you, and besides, it inconvenienced a lot of people. That is our only outhouse."

"So where do I take a leak now?" asked Blond. He looked back and saw a long line of people standing outside the door of the little building. Some were hopping from one foot to another and giving him dirty looks. An old woman by the door was passing out strips of toilet paper. Ames shuddered.

"You can wait until we are on the trail and go behind a bush or a rock," said Abdel who started towing the donkey Kong out of the village. Ames hurried to follow while willing his bladder to hold on for a few more minutes.

Ames strode along beside Abdel as they walked out of the village with the young man leading the donkey. As they passed one of the homes he caught a brief glimpse of a lovely face peering out a window. This startled him and he stopped. He started to say something to Abdel, but by then the face was gone leaving Ames to wonder if he had actually seen what he thought he had seen.

Abdel stopped and looked at Ames. "Is there something wrong," he asked looking in the same direction as Ames.

Ames shook his head and started walking again. Abdel watched him for a moment and then followed after.

In a few minutes the village had been left behind and Abdel stopped while Ames ran behind a bush. The relief felt wonderful. When he returned to the path he saw Abdel staring backward and upward.

Ames turned and glanced at the mountains and could see gray clouds building over the tallest peaks. He looked at Abdel. "Looks like we might be in for a bit of weather."

Abdel looked at Ames and then turned and stared at the mountains again. "That is odd," he said. "This is not the time for rain. It is possibly just a passing weather front."

Ames looked back toward the mountains. "Which one is Ghunda Zhar?" he asked.

Abdel pointed toward a high mountain with the very dense black clouds over it. "That is Ghunda Zhar. It is where the old people say that Shatan lives. Sometimes there are strange noises and you think maybe they are right."

The agent stopped for a moment and scanned the sides of the mountain, but could see nothing out of the ordinary. He started walking again.

Ames stuck his hands in his pocket and stared at the ground as they walked. After a moment he turned and looked at Abdel. "You speak pretty good English," he said. "Just like your sister. Did you both go away to school or something?"

"No," said the Kurd. "My father is getting older and it is our tradition that the sons follow the father in their life's work. My father is the religious and civil leader of our village. When I am old enough, and have learned enough, I will take my place as a learned man of the village. Also I will be a goat herder and general mechanic for the truck. My older brother Gamil was supposed take my father's place. Most of the Imam's in our religion look at the world as it is, not as it will be. My father is different. He wanted me to learn something of the outside world so that I could base my decisions on what the real world is like."

"So he sent you and Fatima away to school?" asked Ames.

"No, he sent me and Gamil to a Christian school in another village where I could learn English. They were supposed to teach us the language and some world history and technology. My sister would walk to the school with me each day and she listened in on the classes. When father found out she was learning English faster than I, he included her in the deal, but always with a chaperone"

105

"So how come she hasn't married her cousin by now?" Ames asked. "I thought girls were supposed to marry early?"

"Fatima is a bit head strong and father tends to give in to her whims. But I should not talk about her. You are not of our religion or our tribe and showing such interest in a girl who is promised to someone else is not seemly."

"So where is your brother, Gamil I think you said? Why wasn't he here to do the translation?"

"Gamil is a sad story. He had a very difficult time learning English and did not do well with religious studies. Eventually he quit school and ran off. He is now a taxi driver in your New York City."

Ames nodded as if he understood. "So Gamil was the oldest and you're the third son. So who's the second son?"

"That was Ibrihim," said Abdel hanging his head. "He died when he was a child. He was playing in the street and got run over by a camel. Very sad." Abdel seemed to lose himself in thought.

Ames looked back down at the ground and let his pace lag slightly so that he was walking behind Abdel and the donkey.

They walked in silence for almost an hour along a path that led through rocky mounds, up and down, but always slightly downhill. Suddenly there was a loud crack from behind them and they both stopped and turned. The clouds over the mountains were much darker now and they could see flashes of lightening. Ames felt something hit his hand and looked to see a small drop of water on his wrist. Another struck him in the forehead.

Abdel looked at the sky with wonder. "This is very odd," he said. "I have never seen rain at this time of the year."

"Maybe we had better set up camp before it gets any worse," Ames mentioned.

"No," said Abdel. "I am sure that this will not last long. This is a very dry region and when there is rain it is very little."

"You don't get much rain here?" asked Ames.

"No," said Abdel. "We get less than 20 centimeters per year and only during the winter months. We also get some snow, but it is rare and does not last, although it does get cold."

At that moment the sky opened up and the rain started in earnest. It fell in large droplets that splattered against the ground, the donkey and the two men. Within seconds all were soaked through. The donkey, Kong, brayed in annoyance at being so wet.

The men ran toward a rock outcropping dragging the donkey behind them. They both huddled under the rock as the rain pounded down. The donkey didn't fit and stood in the rain looking like a bedraggled dog. Every once in a while Kong would look at the two men and sort of whimper. Ames felt sorry for the beast.

Sitting with his back against the rock, Ames watched the water form rivulets in the once hard packed ground. Unbelievably the sun-backed soil was slowly turning to mud. The agent dredged his brain and pulled up a nugget of wisdom. This was the Middle East. It wasn't supposed to rain like this.

Abdel stared at the rain and said, "This is not possible. I have never seen rain like this. I cannot imagine it lasting very long."

"I don't know," said Ames as he peeked a look out at the sky. "Those clouds are deep and black. I think this is going to last for quite awhile."

The Arab looked at Ames for second or two and then hunkered down inside his robe.

The air grew cooler as the rain sapped the heat from the ground. Ames pulled his jacket more closely around himself. Abdel had fallen asleep with his turban tucked under his head. The donkey had finally hung its head and gave up. It appeared to be sleeping and having bad dreams. Every once in a while it gave a snort, lifted its tail and wiggled its backside.

As the day turned to night the rain continued. At any moment Ames expected Noah to come running through yelling about an ark. Suddenly an old man came marching through the rain followed by two zebras. Behind them came two elephants, then two rabbits and two horses. The parade continued with each type of animal moving by in pairs. The animals began skipping and hopping, some appeared to be doing the boogaloo. Two Fatimas wiggled along the path, each wearing sheer silken trousers and veils. Ames watched her dance closer and closer until he finally fell into a deep sleep.

CHAPTER TWELVE

Ames woke up feeling as if every bone in his body was stiff. He reached his arms over his head to stretch, or, at least, tried to. His arms wouldn't move. Neither would his legs – or his head, or anything else. Frustrated and worried, he opened his eyes.

He looked into really ugly brown eyes topping a horribly scraggly beard permeated by seriously bad breath. The mouth smiled, showing scraggly yellow teeth and oozing the scent of used goat.

"Asallam aleikum, sadikie," said the mouth.

He ran his tongue over the inside of his mouth feeling a scummy build up. Looking at the Arab he really wished for a toothbrush. "Uh, sorry," said Ames brightly. "I don't speak Arabic."

The face backed off to reveal a short Arab dressed in a ragged robe with a really dirty turban pulled so far down that his rather large ears were bent over and looked like wings. Behind him stood six more equally ratty looking individuals.

The small character stepped back a pace and said, "Good morning, Joe. I am Salim Muhamet al Jabar. I am leader of Patriotic Rebellion for an Independent Central Kurdistan. I fight against evil king Hussein. We PRICKs are proud of our fight" He grinned even more, if it were possible.

Ames looked up at the strange band. "Ah sorry, dude," he said apologetically. "But I think you're too late. Hussein is gone. The Marines bagged his butt quite a while ago. I think you have a democracy now."

The smile disappeared from Salim. "Hussein gone? Then who do we fight against?"

"I have no idea," answered Ames. "But if you untie me and let me up I can help you figure something out."

Salim pulled out a very long, very wicked looking knife and waved it in the air. With a flourish he stepped forward and whipped the knife downward. Ames tried to duck, which didn't work very well in his present condition. The knife waffled through the air and slashed between his legs, neatly cutting the ropes holding his legs.

He was chilled from the dampness that pervaded his clothing and he noticed that the ground was still wet. He wished the gang would cut his hands loose so he could rub them together.

Two of the ragged Arabs grabbed Ames by the shoulders and pulled him to his feet, bumping his head into the rock overhang. Ames staggered and fell back on the ground getting a mouthful of soggy dirt. He was jerked back to his feet as he spit the dirt out, spraying Salim in the face.

Salim let out a string of curses in Arabic. Ames looked surprised. "Hey," he yelled. " I know what you just said and I won't kiss your butt or eat crap!"

Salim looked nonplussed for a moment and then pulled a rusty looking pistol from inside his robe. Ames absent-mindedly identified it as a Russian Tokarov 10 mm. Salim started waving it in the air and shouting, "I kill you. I kill you right now. You spit on me! Am I animal to be spit on?" He stopped waving the pistol and aimed it at Ames.

Ames looked slightly worried and sputtered, "Whoa there, Ali Baba! Let's not go shooting anyone. We need to make some kind of deal here. You need a cause and I need to get home. Why don't you put that gun down and we can talk?"

The Arab waved the gun in the air some more while yelling in Arabic. With a flourish he swung the pistol down to face Ames again. The gun stopped, but the gun's slide kept going, traveling forward and striking Ames in the groin. Ames doubled over and grabbed his crotch. The slide spring popped into the air and the barrel fell on the ground.

Salim looked at the stub of the gun in his hand, looked at Ames and threw the useless metal into the dirt. Then he dropped to the ground and put his hands to his face. The rest of the men looked down on their leader and back and forth at each other.

Ames was stunned by Salim's reaction. "Hey, hey," he said straightening up and letting go of his pants. "It can't be that bad. Just because that ratty gun fell apart, doesn't mean you should. Look around. Your men aren't falling apart." Ames looked at the other six men. All were looking downcast and shuffling their feet. Two of them were studiously studying the mountains. One had dropped his ancient rifle. "Then again, maybe they are."

Salim looked up at Ames, his face tear streaked, showing clean spots through the dirt. "Who are you," he hissed.

"Oh," said Ames. "I'm Blond, Ames Blond."

Salim's face lit up and he pushed himself back to his feet. "Oh, you are British. We have worked with British before. Many years ago. They will help us." He said something to his men, who started smiling and patting each other on the back. The one who had dropped his rifle picked it back up. All were smiling again.

"Hold on there," Ames interrupted. "I'm not British, I'm an American. You're thinking of that other guy."

"But you are not blond," stuttered Salim.

Ames grew angry. "Don't go there! Just don't go there! Listen you PRICKs, if you untie me I can help you."

Salim muttered something and waved his hand toward Ames. One of his men came over and, using an ornate curved dagger, cut the ropes holding Ames' hands. As the ropes dropped away he rubbed his wrists and looked around. "Where is the man I was with?" he asked.

Salim waved his hand down the mountain. "You mean Abdel? He went to Irbil. He knows our mission and we let him go."

"You mean Abdel and the people in his village support you?"

Salim gave a derisive laugh. "No they do not. They just know we are out here, trying to gain their independence. They have their own ideas of how to rebel against the Satan in Baghdad. No, they do not support us." He shook his head sadly. "They give money to that nutcase Al Raini, but not to honest freedom fighters."

Ames looked at Salim and then turned his head and slowly surveyed the motley group of men. They were dressed in torn and dirty robes with turbans that had needed an oil change at least a year ago. Their weapons ranged from Salim's dysfunctional pistol to a rusty AK-47 and an ancient single barrel shotgun. One man was even carrying an old muzzle-loader. It was beautifully engraved and cared for, but was as useful in modern combat as a sack of rocks.

"You know about Al Raini?" Ames asked eagerly looking back at Salim. "Do you know where he is?"

Salim shook his head. "Sadly I do not. If I did I would get my share of the collection from the villages. He owes us, the dog." Salim spat on the ground. Although they had no idea what was being said, the other six spit too. One man went so far as to gurgle in his throat and hawk up a really green and nasty looking loogie."

Ames walked over and put his hand on Salim's shoulder. "Is there somewhere we can talk?" he asked glancing at the other six.

At that moment it began to rain again.

Motioning Ames to follow, Salim and his band dashed to the north through the rain. Within minutes the rain had turned into a deluge with huge drops of water slamming into their heads and bodies. Their clothing became sodden and heavy, dragging them down as they ran.

The ground turned to mud almost instantly, their footsteps "shlopping" with each step. While the Arabs had turbans to cover their heads, Ames' was bare and each raindrop felt like a lead ball striking him. The impacts were making Ames punchy and soon he was staggering, barely making headway in the onslaught. To make matters worse visibility had dropped to a mere few feet.

Salim looked back and saw Ames lagging. He made a motion and two of the larger PRICKs grabbed Ames under the arms and drew him along, supporting his weight and helping him walk.

It seemed like forever, but was probably just over a mile before an overused tent appeared out of the haze. The party dashed in out of the rain and dropped to the sodden carpets. While the fabric of the tent kept out much of the water, holes here and there allowed continuous streams that poured onto the rugs. Ames looked up and could see the tent vibrating from the pounding rain.

"I thought it didn't rain here much," he said to the ceiling. "This is the second hard rain today. Did you guys do something to annoy Allah?"

"This is very not right," he heard a voice that sounded like Salim. "It does not rain like this. This is very wrong." Ames could hear the others in the group muttering in Arabic.

Ames sat up and looked around. The tent was a faded green with various colored patches here and there. Some of the patches were leaking, allowing water to drip on the rugs. The rugs were old and faded as well. There was no telling what the original colors or designs had been. In one corner, which seemed to be out of the water, was a pile of clothing and bags. A coffee urn sat on a tripod over a circle of stones in the center of the tent where the area was clear of rugs. The wood in the fire circle was sodden and lying a pool of water.

Salim stood and started rummaging through the bags in the corner. He looked over at Ames while holding a bag. "You want some food? I have some food here." His hand dipped into the bag and came out with something that vaguely resembled a piece of mystery meat. He walked over and offered it to Ames.

The meat had a slightly rancid smell. Ames put up his hands and said, "No thank you, I have some here." He reached down to his waist, but found the packet that Abdel had given him was gone. "Well, phooey, that figures," he muttered.

115

Looking up at Salim he asked, "Do you have any dates or fruit or something? I don't think I could handle meat right now."

Salim nodded and smiled showing his yellow teeth, and produced a bag of dates and some canned peaches. He dug out a rusty jackknife and proceeded to open the can, then passed it to Ames.

While Ames was drinking the sweet juice and chewing on the sliced fruit, Salim dug into the pile some more. He produced a dingy brown robe and a length of dull gray cloth. "He handed them to Ames. "These are not as fine as yours, but they are dry. You will feel better in dry clothes."

With some trepidation Ames stripped off his soggy pants and shirt and pulled the robe over his head. The dry cloth felt good until something bit him. Looking down at the tented garment he realized that it was already inhabited. He started to pull it off when Salim stopped him.

"Better to be bitten a little than to be sick a lot." He held up the gray cloth and showed Ames how to wind it around his head to create a turban. It made the agents head warm, but it was also infested. He scratched his head through the cloth.

One of the PRICKs had dug the wet wood and water out of the fire circle and laid a base of dry wood. He pulled out a Bic lighter and started the wood burning. Soon the tent was filled with wood smoke making Ames cough. He moved closer to the entrance for some fresh air. The rain was still coming down hard.

Another of the rebels had filled the coffee pot with rainwater and grounds. It now sat on the tripod. Within minutes it was steaming. Salim produced cups, a can of condensed milk and a bag of sugar. Carefully he filled each cup with sugar and milk and added a little coffee as flavoring, and then passed them around. Ames gratefully took a cup of the steaming beverage and sipped at it. It was so thick and sweet, and heavy with caffeine it gave him an instant headache, but the heat felt good.

As the water in the wood burned off the smoke began to clear and the tent started to warm up. Ames sat quietly sipping at the coffee while listening to the Kurds chatter in Arabic. He was concerned that he was stuck in the middle of the mountains of nowhere with information that might be vital to his country. He needed to get out of this country.

He looked over at the head PRICK. "Salim, I need to get to Irbil. Can you take me there?"

The Arab thought about that for a moment. "No, I cannot take you there. We are thought to be bad people and the government would like to get rid of us. No, you will stay here. You can be a rebel like we are."

Ames thought that was a very bad idea. "I'm sorry Salim, but I must get to Irbil. There is Marine garrison there that can help me get back to the United States. I'm very sure that if we talk to them they will help you, especially if you tell them that you have been fighting against Saddam and want to continue the fight against the insurgents and bandits. And don't forget, Saddam is gone."

"Where did the monster go?" asked Salim

"Well," said Ames. "They had a trial in Baghdad a while ago, but they found there was not enough evidence of corruption or mass murder. They leaked the story that he had been hanged but they had to let him go. I understand he is now living in a condo in the Bahamas."

Salim stared at Ames for a minute and then began talking to the rest of the group. The discussion seemed to take forever and Ames was sure they were talking about girls or cars or something, or maybe how to keep him here.

Eventually the steady drone of the strange language and the heat of the coffee began to affect him and he found his eyes drooping. He felt warm and snug in the dry clothes beside the fire and he was becoming somewhat inured to the insects. Just as he started to fall over in sleep, Salim poked him in the arm.

"We have decided to take you to Irbil, but you must promise us that the Marines will not put us in cages or send us to Canada."

"I think you mean Cuba. They've been sending insurgents to Cuba."

"Canada, Cuba, whatever," said Salim. "As long as they don't send us anywhere."

"I promise," mumbled Ames as he drifted into sleep.

CHAPTER THIRTEEN

The Marine base at Irbil was situated on a plain just to the northwest of the city. It was surrounded by two rows of three high concertina wire and rows of tanglefoot – barbed wire set six inches off the ground and spread in a complex pattern out fifty feet from the concertina. Fighting positions had been dug along the wire and reinforced with sand bags. Towers on tall stilt-like legs with observers and machine guns were spaced along the perimeter. Large concrete barriers, similar to the things used in road work and called Jersey barriers, created a second, inner barrier around the base.

The perimeter itself enclosed a helicopter pad with twelve Blackhawk helicopters, a jet pad with three AV-8B Harriers and a tank and truck park with armored vehicles, including a number of M-1 Abrams tanks and a large group of Bradley Fighting vehicles. There were also some odd-looking things with huge tires called LAV's. A Battery of 155 artillery and smaller 105's were ranged to the north and west of the perimeter.

The current residents of the base were the 2nd battalion of the 8th Marine Regiment plus support units of artillery and aviation. The massed firepower of this small unit was sufficient to decimate most small countries. The other battalions of the regiment were in Mosul and Fallujah to the north and east of Baghdad.

Five hard looking young men in oddly camouflaged tan uniforms with flak jackets, helmets and M-4 rifles manned the single road into the base. A squad automatic weapon poked its nose from a fighting position near the gate and a boxy looking HMMWV with a rear mounted M240 machine gun acted as a sentry post.

When Ames and his rag-tag group of Kurds arrived at the gate, the hard young men waved them to a halt fifty feet from the entrance. The barrels of both machine guns tracked their movement.

Holding his hands where the Marines could see them Ames slowly walked toward the gate. The Marine's rifles were pointed toward the ground but held so they could be rapidly trained and fired if things went south.

One of the guards, a Corporal, walked forward a bit and met Ames. "What do you want?" he asked, not expecting an answer. These looked like a bunch of raggedy A-rabs and probably did not speak English. More than likely they were looking for a free handout. He was surprised when the A-rab spoke.

"I'm an American," said Ames, unconsciously scratching at his robe. "I need to see your commanding officer."

The guard studied Ames for a moment. Ames was dressed in the robe with a turban that had been given to him by Salim to replace the suit that had rapidly disintegrated in the heat and the rain. With his dark hair, seven-day growth of beard and the ratty looking clothes, someone would be hard pressed to tell that Ames was not one of the tribesmen wandering around Irbil.

The guard looked Ames over and decided that, although his English seemed to be pretty good, allowing this Arab and his group into the base might not be a good idea. Insurgents and terrorists still caused problems in the region. Besides, the kitchen scraps from breakfast were gone.

"You can speak to the Kurdish liaison officer in Irbil," said the guard, pointing back down the road. "Go into town and one of the citizens can direct you there. We don't have anyone here who can help you."

"I'm not an Arab," replied Ames. "I'm an American. I've been with these Kurdish tribesmen for the last week. I need to speak to your commanding officer."

"Do you have any identification, sir?" asked the Marine.

"No, my paperwork pretty much disintegrated in the rain. I'm a DORK working with ASSHOLs out of Washington."

The Corporal looked skeptical. "I don't care what kind of asshole you are or whether you're a nerd or a dork or a

121

geek. You don't get on the base. Go into town and find the liaison officer." He motioned at the distance horizon with his rifle barrel.

"Look, Corporal," said Ames with exasperation. "I'm Blond, Ames Blond with the Department of Reconnaissance and Knowledge. I'm an agent for the United States government."

"Yeah, right," said the Corporal with a sneer. "And I'm with SMERSH. If you're going to pretend to be that guy at least get the country right. He's British and the Brit's have a base in Mosul. Now why don't you walk your butt up there and see if they buy into your crap."

Ames rolled his eyes, losing his temper. "Look, dumby, I didn't say I was a British agent, I said I was Blond, you know, like the hair color. I'm Blond, Ames Blond!"

"Real smart there, butthole," responded the Corporal. "Check your dictionary. Blond means light hair. Yours is dark. You should be calling yourself brunette. Now get the heck out of here!"

Ames started to reply, but the Marine had raised his rifle so the barrel pointed in Ames' general direction. The barrels of the machine guns moved perceptibly.

With a disgusted sound Ames walked back toward the small group of Kurds. "They won't let us in. We have to go into Irbil and find the office that deals with freedom fighters," Ames said as diplomatically as possible.

Salim stared at Ames. "They will not help us? You said they would help! Now we have to go to Irbil and deal with bureaucrats? What kind of help is this?"

"No, no," Ames interrupted. "They will help, just not this group. We have to talk to different people. These are fighters. We need to deal with the talkers."

"Ah, I see," said Salim rolling his eyes upward. "We must deal with the panty waists. That is always hard. They do not understand those on the end of the gun. Always they want to spend more on desks and paper than on bullets. I do not want to spend the next two weeks filing out papers, standing in line and being told to come back next week. It could take months!"

"Sorry, but you've just discovered one of the problems with a democratic bureaucracy. Let's head for Irbil and the fat-bottoms."

The group turned and headed down the road toward Irbil. The Corporal watched them go with a smirk on his face. "Bunch of retarded ragheads," he muttered as he turned and walked back to the gate.

As they walked Salim said to Ames, "What about you? Why did they not let you in? I thought you an important American?"

"Apparently not important enough, and besides, do I look like an American right now?"

Salim looked Ames over. "No, you look like a PRICK," he said with a smile. "Like the same as us." Ames smiled back and they continued their weary way toward the city.

Five minutes later a HMMWV rolled up to the perimeter entrance and a Marine with a black bar on his collar points stepped out. The Corporal walked over to the vehicle and touched a finger to his helmet. "Afternoon, sir. Not much going on out here."

The Lieutenant returned the gesture and passed a sheet of paper to the Corporal. He said, "I need to update your general orders. We have a convoy coming in around two o'clock with POL and supplies. Make sure you check the trucks before they come in."

"All right, sir," said the Corporal, setting his rifle butt on the ground and leaning on the barrel. "We always check them anyways."

"And there is an advisory in your orders. It seems Washington has lost one of their spies. An agent by the name of Blond was last reported on a flight out of Baghdad and has been missing for seven or eight days. They think the insurgents might have taken him. We need to keep a look out for him."

The Corporal got a strange look on his face. "Ah, sir, did they say what this guy looked like?"

The Lieutenant consulted the paper. "His description is dark hair about six feet tall at around one hundred eighty pounds. White guy. He gets real annoyed about his name. I'm not sure why, but that's in the description." He looked up at the Corporal. "Why? Does that sound familiar?"

"Sorry, sir. I think I just ran him off."

"What!" yelped the officer in amazement.

"Well, sir. He was dressed in one of them robes and a dirty towel. He looked just like one of them ragheads. He said he was that British secret agent, you know, from the movies. I laughed at him and sent him to the British up in

Mosul. Or maybe he went to the liaison officer in Irbil. He was with a bunch of them camel jockeys."

"Corporal," said the Lieutenant in a low voice. "These people are not ragheads. They are our respected allies. This is their country, not ours and you will speak to them and about them with respect. Do you understand me? Or do you need to spend the next thirty days cleaning pots in the scullery?"

"Uh, sorry, sir," stammered the Corporal bringing his rifle to port arms and coming to attention. "I'll watch my mouth from now on. Um, sir, we don't have a scullery. We get them meal pack things and paper plates."

"So I'll put your butt on everlasting latrine duty. And you darn well better watch that mouth," said the Lieutenant as he turned and ran to his HMMWV. He grabbed the microphone to the radio and started talking.

* * * * * * * * *

Abu turned the rheostat back down to zero and looked over at Sidi. "Stupid thing is still putting out too much power. At this rate Allah is going to bring back Noah just to unscrew the country. Have that Libyan idiot, Mumar or whatever the heck his name is, take another look at the ovulator control circuit. For some reason I have no control over the output."

Behind them there was a heavy whirring sound as the huge disk began to descend from the opening in the mountain. The scissor-like legs slowly closed in on themselves bringing the disk down to the level of the cave. Suddenly there was a grinding sound and the disk stopped halfway down.

A man in a white coat ran over to the legs and began beating them with a sledgehammer. A heavy clanking sound filled the cave. The grinding stopped and the legs moved downward a few feet, then stopped again. The man whacked at the legs some more until they started moving again.

Abu watched these antics until the disk came to a stop in the down position. He waved his hand at the man in white, who ran over to stand in front of the Arab genius. "I hate to ask a stupid question," Abu said to the man. "But why are you smacking the hell out of my creation with a sledgehammer?"

The worker leaned on the hammer, his breath going in and out in heavy rasps, and responded, "The legs became bound up and I had to hit them to get them moving again, oh great one."

"Cut the oh great one bull. Have you ever heard of something called grease? You put it on metal parts so they don't bind up. It lubricates the metal parts so they move smoothly across each other."

The man in white shook his head up and down. "Yes, master. I have heard of grease."

Abu grabbed the man by his lapels and shook him, making the hammer fall to the floor. "Then why the heck aren't you using it you retarded brother of a brain dead monkey?" Abu yelled. "Are you afraid to get your hands dirty or is it more fun to beat the crap out of things?

Where the heck did you get your engineering degree, through some bloody Alabama diploma mill?"

Abu dropped the cowering engineer and turned to Sidi. "Put this screwball on the slop bucket patrol for a few days. Maybe he can keep from screwing that up. And find out what else around here is totally for crap and fix it!"

At that moment a telephone rang in the control room. Sidi rushed in and grabbed it, thankful to be away from Abu when he was in one of his moods. He listened for a moment and called to Abu.

Abu grabbed the handset. "What?" he yelled, then backed off. "Oh, sorry Samir. I thought it was one of those idiots from accounting again. They've been bothering me all day."

Sidi leaned against the doorframe trying to listen to both sides of the conversation. Faintly he could hear the other end. "What the heck are you doing, Raini?" An angry voice said. "Are you trying to drown everyone in the Middle East? You've got enough water to fill the Hoover dam three times over!"

"Settle down, Samir," Abu said waggling his hand in the air. "These are just tests. We'll have the problem straightened out in the next few days. After that we start working on focus."

"Focus? You need to focus on getting your act together," said Samir. "Our investors are getting just a tad worried that maybe they've backed a loser."

"Loser? Loser!" yelled Abu. "You self righteous pimple on a snakes fanny! No one else in the world had the smarts to figure this out and you call me a loser! You can take you're investors and shove them up a camels butt! I'm in charge of Al Shamute. I run this outfit, not that doofuss bunch of coupon clippers you call investors!"

"Settle down, Abu. You just need to get control of things. And cussing me out doesn't help things. And don't forget. I am in command of NERDS. You need us as much as we need you."

"Right, and I can rethink this whole deal if I need to. There are others out there who would be more than happy for a piece of this."

"All right, all right," said Samir in a placating voice. "I'll take care of the investors. You just get control of things over there. At least turn the water down a little before the whole area floats into the Arabian Sea."

"Yeah, yeah, I'll take care of it," Abu stated in a more mollified way. "Just keep your eye on things in the next few days. We're making great strides, very great strides."

"Okay, Abu. I'll check back in a couple of days." The line went dead.

Abu sighed as he replaced the phone. He looked at Sidi. "I guess you heard." Sidi nodded.

"What I want you to do is let the answering machine take the calls from now on. Don't answer the phone. If for some reason somebody wasn't paying attention and does answer, instruct the staff to say I'm on vacation in Alaska or I had to run out to the store for a bottle of goat milk or something. Have them take a number and I'll call back."

"When will you be back from Alaska?" asked Sidi with a pencil poised over his notebook.

"I'm not going to Alaska you twit," stated Abu while smacking his head with his hand. His turban fell off.

"When will you call back then?" Sidi asked, making chicken scratches on the notepad.

"Never you moron!" shouted Abu, knocking the notebook onto the floor and grabbing his turban. "The whole point is to get them off our back until we perfect the process!"

"What if we never perfect it?" asked Sidi with trepidation, poking at his notebook with a sandal-covered toe.

"Then I guess we never talk to them again," said Abu with a bright smile. "I don't think that would bother me too much, now would it?"

CHAPTER FOURTEEN

Ames, Salim and the ragged band of PRICKS trudged down the road toward Irbil. Inwardly Ames was fuming at the stupidity of the Marine. All the dumb son of a gun had to do was call the officer of the day and they could have straightened things out. A single phone call! But nooo! Corporal Jarhead had to be a hard butt. Now they were wandering down the road through the dust under the hot sun, looking for someone who would believe him and get him back to Washington.

Maybe if he could find a place for a shower and a shave, some human clothes to slip into, a tie – something from Brooks Brothers, possibly a manicure and pedicure, a hair cut with styling, a good butt wiping, some baby powder and something for the dysentery, he could possibly, maybe, get somebody to believe he was an American agent.

Back at the tent, while they waited for the rain to stop, Ames told Salim about the US led coalition that had forced Saddam from power and set up a Democratic government in Baghdad. Salim was very happy to learn that the Kurds had been given representation and a voice in the new government. It saddened him to learn that Saddam's trial had gone badly and the former president for life would end up in the Bahamas living his life out in a condominium with other retired oldsters. Apparently some Federal judge had also decided that Saddam was eligible for Social Security and Medicare Parts A and B with the prescription drug option. There was little evidence against him since most of the witnesses were dead, and the rest of the evidence was circumstantial and anecdotal.

The French judge in the case before the international court had decided there was insufficient evidence to prosecute, so Saddam headed for the Atlantic island group with a stop at his bank in Switzerland. There had been talk of giving the ex-dictator a seat on the board of something called AIG, with possibly a shot at the chairmanship. That had fallen through when AIG received a multi-billion dollar stimulus grant from the US government and decided it did not need Saddam's infusion of cash.

Now the lawyers and the news media were talking about a possible lawsuit against the coalition, with the United States as the prime defendant, for unlawful imprisonment, destruction of personal property and violation of religious freedoms. Since all the presidential palaces, wetlands and most of the arable farm land was in Saddam's name, his lawyers felt he had a legitimate claim to those properties, this despite the fact that the lands comprised over eighty percent of Iraq. A Canadian court had offered to sit for the case.

Salim wanted to take his group on a Jihad to the Bahamas or maybe to Canada, but Ames talked him out of it. It might be hard to get at Saddam. Apparently the retired president had stipulated that the condo have a reinforced bunker built under the golf course whiskey bar and a spider hole set in the ground near the ninth hole near the pin. There was also the problem of the lawyers. The Kurds had been named in the lawsuit. Apparently the Kurds were guilty of impeding lawful commerce and violating areas designated for weapons testing. There was also a charge of littering involved because of the corpses left strewn around from some sort of chemical test.

The rain lasted for almost twenty-four hours, causing streams and rivers to over-flow. Ames did not know how the rest of the country was fairing, but the water threatened to topple their rude shelter. The constant drips through the tent made sleeping difficult. The men, including Ames, had spent the time eating rancid goat, drinking really foul coffee and playing Acey-Ducey for camel patties. Ames came out ahead, but wasn't sure if he liked the honor. It would be difficult to exchange camel dung on the world money market. And it would be really difficult to carry the patties in the rain.

The following day they had set out for Irbil, slogging their way along the muddy track. At points where the trail dipped down steep crags, they had made better time by sliding down the hill. The tribesman thought it was fun, but it got everyone muddy and dirty as heck. When they could, they washed off in mountain streams or just stood still in the rain until the crud washed off.

This part of Iraq was comprised of very rugged mountains forming a border with Iran. The ground was very rocky, covered with dark patches of dirt and scrub grass and stunted trees. In their walk they passed a number of small villages all modeled similar to As'al Quarba. The houses and buildings were of pressed mud brick or concrete block with little ornamentation. Camels and goats abounded and the resultant piles all over the place. Ames began to understand the feet problem.

Where crops were being grown, the plants were stunted from poor soil and too little water, although there were some small indications that the recent rains were improving the crops somewhat. The leaves seemed to be greener and the stems a little stronger, or so Salim said.

When they could they begged food and supplies from the villagers. Some had an affinity for the PRICK's cause; others chased them away with thrown stones. In those cases of affinity they were invited in to share a meal. When this happened Salim's group would chatter away with the villagers while Ames was pretty much ignored.

After one session where this happened Ames asked why he was not included and Salim said, "I do not want anyone to know that we are traveling with an American. Some of the villagers do not like Americans because they feel that the United States abandoned them after the Gulf War. So I tell them you are a village idiot who was thrown out of his village. I tell them that we were good enough to take you in and take care of you. That is one of the tenets of Islam. It also helps us get more food, so keep your mouth shut and don't act too bright."

As the sun grew warmer, the mud on the ground turned to steam and the humidity reached over a thousand percent. The sweat dripped off Ames and created puddles in his underwear. He started to get jock rash from the wetness and constant movement, until it was almost impossible to walk. Every time his thighs rubbed together it felt like a saw blade rubbing across raw meat. He asked Salim how he handled the problem, whereupon the Kurd raised his robe and showed him. No underwear.

Ames quickly turned his head away and quietly retched. Later he pretended to needed to take a leak and wandered off to get rid of his now soaked and soiled underclothes. When he came back Salim handed him some goat cheese and told him it would help the rash.

Ames turned around, carefully raised his robe and rubbed the cheese into his groin.

When he turned back he looked on the astonished faces of the Kurds. Salim quietly told him, "You were supposed to eat the cheese."

Surprisingly the cheese helped.

Four days and four more thunderstorms later they had approached the Marine base at Irbil. Fortunately, or not, the last day had been rain free and the ground had dried out to its normal dusty condition.

Now Ames had to reconsider their situation. He was dressed in a mud and dirt spattered robe, wearing a turban with more creatures than the San Diego zoo. His nose had stopped working sometime in the past three days. He needed a shave and bath very badly. His crotch was sore, the cheese was starting to stink and his butt was itching badly. He was determined that toilet paper would be introduced into the Middle East sometime in his lifetime.

The first buildings of Irbil were just coming into sight when a Blackhawk helicopter roared over so close to the ground that the blades kicked the dust into an almost impenetrable wall. Ames and the Kurds threw their hands over their faces and started coughing. They doubled over and hid their faces in their robes when the roar of engines got louder and the big machine settled to the ground.

A group of Marines leaped from the chopper and spread out in a defensive perimeter, their guns pointed at unseen enemies, although there wasn't a chance in twenty of seeing anybody through the dust. A tall Marine Major jumped out of the helicopter and ran toward the group of Arabs as another Blackhawk settled to the ground. "Which one of you is Blond?" yelled the Marine, looking at the group of dark haired people.

Salim looked over his group and yelled, "None of us are blond, we are all brunettes."

The officer smacked his helmet with a hand, "No, which one of you is named Blond?"

Ames raised his hand and the Marine grabbed him by the shoulder. "Come on, sir. There was a mistake at the gate. We need to get you back to the base." He started pulling Ames toward the bird. Then he got a strange look on his face, his nose twitched, he dropped his arm and he backed off a couple of steps.

Ames pulled back as well. "What about them?" he asked pointing at the Kurds.

"They can go on to the Arab liaison in Irbil," yelled the Marine over the roar of the helicopters, waving his hand in front of his face. "And what the hell is that smell?"

"The smell is probably me and I can't go with you until they are taken care of. I promised them help," Ames yelled back.

"Don't worry, sir. They'll be well taken care of."

"Then give them a ride into Irbil. They've helped me out a lot over the last few days and deserve a reward."

"I can't do that, sir," the Major yelled. "I have orders only for you."

Ames considered it for a moment, and then yelled back. "You're going to have a problem then. I don't go with you unless you take care of those guys."

The Major stared at Ames before making up his mind. He ran over to the second helicopter and grabbed one of the Marines in a flight helmet and spoke to him. There seemed to be a mild disagreement with much hand waving and yelling. Finally the second Marine slammed his hand into the side of the helicopter.

The Major ran back to Ames while the other Marine ran over to Salim.

"That chopper is going to take them on in to Irbil," the Major hollered taking the agents arm. "Is that okay with you, sir?"

Ames nodded and pulled his arm away again and moved over to Salim. "I have to go with these men," he said. "You're to go with the Marines on that helicopter. They have promised me you guys will be taken care of. I'll check back and make sure they kept their word."

Salim looked at the helicopter with a troubled expression. Looking back at Ames he asked, "Are you sure that thing is safe? I know you Americans ride around in them but you guys are nuts anyway."

Ames laughed. "No problem Salim. It's as safe as a camel in heat. You can ride it but be careful trusting it behind your back."

Salim looked at Ames for a moment then smiled and nodded. "Go with God, my friend," said the little Kurd. "It is his will that we have helped. You will always remain our friend." He held out his hand to Ames.

Ames grasped the hand and, in a choked voice, said, "You go with God also, my friend. Salaam alaykim, sadikie." He shook hands with each of the rebels before turning back to the tall Marine. "Okay, General, let's go."

As they climbed into the chopper, the Marine said, "I'm only a Major, not a General."

"Whatever," said Ames as he leaned back against the chopper wall and closed his eyes against the dust. He felt a tap on his shoulder and opened his eyes back up. The

Major was handing him a pair of earphones. Ames slipped them onto his head as he watched Salim and his six PRICKs climb aboard the other Blackhawk. He waved and the Kurds waved back.

With a roar the machine leaped into the air leaving Ames' stomach on the ground.

He heard static through the headphones and then a voice. "Sir, could you sit over there?" The copilot, a Captain, was pointing at a lone seat in the rear of the chopper. The rest of the assault force was crammed into the forward seats, some sitting on each other's laps.

Ames pulled the boom microphone in front of this mouth. "Why back here?" he asked as he slid into the seat.

"Sir," said the Captain. "I'm sorry, but your butt stinks. What the heck have you been doing, rolling in camel crap?"

"It's a long story," said the agent as he sat in the rear seat, leaned back and closed his eyes again. For the first time in weeks he felt relaxed. This lasted all of ten seconds until the friends in his robe started having lunch. Apparently the vibration of the helicopter upset them and Ames had to start scratching beard, head and other body parts. With a muttered, "Crap", he grabbed the turban and threw it out the door.

Despite the bug bites Ames started nodding off and was almost asleep as the helicopter came to a landing inside the Marine compound. As Ames dropped out the door the Marines ducked out through the door on the other side leaving the agent standing alone by the chopper as the engine whined down to a stop.

The pilot and crew chief jumped down, giving Ames a dirty look before they walked past the aircraft and toward a group of tents and Conex boxes away from the field.

A HMMWV pulled up near the helicopter and a young Lance Corporal and an even younger looking second Lieutenant got out. "Are you Mister Blond?" asked the officer.

"Yeah, I'm him," said Ames as he walked over to the Hummer.

"I'm here to take you to the CP. Climb in." He opened the door to the vehicle.

As Ames passed the Corporal, the Corporal reared back and held his nose. "Sir," he called. "Begging you pardon, but that ain't getting in my vehicle!"

The officer looked at the Marine and started to say, "What are you talking . . ." At that moment Ames started to get in the machine. The Lieutenant backed up and said, "Whoa there, sir. I think it might be a better idea if we walked. It could take a week to fumigate that Humvee and we might need it."

Ames scratched his beard and grinned. "No problem LT. Wouldn't want to cause the loss of the war for the loss of a camel. Lead the way."

CHAPTER FIFTEEN

Lieutenant Colonel Horatio Ezekiel Round, better known as "HE", commanded the 2nd battalion of the 8th Marine Regiment and was responsible for the training and deployment of his Marines and attached air and supply assets according to doctrine set down by the Department of Defense and Coalition Forces Command. He considered his Marines to be the best trained and toughest in the Corps, which, of course, made them the best in the world. If the United States Marines were the best fighting force in the world, and his were the best of the Marines, then God help anyone who got in their way.

H. E. Round had started as a boot Lieutenant during Desert Storm when he was a platoon leader with the 26th Marine Expeditionary Unit where he earned an impressive array of chest hardware including a Silver Star, a Bronze Star, and a Purple Heart amongst other campaign and service medals. During subsequent actions in the Philippines, Central America and Afghanistan he had added another Silver Star, a second Purple Heart and a Navy Cross, all of which helped his rise to Colonel in the best trained fighting force in the world.

Now he sat in his office, which was a fancy title for a blocked off area of a Base-X command tent. The tent itself was an off olive green on the outside with white canvas walls inside. The office contained a table with a two laptop computers on it, three chairs commandeered from a burnt out house and a small stand with a coffee maker on it. Light was provided by fluorescent strung on either side of the tents ridgepole. A number of map boards lined one wall and a generator could be heard chugging away somewhere outside the tent.

At the moment the sides of the tent were rolled up and only the side netting was down, so the space seemed bright and open, as well as hot and dusty. A fan tried its best to cool things off, but only succeeded in moving the dust around. Behind the desk crossed flags, the American standard and the regimental colors, stirred slightly in the diminutive breeze.

In front of him stood a civilian, in a nasty looking robe and with an aroma that would have knocked out a camel, who professed to be an agent for some ultra-secret government agency. The individual smelled of rancid cheese and goat droppings and for some reason he kept scratching his crotch and butt. As the Colonel watched

Ames, something small and dark wandered out from under the greasy hair on his forehead, crossed the forehead and ducked into the hair by the left ear. No way was this person going to sit in one of his chairs.

"First off I apologize for the air conditioning in here. The thing is on the fritz and as it stands with your aroma I'm grateful for that. Look, Mister Blond," said the Colonel in a gruff voice that matched his muscular bulk. "I have a message here that says that I should try and locate you. Once I find you I am to notify Washington. It doesn't say a damn thing about giving you one of my helicopters, a pilot and a security force to get you to Baghdad. I have sent the message that you have been found and now we wait for a response."

"But, sir," replied Ames. "I really need to get to Washington. I am tracking an international terrorist and I need to get the information to my office."

"Let me tell you how it is," said Round as he stood up and moved around to the front of the desk. He leaned back and sat on the table with one foot on the floor. "You match the description of Blond - vaguely. I have no idea who you really are and I am damn sure not letting you run around loose on my base. For all I know you could be a terrorist who has killed Blond and taken his place. For now you're under close supervision until I get confirmation of your identity."

Blond crossed his arms and stared at the Colonel, then uncrossed them and reached around to give his bottom a scratch. "What exactly does close supervision mean?"

"It means that you get to travel with an armed guard with orders to shoot your butt if you do something odd. If you are Ames and you turn into cold meat, I get to write a report describing my grievous error. If you're not and I get my base blown up, then I write a report and a bunch of letters to wives and mothers. I would rather write the former and not the latter."

"So what happens now?" Asked Ames, still scratching his bottom, his fingers seeming to dig a hole into his nether region.

"First we get your finger prints and FAX them to Washington. Second the guard takes you out and hoses your down, cleans the freaking bugs off you and puts you into some clean clothes. My God man, I've heard of going native, but didn't you go just a little overboard? Even Lawrence of Arabia took baths."

Ames hung his head as the Colonel yelled at him. "But we've been on the road for a week and it's been raining and dirty and I had a rash and then Salim offered me the goat cheese and how was I supposed to know I was supposed to eat it and, and." And he ran out of breath.

"You sound like one of my troops trying to get his butt out of a crack. Secret agent, my aunt's fanny. Sergeant!" He bellowed the last and a Marine in body armor carrying an M-4 pushed through the door, a worried look on his face.

Pointing at the agent the Colonel said, "Take this piece of crap over to G-2 and get him finger printed and then get him a shower and some clean clothes. Better yet get him the shower first. I'm not having my operations center smelling like a New Jersey dump. From there, go to Doc's tent and have the corpsmen check him and see if they can do something about those bugs."

"Aye, aye, sir," said the Sergeant, grabbing Ames by the arm. He quickly dropped it and stepped back two paces. With a vague motion at the tent flap he said. "If you'd go through there sir, we'll get you started."

"Oh, and Sergeant," called the Colonel, "Keep a close watch on this character. If he tries anything, shoot him, but try not to kill him. He may actually be important to someone."

"Aye, aye, sir," responded the NCO, following Ames from the tent.

The Colonel looked at the closing door and muttered, "Why did that twit have to show up in my command?"

Ames and his newfound friend, a Sergeant Jenkins, were making use of the facilities at the enlisted shower point. This was comprised of a tent with a floor of rubber mats on top of pallets. Poles with four showerheads were spaced in two rows along the mats. The poles connected to hoses that ran out of tent. Somewhere behind the tent a ten thousand gallon tank trailer was connected to a pump and water heater unit. At the moment Ames was making liberal use of a borrowed bar of soap while standing under the hot water. His "friend" was standing near the tent entrance holding his rifle with the barrel in Ames' general direction.

Ames had already scrubbed his hair until his head felt raw, but clean. At present he was scrubbing and scratching at the cheese on his groin. For some reason the cheese was being very difficult about being removed. It clung in gobs to his hair and he had to work hard to get it loose.

The Sergeant watched him scrub for about five minutes and finally asked, "What the hell have you got there that you've got to scrub your groin so hard? You got the crabs or something?"

"Yes and no," snapped Ames. "I've got goat cheese on my groin."

"Goat cheese? What the heck, is that some kind of religious thing?"

"No, I had a rash and rubbed the cheese on it to ease the pain."

The Sergeant scratched his head under the helmet. "You ever heard of aspirin or Tylenol or maybe some lotion?"

"An Arab," replied Ames, still scrubbing. "He told me to use the cheese. Well, actually he told me to eat the cheese, but only after I had already smeared it on. Never mind, it's a long story."

"I'll bet it is. Can I give you some advice?" Ames nodded. "Try shaving the hair off. It will take the cheese off and the fur will grow back. Might make your wiener less sore. Just be careful with the blade or you could end up a soprano."

Fifteen minutes later Ames buttoned the last button on the BDU's the Sergeant had pulled for him from the supply tent. These were green and brown as opposed to the white and tan that the Marines were wearing. Ames figured it was so they could tell who was who. He had gotten new socks, boots, underwear and the BDU's to replace the robe and turban that Salim had given him. The Sergeant had used a stick to pick up the old clothes and deposit them into a trashcan.

After he'd finished the shower a corpsman showed up with a bottle of RID to dispose of the insects. The medic had literally doused Ames in the chemicals and then made him shower again. Then the doc had left after handing Ames a second bottle of the stuff in case of a relapse.

Fully dressed and feeling a whole lot more human Ames looked at the Sergeant. "So what's next on the agenda? Do you lock me in a cage until the Colonel gets the word?"

The Sergeant shook his head. "Nah. The Colonel is just covering his rear until you get cleared. He knows as well as I do that you're an American. He just wanted to pull your chain for a while."

Ames thought that over for a moment. "Okay, let the Colonel get his jollies. What do we do now?"

"First we go over to G-2 and get you fingerprinted and have them sent to Washington. Then we go get something to eat. I imagine you've been eating that Arab stuff and would like something better in your stomach even if it's MREs."

G-2 was in another Base-X medium tent, but the agent did not get to see much. The tent opened into a small space that had a flap of canvas separating the small front section from the larger back. The small section had a two field tables set side by side. Sergeant Jenkins used a field phone to talk to someone on the other side of the flap.

A couple of minutes later another Sergeant came out from behind the flap and started the process of taking Ames' fingerprints. This involved putting one finger at a time on a small electronic pad. The pad would buzz for a moment and a dim light would flare. The Sergeant would then move another of the agent's fingers onto the pad. Within minutes all ten fingers had been done. The Sergeant had not said a word during the whole process.

They walked out of the operations tent and headed for the mess tent. Ames walked with visions of hamburgers and fries dancing in his head.

At the mess tent Ames was handed a paper plate and he took his place in the chow line. He walked in front of a steam table and a messman in whites dropped a piece of meat with a white topping onto his plate. Ames looked at it suspiciously. "What the heck is this?"

The troop smiled at Ames. "You're in luck. We're having the cook's specialty today, boiled goat with goat cheese topping. It's real good, better than the heat and serve combat rations."

Ames' face turned slightly green as he dropped the plate and ran from the tent.

The Sergeant caught up with him outside next to the garbage cans. Ames was loudly retching with his face stuck inside one of the cans. "Don't like military chow, huh," Jenkins said nonchalantly.

As Ames stood up and wiped his mouth, water droplets pattered down and started spotting the uniforms of the two men. The Sergeant looked at the sky, which had darkened considerably in the last few minutes. "Come on, we'll head over to the command tent before this gets any worse." He waved at Ames to hurry along.

The two men ran towards the headquarters tent as the rain increased in intensity. By the time they ran through the flap into the tent the rain was coming down at such a furious rate that it was almost impossible to see through. The two started shaking their arms and heads to get rid of the water.

"Hey, dumb! Watch it!" Shouted a Corporal hunched over a laptop, trying to protect whatever he was working on.

Seeing whom it was he stood up and said, "Hey, the Colonel's been looking for you. Wait right here and don't go anywhere." He walked over and parted the divider to the Colonel's office.

A Gunnery Sergeant stood at the netting looking at the falling water. He turned as the Corporal went by and looked at the two rain soaked men. "This is bullcrap. I been in this bullcrap country six times now and this is bullcrap. Effing Noah would need an ark to get through this rain. Bullcrap!"

The Sergeant looked at the Gunny. "This is my third tour and I ain't never seen rain like this. Where the eff is all this rain coming from?"

At that moment the Corporal rushed back in. "The Colonel wants you in his office right now. He doesn't look happy."

The Colonel was standing as they came into his office. "Ames, you're more trouble than your worth," he said in a loud and gruff voice. "Washington has confirmed you're who you say you are and I have to give you anything you want. And they stressed anything. As if I don't have enough problems."

Ames walked up to the desk. "I'm sorry about your problems, but I really need to get to Washington. If you could get me a chopper or something to Baghdad or Mosul so I can catch a plane, I'll get out of your hair."

"Listen to me son," the Colonel said, lowering his voice. "I've got raghead insurgents from every country in the Middle East causing hate and discontent and that's stretching my resources. This damn rain is causing problems you wouldn't believe. Streams and rivers are overflowing, causing massive flooding that's pushing people out of their homes and screwing up logistics. Not only do I have to fight off the foreign ragheads, I have to find a way to feed and take care of the refugees and the Iraqi government doesn't have the resources to help a hell of a lot. I'm running out of options, people and equipment and you want to steal one of my birds."

"Does this mean I don't get out of here?" asked Ames.

"Right now everything I've got is grounded and I'm getting calls for help from stranded people who will drown unless I get something into the air. The roads are so screwed up I can't get vehicles through. People are dying and there isn't a hell of a lot I can do to help, so don't plan on getting out of here for a while. I don't give a rats tail about you or Washington. You leave when I can get you out without compromising my mission."

"So, I'm stuck here," stated Ames.

"Until this rain stops and we get slightly caught up you're here for the duration. Sergeant, you get to nursemaid our boy for a little while longer. See that he gets someplace to sleep and some dry clothes. Oh, and the shoot order is rescinded. We can't have a valuable agent with holes in him."

CHAPTER SIXTEEN

Ames watched through the window of the airplane as the lights of Washington grew closer. In a few minutes the plane would land at National Airport and he would be home. Or at least he would be in the right city and country. In all probability his first stop would be DORK, not his apartment.

In Iraq it had been three days before he had been able to leave, and it rained twice more. Heavy downpours just like the ones he had already been through. The area was getting more and more soggy despite the sun and heat.

During that time Ames had helped the Colonel and his troops where he could, driving a vehicle, pulling people from the water or mud and generally trying not to get in the way. He ended each day feeling tired as hell but good about himself.

The evening meal the second night had made Ames' stay worthwhile, at least as far as his stomach was concerned. Hamburgers and fries! It did not seem to matter that they came from a military heat and serve tray, nor that the hamburger was like cardboard, the bun pasty or the fries greasy and hard. It wasn't made of goat.

Sergeant Jenkins watched in awe as Ames wolfed down three of the burgers with a half a gallon of milk, military, reconstituted and then pointed at the burger still sitting on the NCO's plate. "You going to eat that?"

When Jenkins shook his head the agent grabbed the burger and stuffed it into his mouth, munching happily with his cheeks looking like a chipmunk. "You know," the Sergeant put in, "If you want more all you have to do is go back through the line. They give you all you can eat."

Blond shook his head and muttered, "Mo anks. Ish fhlenty. I'm ettin shtuffet." Crumbs dribbled down his chin. He gulped loudly and took a swig of milk and swallowed hard. "After all that goat this stuff tastes really good." He belched loudly and slouched down in the chair while holding his stomach.

Unfortunately the side effect of the burgers was a horrible case of gas. Ames slept fine in the officer's tent, but the brass was forced to find different accommodations. Ames became the hit of the camp the next morning, at least with the troops, when the story got out that he had single handedly cleared the tent and gave the senior people a bad nights rest by giving off a green gas cloud that would have made Hiroshima seem small.

As he had climbed aboard the Blackhawk the third afternoon to leave, the Colonel had grudgingly taken his hand and told him he might not be such a candy-ass after all. The Colonel and Sergeant waved to him as the chopper lifted into the air. The enlisted troops waved and the officers cheered.

The flight to Baghdad in the helicopter was uneventful, except for the occasional ground fire that tinged off the fuselage. A clerk from the embassy met him at the terminal building and drove him to the embassy. The ambassador received him in his office and offered him a drink.

Ames responded, "Yes, sir. It's been a rough week and I deserve a drink. I'd like a vodka martini. Don't shake it, just stir the heck out of it."

The ambassador went to sideboard and began making the drink. "I'm extremely sorry about the inconvenience to your mission. I really should have been more help in getting you out of the country. United or ElAl would have provided better flights, but your boss said the budget was tight. Then again you would not have been able to take such an in-depth tour of the countryside. Just imagine, tourists would pay thousands to go and experience what you did."

"Sure thing," said Ames. "I'll be sure to stop at the travel agency and recommend the trip. They can list it as a delightful stroll through the elegance of third world living, complete with camel crap and goat meat. They can say the accommodations are rustic and the people are friendly and warm. They might add an advisory to include toilet paper and about a ton of moist towelettes to their luggage." The agent scratched his groin for emphasis.

"You don't need to be sarcastic, Mister Blond," said the ambassador as he handed Ames the drink. "We all make mistakes. You're on a flight out of Saddam International at five, direct to Paris with a changeover to Washington. That should correct the mistake. In the mean time I think we can scrounge up some clothes to replace those army things."

Ames took a sip of the martini. "Is this another flight on Iraqi Air or do I get to go by camel caravan this time?" He waved aside the ambassador's objection. "I need to know a few things. First, does it always rain this much in this darn country? What're the odds of getting a weather forecast that's worth a spit? I thought the Middle East was supposed to be dry and hot as heck."

The ambassador chuckled. "No, it actually is dry and hot here. The guys in meteorology say that we are experiencing an unusual wet spell, they're not sure why. The environmental nuts are saying it's due to the ozone layer, the wacko's are saying its space aliens and the conspiracy theorists are saying the government is responsible. And that's just here in Iraq. I'm not sure what they're saying in the states."

"Probably blaming the President, the CIA and the military for conducting experiments in weather control," said Ames. At that moment a strange look crossed his face. "Bat buggers!" he shouted. "I'm a real dumb fart. It's been right there the whole time and I've missed it. Damn! I need to get to secure phone right now!"

The ambassador pointed to the phone on his desk. "Use this one. We're pretty sure the only ones who listen to it are the Russians and the Chinese. And maybe the terrorists and insurgents, but we're not sure about them."

"What the heck kind of phone system is that?" asked Ames in astonishment.

"Hey, everybody in the world has computers and they're all hacking anything that moves, communicates or has wires," explained the ambassador. "We had a pretty good system, but it got hacked about two months ago and they haven't come up with anything better yet. Congress is on another budget kick and there's no money for security - again. As it stands, we make calls and just watch what we say."

"Well, heck," said Ames. "This isn't going to work. I'll just have to wait until I get back to Washington."

"We have some spare clothes here," said Hardiman changing the subject. "I think you can change out of those BDU's and get into something more appropriate for an airline flight. I'll get my aide to help you out."

He was taken to a room in the embassy and offered everything from a Chinese mandarin costume to knickers.

Holding up the short-legged pants he asked the staffer, "Planning on infiltrating the 1890's? I'll just take that suit and a shirt. Do you have a tie?"

The kid passed over a dark tie with mice on it. "Mickey Mouse," said Blond, "Well that about matches the situation here."

The flight out of Baghdad had taken off on time. The embassy passport officer had issued Ames a new passport to travel on. It wasn't in his own name and the picture looked rushed, but it got him through Orly in Paris and on the flight to Washington.

Now the plane was taxing to the terminal and the passengers were collecting their carryon baggage, turning the aisles into a confusion of humanity, bags and used cups and trays. The stewardess' were doing their best to try and get people to sit down until the plane came to a stop, but the cattle ignored the sensible and continued to prepare to stampede. The flight had been long and the herd was ready to move.

Rather than get caught in the crush, Ames remained in his seat until he was almost the last one left. He then stood and leisurely made his way forward and out the door. The stewardess gave him a warm smile and a quiet thank you as if she appreciated him being one of the few sane ones on board.

Ames was walking through the terminal headed for the cabstand, after passing through immigration, when a young woman from DORK holding up a sign that read "BLOND" intercepted him. She appeared to be fending off every male in the building by swinging the sign back and forth. She clipped one pudgy character and sent him sprawling, his bags and butt sliding across the floor.

He vaguely remembered her as a Sylvia or Sheila or something. She was quite good looking with blond hair, sparkling blue eyes and a very pleasing figure, which might explain the attention the sign was getting.

As he walked up to her she started to smack him with the sign and then her eyes opened wide in recognition. She lowered the sign, flipped her identification at him and said, "N sent me to pick you up. I have car outside waiting."

"You're picking me up?" asked Ames with a grin. "Does this mean drinks and possibly more later?"

She gave him a nasty look while lifting the sign back up and said, "I assume you've heard of the sexual harassment policy? I'd hate to have to report you for making uncalled for remarks."

"Bloody heck," Ames muttered, no longer grinning. "I suppose now I'm supposed to turn into a meek and timid wimp who goes along with your every suggestion rather than have a black stain in my record and possibly miss the chance to spend two minutes in your presence. Sorry, it doesn't really work that way. I really have too much on my mind to worry about whether you have on pink or black panties. Just show me to the car and get me to the office."

"Panties!" Okay, that's it." She scowled, making her face a whole lot less pleasing. "I'm filing a sexual harassment report and you can kiss your job good-bye.

The government won't accept this kind of abuse," she said smugly.

Ames just looked at her. "Sweetie, I hate to tell you this, but your view of life is just a tad skewed. Do you honestly think that the government is going to dump someone who has information about a global threat just so they can placate a temporary intern? You better show me to the car before you step in any more doo-doo. He grabbed her shoulder and turned her to face the door, then gave her a little shove.

She glared back at him with a face that would have frozen a daiquiri and turned and marched through the terminal doors, nearly colliding with them when they failed to move fast enough. A male passenger, just entering the door, jumped backward to get out of her way. As Ames followed Sheila, or Sylvia or whatever, through the door, he heard the passenger mutter, "Somebody ain't getting nothing tonight!"

Ames nodded and smiled at him. "Careful," he muttered in an aside to the passenger. "She might hit you with a sexual harassment suit." The passenger shuddered and scurried through the door.

Sheila, or Sylvia or whatever, led him across the drop off road and into the short term parking where she found a light blue Lexus, unlocked the driver's door, tossed in the sign and got in. Ames tried the passenger door, but it was locked. He tapped on the window, but the girl just glared at him. He crossed his arms and stood there for a moment staring at her until she finally caved and pressed the unlock button.

Sliding into the seat, Ames looked at her. "Well, there goes the honeymoon. We've had our first fight. Can you start this thing and get going or are you to mad to drive straight?"

She jammed the key into the ignition with a snarl and turned it so hard that Ames thought she was going to break it off. She jerked the transmission into reverse and backed out of the space, darn near hitting two cars and an old guy in a wheelchair. She dropped it into Drive and squealed the tires, leaving behind smoke, honking horns and the sound of the buzzer on the old guy's wheelchair. There was a streak of about two inches of tire tread on the pavement. It was only at the last minute that she remembered the gate and slammed the brakes, barely missing crashing through it. The attendant reached out for the payment and she threw five dollars at him.

As the attendant grabbed for the money Ames leaned across and yelled, "PMS!"

The attendant smiled and raised the gate while handing Sheila, or whatever, her change. Ignoring the money, the girl stomped the gas and destroyed the tires a little more. A dense cloud of rubber smoke followed them from the lot. Ames was sure the EPA would file a complaint.

The ride to DORK was quiet, but the atmosphere in the car could have started World War III. At the door Ames got out of the car and turned to lean back in. "I don't suppose you'd be available for dinner tomorrow night?"

The girl growled and pulled away so fast that Ames barely had time to pull back and slam the door. With a grin he watched the car roar away, barely missing running over three spies and a mole (the furry kind).

When Ames entered the building the security guard at the desk made Ames go through an electronic fingerprint and retinal check before he would even speak to him. When the tests passed the guard said, "It's about time you got back. N has been driving everybody crazy looking for you. I think he has every agent in the world trying to locate you. He said that when you get in you're to go right up to his office."

Ames thanked him and headed for the elevators, carefully keeping his eyes on the automatic machine guns mounted in the corners of the ceiling. Another guard in a glass booth checked Ames' physical description and made him press his palm to a hand scanner. The elevator door finally opened and Ames stepped in. A purple light blinked on and scanned Ames' body. Somewhere a computer matched Ames' thermal image to a stored thermal image. When that passed, the elevator doors slid shut. Ames knew that if the check had not passed the doors would have closed and a grenade would have dropped from the ceiling.

At the fourteenth sub-level Ames left the elevator and crossed the hall to a plain looking door with the words "Broom Closet" on it. The agent carefully turned the doorknob twice around to the left and once around to the right before pushing the door open and stepped into a closet complete with brooms, mops, pails and rags. He pushed aside one of the buckets and pulled on a coat hook on the wall. A panel slid open.

Ames stepped through into an ornate anteroom with a couch, an overstuffed chair and a desk. The walls were painted a muted tan with pictures of the president, the vice president and Mickey Mouse in oak frames. An ivy plant sat in a pot on a small table between the couch and chair, providing a spot of greenery. At the desk an older woman was poking at the keyboard to a computer.

The woman was somewhere in her eighties with blue hair and really ugly tortoiseshell half-glasses perched on the end of her nose. She wore a turquoise pantsuit that set off her hair rather nicely. She looked up as Ames came in.

"Good evening, Miss Pinchpenny," said Ames as he sat on the desk and picked up a pencil.

Pinchpenny glared at him and grabbed the pencil. "You'd better get your butt in there if you know what's good for you! The old man's really upset at you taking an extended vacation on company time. And what the heck did you do to Sheila? That girl is really teed off. She's talking harassment suit, lawsuit and she wants you personally to be hung and neutered. She wasn't clear as to what the order would be in."

"Hey," responded Ames standing up and holding up his hands. "First, it wasn't a vacation, I was working! And how the heck did you find out about Sheila? It's been less than ten minutes."

"You ever hear of email, dummy?" Pinchpenny responded, looking at him over her glasses. "Get on in there. And ask him to leave the intercom on. I want to hear him fry your fanny."

CHAPTER SEVENTEEN

As Ames walked into the General's office that officer was seated at the desk shuffling papers from one side to the other as though he were looking for something. Looking up he spotted Ames and stood up. He glowered at the agent and yelled, "It's about time you got back from your vacation. Did you ever think to check in now and then? What the heck did you find out?"

Ames pulled a chair from the wall and sat down. "Well I found that Al Raini might have been doing something near the village of As'al Quarba. The villagers say that some of his men have been collecting money from the locals, but this apparently stopped some months ago. There have also been trucks and aircraft in the area of a mountain called Ghunda Zhar that's near the village. I don't know if that has anything to do with Al Raini, but something is going on in that area."

The General stared at Ames. "Do you have anything concrete like a sighting of the man himself?"

Ames reached into his pocket and pulled out a crumpled and faded piece of paper. "No there were no actual sightings, but I did get this," he said handing the dog-eared document to N.

The General snatched the paper and carefully unfolded it. "What the devil is an ovulator? It sounds like something vaguely obscene. Are those bloody Arabs working on cloning or something?"

Ames looked up and said, "I'm not sure. Hassim gave that to me and I thought maybe R should take a look at it. It might be nothing. It was found stuck in the dirt along the Tigris."

N looked at the document again and pressed a button on his desk. A moment later Pinchpenny came in. "Have somebody take this down to R. Have him analyze it and see if it has any meaning. Tell him to get back to me when he's done."

Pinchpenny gave Ames a dirty look and then left. N focused his attention back on Ames. "We really need to know what Al Raini is up to," he stated. "I'm thinking of sending you back over there. I think we can set you up as an Arab or something – put you in a robe and a turban, smear some camel dung around. Feed you some goat cheese. Maybe you can pick up on something."

Ames was alarmed at the thought of going back into the field as an Arab. Just the thought of getting that dirty again, brrr! And the goat cheese! He felt his lunch rising in his throat and his gonads crept up into his body. "Ah, sir. I don't think that would be that good an idea. I don't speak Farsi and I don't really look Arab. Maybe you should send someone else."

"Nonsense. You've already been there and you know the culture. You can pretend you're a deaf mute or something. Maybe you could be the village idiot or a mute holy man. We'll think of something or other. That would get them to talk around you."

"If I'm a deaf mute that might work, except I would have no idea what they are saying."

"Did somebody just mention deaf? Unable to hear? No knowledge of the language? Oh, wait, that was me!" exclaimed the General.

"No need to get sarcastic."

"We'll have to work on that. So tell me everything that happened from the time you left here. Wait a minute while I turn on the recorder."

The General turned on a small tape recorder and set it on the desk. For the next two hours Ames took N through his escapades in Iraq with the General stopping him every now and then to ask a question.

Since you never knew what was important and a good agent told all the details regarding a case, Ames left nothing out. When Ames related the part about the cheese, Ames had to halt his story long enough for the General to get control of himself.

The same thing happened when the part about the shower and razor came up. Ames sat and drummed his fingers on the desk while Tenstars whooped and coughed. The agent could hear loud laughter from Pinchpenny's direction in the outer room. Apparently she had the intercom on.

When the General stopped laughing, Ames continued his story, finishing with the flight out of Baghdad.

With the story finished the General rewound the tape to check that he had gotten it all. Only, the recorder wouldn't rewind. The General snapped the top open and found that there was no tape in the machine. With a, "Well, drat!" N reached into his drawer and took out a blank cassette and snapped it into place.

"Okay," he said. "Let's try that again."

Ames looked aghast at the idea of repeating the whole story all over again.

With a swipe of his hand, the General slid the recorder into the top drawer. "Forget it. I'll just get the copy from Pinchpenny. She has my office bugged and records everything that goes on in here. I think she's a plant by the CIA or NSA or something."

"Why don't you get rid of her then?" asked Ames

The General sighed. "I can't. The blasted Federal employees union would have a fit and I'd probably get sued for replacing a woman, although I'm not sure Pinchpenny is one."

Ames looked down at his lap. If the General was afraid of lawsuits, what were his prospects with Sheila or Sylvia or whatever?

"Tell me more about the rain," said the General, changing the subject.

"Well, it was raining about every other day, and raining hard," said the agent, trying to ignore thoughts of the intimidating blond. "When we were trekking out of the mountains, we had trouble crossing streams that were swollen and overflowing the banks. At some points we had to go up or down stream to find a place to cross. Then when I was at the Marine base it rained again. When I got to the embassy in Baghdad the ambassador made a joke about weather control. Is it possible he was right?"

"According to the meteorologists that area has an average annual rainfall of less than ten inches. In just the last two weeks they've had over fifteen. And our people tell me it's raining again today. "

"So you think that whatever Al Raini is working on may have something to do with this change in weather? That he might have weather control?"

"You're talking about something the smart boys say is impossibility with our current technology."

"But Al Raini, according to his dossier, took degrees in electronics and meteorology. He also took one in fondue dishes, but I don't think that one applies. Do you think that maybe he has made some kind of breakthrough?"

"I have no idea, but you're going back over there and find out."

"As what, an Arab deaf mute?" said Ames with a chuckle.

"Actually, yes," replied Tenstars with a grin. "I'll pair you up with Hassim. He can be your brother or something. He interprets. You nose around. Get down and see the ASSHOLS and get fixed up as an Arab. I'll contact our Baghdad office and set things up with Hassim."

Ames stood up and headed down to ASSHOLS. As he started to pull the door open to Dirty Tricks he stopped and gingerly reached out and lightly tugged on the door handle. It didn't come off in his hand. With a sigh of relief he pulled the door open, only to find himself thrown backward, slamming his head against the wall.

A familiar face popped out the door. "That was even better than the last one," crowed R. "I installed a delay and a heavier spring. Makes a heck of a bang when it goes off. Great, huh?" He ducked back into the room.

Ames stood up and shook his head to clear away the stars. "Crazy son of a bitch," he muttered as he reached for the door. With a start he pulled his hand back, then carefully reached out and yanked, while stepping quickly to the right. A second later the door crashed open and Ames slipped through before it could close. The door thumped shut behind him.

The room in front of Ames was still crowded, only this time it looked like the set from a Frankenstein movie. The center of the floor had a long table with massive looking ceramic electrodes reaching to the ceiling. Wires were strung everywhere and a huge control panel that looked like it came from the Starship Enterprise sat against one wall. Colored lights were flashing in rows up, down and across. It was actually kind of pretty. Sort of like a house on Christmas.

Ames ducked under the wires and worked his way across the room to the opposite doorway. He had to dodge strange looking poles and conduit to get there.

Inside the next room he found R tinkering around with some sort of small device. As Ames walked up R suddenly straightened and hid whatever it was behind his back.

"Hey, Ames," called the old scientist. "N called and said you were going back to Iraq. You must have had a good time to want to go back so soon. I hear everybody else is trying to get the heck out of there. Something about violence or crazy religious fanatics or too much water. Whatever."

"I checked out that paper you sent down," he continued. "I scanned it into the computer and did an enhancement on it and translated the Arabic into English. Your ovulator is a part of what appears to be a machine to control the weather. It seems to alter the ionization of the atmosphere to draw water molecules. When a sufficient volume is brought together the ionization is switched and the water disperses, dropping as rain."

"So Al Raini has weather control!" declared Ames with awe. "Damn, that's a heck of a weapon. You could destroy a countries economy by changing the weather, destroying crops, making outside work all but impossible."

"Actually, the best part was in the Arabic. It gives us a possible location," said R with a huge smile.

"Where?" asked Ames.

"Well, if you recounted your journey in Iraq properly and you got the name of the village right, you were only about twenty miles from it. It's near Ghunda Zhar, the highest mountain in the range." R took Ames to a table with a map on it. "This is the village you were in," said R, pointing at the map. "This is Ghunda Zhar here to the North East."

"So I have to go to the mountain and find Al Raini and his machine." Ames said it as a statement rather than a question. "So when I get over there I at least have an objective, which is more than I had the first time. N says I need to look like an Arab deaf mute. I suppose that means I'm back into a dirty robe with no underwear and a turban." Ames' shoulders hung in resignation.

R cackled. "Oh, I think we can do better than that. " He walked to a cupboard and opened it, revealing a long dark brown robe and a light blue turban. He took the robe down and turned back to Ames.

"This is the robe you'll be wearing. It's actually called an Abaya, but robe will work. This one has some special features. It resists dirt and water so it shouldn't get dirty and its more light weight than an Arab robe. That should make you more comfortable. It is also bullet proof. The army lab in New Jersey has come up with this stuff that they spray on cloth and bullets don't go through. I have no idea what the stuff is, suffice to say it works."

"So it's like body armor?" asked Ames.

"Yeah, except for one small problem. The stuff doesn't reduce impact. You get hit with a bullet that's traveling at nineteen hundred miles an hour and you're going to get knocked on your butt. I can guarantee that it'll leave a heck of a bruise and maybe some broken bones. So try to avoid getting hit."

Ames took the robe and fingered the material. It felt like a robe, nothing strange about it. The bulletproof stuff must be pretty good, but he wasn't sure he wanted to try it out.

"What about the turban?" he asked looking into the cupboard.

R took it down and passed it to Ames. "This is treated the same way as the robe and should protect your head. However, the first shot will probably knock it off and give you a serious headache, if not a concussion.

"It also contains a radio transmitter that sends a long range microwave signal when you press the button inside. The button looks like a button not a button. I mean a button like on your shirt, not a button like on a radio. Did I say that right?"

"Yeah," responded Ames. "It's like a locator beacon."

"Yeah, yeah. That's it. A locator. Just the thing," muttered R. "I also have a glue on beard for you. Don't worry it looks really good. We took it off a dead Arab, so it really looks real."

Ames wasn't so sure about having a dead guys beard stuck to his chin, but resolved to make the best of it.

Then a thought occurred to him. "Say, what's all that stuff out in the other room? Is it some kind of new interrogation technique?"

"That stuff," chuckled R. "Heck no. That's for a remake of Frankenstein. The car commercial went over so well we thought we'd make a movie and see how that went. Got' a remember, the budget is tight. Speaking of which, where are my car and watch?"

"Uh, sorry. The watch kind of got lost along the way and the car got traded to a bunch of guys in Baghdad."

"Oh," said R "Misuse of government property. I'll just make a note of that and they can deduct them from your pay." He pulled out a notebook. "One watch at nineteen dollars and ninety five cents and one Pinto car at twenty two hundred dollars."

"Whoa," chirped Ames. "There is no way that screwed up car is worth twenty two hundred bucks. That sucker was rusted out, falling apart, wouldn't run and is almost thirty years old. Ten bucks maybe, but no way twenty two hundred!"

R looked at strangely at Ames. "You haven't bought much through government procurement have you?"

At that moment R's cell phone beeped inside his pocket. R took it out and flipped it open. He turned away from Ames who could hear nothing of the conversation. After a few seconds R flipped the phone closed and said, "N wants to see you in his office when you're done here."

"Are we done here?" asked Ames. "You don't have a car or some other neat gadgets for me?"

"Not hardly," said R. "You dumped a watch and a car on me already. You're lucky you're getting a robe and a turban. Get out of here."

Ames bundled up the robe and turban and headed for the door.

"And stop wadding those things up," shouted R. "I just had them pressed!"

The agent flipped the finger at him and walked out the door.

Ames found the General in his office tapping his fingers on the desk. "You wanted to see me, sir?" asked Ames when he stood in front of the desk.

"Do you know a Sheila Bitz?" the General asked without preamble.

"I met a Sylvia or Sheila or something on the way here. She drove the car. Blond, good figure, sort of cute, why?"

"She has filed a sexual harassment complaint against you is why. What's that all about?"

"She made a crack at the airport and I cracked back."

"Blast it, Ames," said the General shaking his head. "You should know that ever itty-bitty group in the country, from women's lib to dwarf Methodists have lost their sense of humor and are suing everybody for everything from dirty jokes to dirty fingernails."

"Yeah, I know. It's just all this whining gets to me and I want to do some whining of my own. You know, like those damn homeless people who spit on your windshield and smear it around with a dirty rag? I'd like to get out of the car and spit all over them. But I'd probably get sued for violating their rights or something."

"Yeah, I understand that."

"Or those people in the checkout line who don't start writing a check until they get the final total, and there are like forty people in line behind them. I'd like to shove a pen up their bottom half and scribble all over their esophagus. "

"Okay, I can feel that."

"Or the people who drive slow in the left hand lane. They should have tire tracks branded across their butts and a tire iron shoved up their nose. Yeah, get them suckers!" Ames started rubbing his hands together.

"Okay, Ames I get the picture."

"Or maybe those retards who. . . "

"Ames, shut the hell up!"

"Sorry, sir. I got a little carried away there."

"The way this is going to work, you're getting on a plane to Iraq. You will meet with Hassim and straighten out this thing with Al Raini and the NERDS. Get to Ghunda Zhar and find that nut. I'll take care of Miz Bitz. And watch your mouth from now on!"

CHAPTER EIGHTEEN

Ames waved to the guard as he left the DORK building and headed for the parking lot to get his car. His flight back to Baghdad did not leave until the following afternoon, so he figured he would get some sleep in his own bed and see if his plants had died while he was away.

He had been thinking about this next trip to Iraq and thought it might not be as bad as last time. After all, he would have Hassim as a guide and surely the CIA agent would have access to a car or truck or something to get to the village. He had Iraqi clothes, but they were of good quality and he would be taking some food and things with him, so he would not have to live off the local economy, which meant no goat.

Spend a few days poking around in the hills and then catch a flight home. He might even get to see Fatima. Sure she was young and might be married by now, but she was a nice kid and not too shabby to look at. Her brother seemed nice enough and maybe he would help out, possibly acting as a guide into the mountains. Yeah, this trip should be something of a piece of cake. He even knew some Arabic now from spending so much time with Salim and the guys.

Maybe he'd get a chance to look them up too, and find out if the Marines had done right by them He started whistling as he began to think of the upcoming trip as sort of a vacation with some minor work thrown in.

He unlocked his car, a four-year old Honda Accord, climbed in and started the engine. It rattled slightly reminding him that the car was due for a tune-up sometime in the near future. The oil light flickered on and off. He would have to get an oil change at the same time.

Putting it in gear he backed out and headed toward the gate to the lot.

He pulled up to the gate and put the car in park. Two guards came out of the gatehouse and started inspecting him and the car. One guard patted him down, the other pawed through the trunk, looked under the seat and dashboard. Using a mirror, one of them scanned the underside of the car. Finding no Top Secret documents, disks or unused candy bars, the guards pocketed the change from under the seats and ashtray and waved Ames on his way.

Ames waved back and pulled out onto the street, turning left to head for his apartment on L Street NW. He had gone only a block when he stopped at a traffic light and looked in the rearview mirror and saw a car pull away from the curb and stop directly behind him. A passing car on the cross street momentarily lit the interior of the other car and Ames noted that the driver and passenger both with a Middle Eastern look to them.

As he waited for the light to change, the passenger in the other car got out and walked toward Ames car. He held something in his hand. Ames started to get worried and reached across and snapped the door locks.

Just as the man reached the rear side door, the light changed and Ames moved forward. The man raced back to his own car. On a hunch the agent made a right at the next street, just to see what the other car would do. It followed him through the turn.

Suspecting he was being followed. Ames took the next left. Sure enough, the other car followed. Ames increased his speed and took the right at Minnesota Avenue without stopping, running the red light and startling an oncoming driver who slewed to a stop. At Pennsylvania Avenue he rushed into the left lane and spun around the corner, accelerating to cross the Sousa Bridge. The other car stayed with him, running two red lights in the process.

Racing the traffic lights, Ames spun around Barney Circle and whipped the car right onto 13th Street and immediately hung a left on E Street. In his rearview mirror he spotted the other car as it made the turn onto E. He cranked the wheel over and spun down 12th Street, hooking an immediate left on Independence Avenue. The pinging in the Accord's engine increased as he stepped on the gas and roared up the avenue. The tires screamed when he rounded the corner onto 11th Street, crossed Pennsylvania Avenue, running the red light and scaring the crap out of half a dozen other drivers.

As he jerked the wheel to turn at G Street, Ames looked around for a telephone to contact DORK and let them know he was being chased. Unfortunately, with the advent of cell phones, pay telephones were disappearing and the agent could not find one.

With trepidation Ames screamed to a stop at Garfield Park and then turned right onto 3rd Street, then took a left at Folger Park. At Canal Street the other car was so close the bumpers collided and Ames' neck snapped backward. He stomped on the gas and roared up the on ramp to the Interstate 395 beltway.

The other car accelerated and pulled into the right lane. Seconds later, the other car, a dull blue Acura, pulled alongside Ames. The agent glanced over to see the dark skinned passenger gesturing at him and waving his hands. Ames jerked the wheel and the front fenders kissed with a loud bang. The other car dropped back with the passenger flipping Ames the bird through the open window.

Ames dropped his speed after crossing the bridge and turned down onto the George Washington Parkway. He pushed the Accord hard, the engine pinging and whining.

Smoke started coming from the tailpipe and oil light came on a solid red. The car was hesitating as he looped up to the Arlington Bridge and crossed back into the District. The Acura pulled up beside him again and the passenger started yelling at him and waving his hand.

Ames vaguely heard "Pull the damn car over," as he gave them the finger and looped around the Lincoln Memorial to swing onto Constitution Ave. The other car dropped back. A police car turned on its lights and sped after the two cars when they roared through a traffic light.

At Pennsylvania Avenue the procession slewed around the corner and sped down the wide avenue, passing historic buildings and gaining two more police cars. Red and blue lights winked off and on and the howl of sirens filled the air.

Ahead Ames could see a police roadblock and he yanked the wheel over to turn onto 3rd Street. The car was smoking badly now and the oil light was shining redly at him. With a muttered "Damn," he pulled to the curb in front of the Reflecting Pool and ran back to the Acura that had pulled in behind him.

He yanked open the driver's door and grabbed a small man in a dark colored suit and yanked him out of the car. With a heave he clouted the man on the chin, sending the man to ground. Ames leaped across the hood of the car to get the passenger who had just climbed out. Ames grabbed him by the lapel and tossed him on the ground. He had just raised his fist to hit him when the agent was grabbed from behind by a police officer.

"Who sent you!" yelled Ames as he was pulled off. "Why the devil are you following me?"

Ames felt handcuffs gripping his wrists as the man pulled a paper from his pocket and thrust it at him.

"I'm a process server, you moron!" the man yelled as he dropped a subpoena at Ames' feet. "You've been served!"

* * * * * * * * *

Ames thrust his wallet into his back pocket and reached for his car keys as T, the representative from the DORK Legal Information and Rehabilitation department finished signing the release papers. The attorney from LIAR pushed the paper back to the desk sergeant, slipped the pen into his jacket pocket and turned to Ames. The sergeant tapped the lawyer on the shoulder and made a come on gesture with his fingers. T gave a smile and handed the pen over.

The sergeant turned from the counter with the paper and T said to Ames. "You've been charged with reckless driving, failure to stop at a traffic signal, speeding, operating an unsafe vehicle, avoiding arrest, public endangerment, pollution of the air, assault and battery, leaving the scene of an accident, and possibly, operating a motor vehicle without a license."

"But I have a driver's license," said as he pulled his belt through the loops in his pants. "I just had it renewed last year."

178

"Actually, no you don't," said the lawyer. "In essence you are an intelligence agent for the United States government and, as such, you don't exist. If you don't exist, you don't have a license. What you have is a document generated by a computer program designed to create an alias for you and allow you to operate a motor vehicle."

"If I don't exist, how come I get paid? How come I have a bank account and an apartment?" asked Ames looking slightly miffed.

The lawyer took Ames' arm and led him out of the police station. "No, you don't get paid and you don't have an apartment," the legal beagle explained. "You have an account at a bank that thinks you're a minor government agency and your apartment is rented through a dummy corporation."

With a startled look Ames asked, "What if I want to get married or change jobs? If I don't exist how can I do that?"

"In that event we would create a cover for you and you could be an accountant or something to allay the little ladies suspicions. As far as taking another job, do you know the creed of the Mafia?"

"Sure," said Ames. "Once in, never out."

"There you go," replied the attorney. "We can pull you in and give you another job, but you'll always be a DORK."

Ames thought that over for a moment and let out a sigh. "So what happens now?"

Ames and T got into a non-descript gray government car before the lawyer answered.

"The subpoena is from Sheila Bitz, or rather her attorney. She wasted no time in bringing her harassment suit against you and sending Alan Mohamet out to serve you. She apparently hired one of those fly-by-night twenty-four hour legal services. Interestingly she also names DORK as a correspondent in the suit. That pretty much makes the suit worthless, since DORK doesn't exist either. She is essentially suing nobody, and retaining a lawyer at three hundred dollars an hour to do it." He chuckled at the thought of a lawyer's dream – to get paid lots of money to do nothing.

"Any way," he continued. "N is really pissed at you. He wants you on a plane and out of the country before morning. You're on a flight out of National in forty five minutes. We're headed there now."

Ames jerked in his seat. "What about my clothes, my bed, a good night's sleep? What about my plants? I need to pick up some supplies for the trip, a Big Mac, some fries! And what about the robe, turban and beard, I need those before I go!"

"Forget the supplies, you can get a cardboard burger at the airport. The robe and stuff have been picked up by clandestine services. They broke into the impound lot and hijacked them from your car. They'll meet us at the airport."

Ames almost started to cry. This trip was not working out as he envisioned it. What else could go wrong?

180

CHAPTER NINETEEN

Ames descended the stairs from the plane into the heat of the Baghdad summer. Unlike his previous trip, the humidity was very high and the robe he was wearing became instantly sodden with sweat. At the same time his Right Guard gave up the ghost and the smell of ripe goat emanated from under his arms and the purpose of the turban became clear. It was a mop to absorb the buckets of sweat from his head. He wondered what they did about damp underwear. Since he was not wearing any the question was moot.

In Paris he had changed from business attire into the robe and turban of a Muslim. The fake beard completed the ensemble and was so good that he had trouble with the security personnel at the airport. They detained him for six hours poking into every orifice on and in his body, combed through his hair and beard, checked his underwear and discovered the loss, shoes and socks looking for explosives or possibly just to get a kinky thrill. The security personnel caused him to miss his flight. Only threats of a discrimination lawsuit had forced them to release him to catch the next plane out. The uniformed cop wanna-be's stood near the gate smiling and giggling as he boarded the plane.

In the terminal in Iraq the large figure of Hassim stood out like a destroyer among rowboats. When Ames walked up to him Hassim grabbed him in a bear hug. "Ah, my good friend. We will now have a great adventure together!" Ames pushed against the big man, not to escape the embrace, but to distance himself from the seemingly months old scent of an unwashed body. Hassim would have made an excellent advertisement for under arm deodorant.

"Holy month old catfish, Hassim," squeaked Ames. "Did you ever consider taking a bath?"

"Ah, now, no talking," said Hassim in gruff voice. "You are a deaf mute. You must not let our enemies know you are an infidel, even though you are."

Ames glared at Hassim as the Arab took him by the arm and led him out of the terminal. "I have a car waiting. We can go most of the way by road."

They reached the car park and Hassim pointed with pride. "There is the car we will use. Is it not beautiful?"

Ames' mouth dropped open. Sitting in front of them was a light blue Pinto. The roof was more dented than before and there were bullet holes along the side. The glass in the side windows was gone and the windshield was marred by jagged cracks. On the dashboard, the hula girl swayed her hips to some inner beat.

"You've got to be crapping me," said Ames. "Where did you find this piece of junk?"

Hassim looked at Ames with disdain. "This is a handsome car. It belonged to a thief of Baghdad named Ali Baba. He and the forty thieves he worked with used to be the scourge of the city until Chief of Police Aladdin Al Hourti put him out of business. I picked up the car in a police auction."

"And this junk heap is supposed to get us, what, a hundred and fifty miles?"

"More like three hundred with the conditions of the roads, and we'll have to walk part of that," said Hassim. "Your department does not have much of a budget to support clandestine operations. I was lucky to have the seven dollars the car cost."

"Good grief, and that twit R wants twenty two hundred for it" muttered Ames in shock. "Three hundred miles and look at the tires! The suckers are bald! I don't suppose this thing has a spare?"

"Hey, don't worry," said the Arab. "I put extra fuel in the trunk and I have a spare tire strapped on the back. We'll make it, no problem."

183

"How much fuel have you got?"

"I put in eight jerry cans."

"So we're going to run around in a country full of bullets and IED's in a car with forty gallons of gasoline protected by a sheet of rusty metal. Sounds like a plan to me."

The car groaned sadly as the two men climbed into the car and Hassim turned the key. The engine whined and coughed. Hassim pressed the gas pedal four or five times and tried again. The engine coughed, whined and then back fired with a loud bang. The hood flew open.

Hassim smiled. "Do not worry. It does that. I think it just wants to get our attention." He climbed out of the car and slammed the hood down.

Inside again, he pumped the gas and turned the key. The engine coughed, whined, coughed again and growled into operation. The hood flew open again.

Hassim released the key and the engine settled down to a low rumble with a light pinging sound. Dark smoke drooled from the exhaust. Hassim got out of the car to close the hood. The engine quit.

Rather than go through the whole rigmarole again, Hassim had Ames hold the hood closed while he started the car. The car whined, coughed and started. Hassim held the gas pedal down while Ames got back into the car.

The Arab put the car in reverse to back out of the parking space. There was a clunking sound but the car did not move. Hassim looked over at Ames. "Would you be good enough to get out and push on the front? Sometimes this beautiful car is a bit cranky."

Ames looked at Hassim in amazement and then got out again. He pushed on the hood while Hassim sat in the car. Hassim was jerking his body back and forth while yanking on the steering wheel. It looked like he was trying to physically move the car while still seated in it. The car groaned and moaned as the car swayed up and down on tired springs.

Slowly the car started inching backward. Ames pushed harder. The turban reached maximum water density and sweat dribbled down his forehead and into his eyes. He felt like he was wearing a wet towel on his head.

Finally the car moved out of the parking spot and Hassim waved for Ames to get in. With Ames inside Hassim put the car in drive, jammed the gas and the car crept toward the parking lot exit blowing black smoke.

On the street Hassim coaxed the car to go faster and Ames noticed a wobble coming from the back. Looking at Hassim, he asked, "Why does it feel like the tire is going to fall off? And what is that smell?"

Hassim laughed. "The tire is not going to come off. It is just a little off center from the land mine."

"What land mine?"

"The land mine the car ran over when Aladdin captured Ali Baba. The mine did not go off right away, but it did pick up the back of the car and slam it down on the curb?"

"So the wheel might fly off at any time," said Ames. "Swell! What about that smell."

"Oh that is from the cheese. Ali was hiding his cheese in the engine compartment and it got too hot. It melted and then caught fire and then turned black. Don't worry. The smell will go away. I do not even notice it now."

"Why in the world would you hide cheese in an engine?"

"How far do you think a half kilo of cheese is going to go with forty guys?"

Ames stared out the window as he thought that one over. The city crept by as Hassim guided the car to the north and then turned northeast to cross the Tigris. The road was good macadam and four lanes wide with a grassy median in between the lanes, although they had to dodge random holes in the highway. They passed clusters of homes and businesses and, after an hour or two, they reached the city limits and turned onto the route three expressway. After leaving Baghdad behind, the scenery slowly gave way to scattered buildings and open fields.

Ames was astonished by the amount of greenery. The last time he was here he recalled that most of this area had some greenery, but not like this. Now there were large bushes and trees with fields of tall grass. Somebody should be selling lawnmowers here.

The drive was pleasant enough except for the occasional camel or donkey who passed them and their riders yelled things about blocking the road. After a couple of enjoyable miles, except for the smell of burnt cheese and leaking gasoline, Hassim pulled off the expressway and headed up a semi-paved road paralleling the main highway.

Ames looked at Hassim with a worried look, "What did you leave the main road for? I looked at a map and the highway north is pretty good in most places, almost like an American interstate."

Without looking at Ames, Hassim replied, "The expressway is for Mercedes, BMW's and Cadillac's. We would be very conspicuous driving there. Did you not notice that many of the drivers were screaming and yelling at us?"

"No," said the agent, "I thought that was normal here. Rather like Frenchmen driving fast with one hand on the wheel and the other with middle finger held out the window."

Six hours and one hundred miles northeast of Baghdad they stopped for the night at a roadside inn. The headlights did not work.

The inn was run by a Pakistani who required extensive ID from both of them before he would give them a room at inflated prices. The rooms were done in a fake American southwest motif with hot and cold cockroaches and very lumpy beds. Ames found the standard Koran in the drawer of the night stand and the hot water did not work in the shower. The agent had to pay cash because the Pakistani wouldn't take Visa. They charged extra for blankets and clean sheets. Ames paid the extra.

The following morning they had a light breakfast of watery coffee and a two-day-old cinnamon Danish. Ames passed up the goat cakes with butter sauce. Hassim made a waffle with whipped cream and some kind of berries. The lobby smelled like burnt flour.

Outside Hassim attempted to start the recalcitrant car only to be rewarded with squeaks, thumps, rattles and an occasional puff of black smoke. After half an hour of cranking the car and cussing the battery died. An hour later they got a jumpstart from a helpful Abrams tank. They set off for Irbil traveling north on the bumpy road. Behind a pleasant row of trees Ames could see cars whizzing by on the expressway.

As they went further north the terrain changed and became more mountainous, going from flat plains to hills with the mountains in the distance. Far away Ames could vaguely see the peak of Ghunda Zhar through a ring of dark clouds. The going was fine until the hills became steeper. They rarely met another car or person except for the occasional pilgrim returning from Mecca. These staid zealots would walk past them, waving and smiling with the occasional pilgrim offering cheap Chinese made images of the holy shrine at Mecca, all while the car chugged and smoked.

Twelve hours later, with a one-hour stop for lunch, they rolled into Irbil. They had planned on continuing east toward Ghunda Zhar, but were stopped at the Marine checkpoint just south of town. There were two HUMMV's parked partially blocking the road with three US Marines standing behind them. A third HUMMV with a pedestal mounted machine gun sat to the side of the road about fifty feet away.

As Hassim brought the car to a stop, the Marines split up, with one leatherneck going to the passenger door and the other two going to the driver's side. All three had their M-4's in the ready position.

One of the Americans spoke to Hassim in Arabic while the other two kept a close eye on Ames. The non-speaking Marine, on the driver's side, looked closely at Ames, then stepped back and pulled some papers from his pocket. He flipped through the sheets while glancing at Ames. Ames watched him and wondered what the heck this was all about.

He started to lean to Hassim to say something to the guard when the Marine with the papers stepped back and lifted his rifle. "Code one! Step out of the car!" he yelled as Ames heard the safety on the rifle snick off. The other two soldiers instantly stepped backward away from the car and raised their rifles. Ames rapidly turned his head from side to side and saw the machine gunner pull back on the charging handle while pulling the stock into his shoulder.

Both Ames and Hassim lifted their hands where the troops could see them.

The translator yelled something in Arabic and Hassim carefully opened the door and slid out onto the ground, his face in the dirt and put his hands on the back his head. Ames quickly followed suit even though he did not understand the command.

Still shouting in Arabic the translator laid his rifle on the ground behind him and stepped toward the two men on the ground. Being careful to keep out of the line of fire he pulled out some plastic ties. He quickly and expertly pulled the men's arms down and wrapped them tight behind their backs. He then rapidly ran his hands over their bodies checking for weapons or explosives.

Struggling to turn his head to see his captor, Ames croaked, "Wait, you're making a mistake. I'm . . . oof" A kick to his side effectively shut him up. The senior Marine, a Corporal, produced cloths and slipped gags into their mouths tying them behind their heads. The third sea soldier brought sacks from the HUMMV and hoods were slipped over their heads.

Ames felt himself flipped over on his back and hands run over his front. He was then yanked to his feet and pushed forward. After about twenty steps he was forced to the ground on his knees again. He could hear the creak of the door on the Pinto opening and conversation too low to be understood. Then he heard a yell. "Hey Sarge, look at this!" There was scuffle of feet and steps came closer. A few moments later he heard a voice in Arabic and a muffled answer from Hassim. Ames tried to speak but the gag made his words come out slurred and distorted. After a minute the footsteps went away.

Ames' world dissolved into darkness, the heat making sweat drip down his forehead. An itch developed on his nose that was slowly driving him crazy. The turban scrunched down on his head did not help a bit.

He could feel a cramp building in his knees as he listened to the sounds from outside, the occasional noise of a car, muffled conversation, footsteps.

Just when he thought he could not stand it anymore he heard the rumble of a heavy truck and the grumble of the engine as the driver downshifted. He heard footsteps coming close again and he was suddenly grabbed under the arms and lifted to his feet. There were stabbing pains in his knees as the blood rushed back toward his feet. He tried to stand and almost fell over. The arms half supported him as he was pulled forward. More hands grabbed him and he was pulled onto a hot metal surface, his face scrubbing across the metal through the hood. When he stopped moving he could hear another body being pulled up beside him.

Metal slammed against metal and the sound of chains. The truck grumbled to a start and moved forward, Ames' body bouncing against the metal. He could hear Hassim groaning beside him.

For what seemed like an intolerably long time the truck jounced and bounced along. More than once Ames' head smacked down against the bed of the truck. He wished the guard or whoever was in the truck would at least help him into a sitting position. He heard and felt Hassim going through the same experience. Occasionally the two would bounce into each other.

After a considerable time the truck came to an abrupt stop forcing both men to slide forward and strike the wall of the truck. The driver started out again and they slid backward toward the rear. This happened more and more frequently and Ames assumed that they were going through city traffic. His head, arms and back felt like he was being run through a food processor.

Finally the truck came to a complete stop and Ames heard the driver's door open. There was a rattle of chains and a metallic slam as the gate of the truck was dropped.

His feet were grabbed and he was dragged from the truck, a pair of hands grabbing him just before he would have hit the ground. He heard an "oof" and a thump as Hassim was pulled out. From the sound it seemed that the hands missed and he landed in the dirt. Ames could hear muffled curses from Hassim. Whoever was doing the grabbing yanked Ames to his feet.

A rope was knotted around his neck and he was led forward, his feet tripping over stones or whatever was on the ground. He skipped forward on a particularly high obstacle and almost landed on his face. Thereafter the ground felt harder, like concrete. Ames assumed they had entered a building. The sounds had a different kind of echo.

After a short time, he was pushed forward and he heard the clank of a door closing. He was pushed a few more steps and then the hood was pulled off. He blinked at the sudden light, his eyes tearing from the brightness.

He was in a white walled room with three people. Two were Army soldiers with rifles. The third was in slightly different uniform that Ames recognized as brown colored tiger stripes Why tiger stripes, Ames had no idea. There weren't any tiger's in Iraq that he knew of. This man had a pistol in a holster slung under his left shoulder. His insignia indicated that he was a Captain.

The Captain reached behind Ames and undid the gag, allowing it to fall to the ground. Ames moved his tongue around in his mouth trying to get moisture to the desert that his palate had become. He flicked his tongue over his lips and along his teeth.

The Captain said something in Arabic and Ames squeaked out, "I don't speak that stuff."

The Captain stepped away from Ames and said in English, "Okay, if you want to play it that way. Walid Rhamin, you are accused of terrorism and acts of sedition here in Iraq. You're crimes consist of acts against the people, schools and cruelty to animals. You have fomented riots and created a public nuisance. Specifically you are accused of plugging up the toilets in two elementary schools in Baghdad and you are accused of camel corking in at least three cities including Baghdad, Mosul and here in Irbil. Do you have anything to say?"

Ames started to say something but his mouth was so dry that all that came out was a croak. He wet his lips and ran his tongue around the inside of his mouth again. "I am not Walid whatever," he began. "I am Ames Blond of DORK out of Washington."

The Captain looked skeptical. "Of course you are," he said. "A dork, I mean, to think that we would accept such a plainly false statement. According to your dossier you were educated at the Farmers University of Central Kansas in the United States. While you were at college you learned excellent English skills and found out considerable information about the workings of the US government. So don't try any of that I'm an American crap."

"But I am an American!" Ames insisted. "I'm undercover. I'm here to locate Abu al Raini and discover what dastardly plot he has going here in Iraq!"

"Sure," the Captain answered with a smile. "I've been here long enough to have heard it all. You're an American and you're with the CIA or the NSA. You're with Halliburton or Pizza Hut. You're the Roto-Rooter man. I don't give a hoot. You look Arab, you smell Arab and you match the description of a known terrorist.

"The toilet plugging was bad enough, but camel corking! My God, man, how insidious can you get? Do you realize what it's like trying to uncork a camel? And what happens when you finally get the cork out? Those cities will stink for weeks! And how the heck do you do that? What, you push the cork in or do you use a hammer? Get this slime ball out of here."

The older guard smiled at the joke and pushed Ames out the door and along a corridor to a steel door. The younger soldier opened the door and the two of them pushed Ames inside. After his hands were released he shouted, "Wait! Look, my beard is a fake." He grabbed the black mass and yanked. Nothing happened. The beard remained firmly attached. "Blast it," he muttered, and gave the beard another yank.

"Ow," he cried. "Stupid glue!"

The two men stood and watched Ames' antics, the soldiers obviously trying very hard not to laugh.

"Are you done yet?" asked the Sergeant.

Ames lowered his arms with a sigh.

The Marines backed toward the door laughing and the door was slammed shut. Ames found he had an excellent view of three blank white walls and a barred doorway that opened onto another blank white wall.

The room itself was not much better than the walls. There was an iron cot bolted to the floor with a dirty mattress on the frame. A stained commode sat in one corner and a steel sink was hooked to the wall next to it. A single bulb, inside a mesh container, lit the room from the ceiling.

The agent went over to the sink and using his hands as a cup, drank some of the brackish water. It tasted like twice used spit, but it made his mouth wet and eased the dry ache in his throat.

It had been a long day and Ames said to heck with it. Pulling his robe around him, he lay down on the cot and tried to sleep. Almost immediately the door banged open and the Sergeant poked Ames with his rifle barrel. "Get your butt up Walid. You're taking a trip."

Ames climbed to his feet and was pushed out the door. His hands and feet were bound with steel cuffs with a chain connecting them down the front. He was then pushed out the door to another truck and forced into the back. He saw no sign of Hassim.

As the truck drove off a dark figure slipped along the wall of the building and climbed the fence into the camel corral. Moving quickly the figure snuck up on an unsuspecting camel and lifted its tail. Inside the building the Captain heard pounding and the scream of a camel.

CHAPTER TWENTY

The cell measured eight feet by eight feet with white walls made up of white washed cinder blocks. The bed was a steel shelf attached to the wall with a foam mattress encased in blue plastic. There was a small stainless steel sink in the corner and the toilet was a hole in the floor. He had been issued an orange jumpsuit and a pair of black slippers. A blue blanket lay on the bed. A Koran at the head of the bed completed the décor. All in all, it was very depressing.

Ames had arrived at the United States Naval Base at Guantanamo Bay, Cuba the night before. It had been a long flight from Irbil, sitting in a mesh seat with his hands and feet handcuffed. The plane had landed twice at unknown airfields. The windows in the plane were blacked out so Ames had no idea where they were headed.

The in flight meal had consisted of a couple of baloney sandwiches and a bottle of water. The two prisoners with him had looked at the baloney with confusion. Islam excluded the eating of pig and the two were unsure if the slab of pressed red whatever contained any of the evil beast. The problem appeared to be solved when Ames chomped down on the sandwich and ate without disappearing in a puff of sulfurous smoke. The other two saw this and dug in.

One of the two started talking to the agent, but, getting no reply since Ames spoke no Arabic, Farsi or other Middle Eastern language, gave up, assumed Blond was a twit and lapsed into silence. The other said something to the first and surreptitiously gave Ames the finger.

After that the flight had devolved into a limbic experience, staring at the cabin wall and listening to the drone of the engines. Eventually Ames fell asleep with his head hanging from the seat restraints. When he woke up for the final landing he had a headache, a sore neck and the beard was covered with dried drool.

The plane had made a wide circle over the field, actually crossing into Fidel's side of the fence, and then took a steep descent to the landing. He and his fellow Arabs had been hustled out of the plane and into the back a closed truck. The vehicle drove a short ways and then sat for a long time while the two Marine guards watched him and the two Arabs shackled with him.

Finally the truck moved only to stop again a short time later. There was the sound of other vehicles and the roar of a large engine. Ames felt the truck swaying and smelled salt water. He suspected they were on a boat of some kind. The boat rocked for about twenty minutes while Ames started to fall asleep. His eyes were drooping when the truck started moving again.

There was another short ride with the prisoners swaying as the machine went around corners and then the truck stopped again. The rear flap and tailgate were opened and Ames and the two Arabs were prodded out onto the ground. He was facing a long enclosure with ten foot cyclone fencing topped with concertina wire. A gate stood in front of him.

He was herded through the gate and into a building where he was expertly frisked and forced into a chair. A Marine officer gave a short speech in Arabic that Ames did not understand. He was then led into another room with two other people. A different Marine officer, this one a second lieutenant, sat in one of the chairs. A second Marine with an M-4 stood behind the Lieutenant. Ames was pushed into the remaining chair and the guard moved back against the wall by the door holding his rifle by the handgrip.

The Lieutenant came right to the point. "Walid Rhamin, you are accused of acts against the government of Iraq and the coalition forces in Iraq. Give us the names of the other members of your group and I'll see what I can do about getting you out of here." The Marine behind him translated the speech into Arabic while the

Lieutenant spoke, the dual languages sounding slightly confusing.

"First off Lieutenant," said Ames. "You don't need the interpreter. I speak English. Heck I probably speak it better than you do. I'm an American. I work for the Department of Reconnaissance and Knowledge in Washington. I am a field agent, under cover, looking for the terrorist Abu al Raini."

"Uh huh," said the officer, staring at Ames. "I'm quite sure that you're an American and I'm a Martian. I'm only here to see how many of your women I can get, just like in that old movie. Let's cut the bull and you tell me who you had working with you, who your boss is and where we can find him!"

"Are you people dense," yelled Ames, standing up and rattling his chains. "I'm an American! Is that so blasted hard to figure out? Run my finger prints through the FBI computer, for Pete's sake." His tirade ended when he felt the barrel of a rifle against the back of his neck.

"Sit down Mister Rhamin," said the officer in an even voice. When Ames had retaken his seat, the Lieutenant continued. "That was the first thing we did. Your prints came back without a hit, just what we would expect if you were an enemy combatant from somewhere in the Middle East. Now simmer down and let's discuss this like intelligent people. Who were the people working with you? Who was your boss and who planned your missions?"

"Damn it," shouted Ames. "They've got my records on ice because I'm under cover, you dumb twit! Contact

DORK and they'll tell you. I'm an American! I'm on your side. Contact General Manystars, he'll tell you!"

"Uh huh," said the officer. "I'm quite sure there is a General officer named Manystars. With a name like that what else would he be? Who's your boss and who plans your missions?"

Ames lunged across the floor at the Lieutenant and felt a stabbing pain in his head as the guard slapped him in the head with the rifle. The turban cushioned the shock and kept him from losing consciousness, but he was forced down against the floor. The Lieutenant hadn't moved.

"Get him out of here, Corporal," said the Lieutenant looking at one of the Marines. "Stuff him in one of the cages and give him some time to think things over."

The Corporal grabbed Ames by the arms and pulled him off the floor and stood him up. The agent was shoved through the door and down a corridor and through another door. He was led outside and along a path to a large white building. Inside there was a hallway with steel doors spaced along each side.

Three quarters of the way down he was pushed into a cell, the one he was now in, his handcuffs removed and the door closed and locked. He moved over and sat on the bed trying to figure out how to get out of this, then lay down and closed his eyes. He was instantly asleep.

He was awoken minutes later with a Marine poking him and yelling in Arabic. A second Marine stood in the doorway. Both were armed with short club-like nightsticks.

Tiredly Ames said without getting up, "I have no idea what you're saying. I don't speak that stuff."

The Marine backed up and regarded Ames while tapping his hand with a nightstick. Finally he said, "Get your clothes off and put on the orange suit and slippers. Lay your old clothes in the middle of the floor and then back up into the corner." He pointed with the stick.

Ames started to pull off the robe, then stopped and asked, "Aren't you going to turn around or something to give me some privacy?"

The Marine laughed. "Yeah, I'm sure going to turn around and give you a chance to jump me. Just change your clothes!"

Reluctantly Ames pulled the robe off and changed into the orange suit. The guard kept his eyes on him the whole time, checking to be sure Ames did not have a weapon of some kind, or that he did not hide anything on his person.

The guard told him to again stand in the corner, then reached down and picked up the bundle of clothes. As he backed toward the door the Marine said, "You get a shower once a week, like the Lieutenant said. Dinner is in about an hour." He left the room and started to close the door, then swung it open again.

"How come you don't speak Arabic?" he asked.

"Because I'm an America," said Ames. "Please tell your Lieutenant or whoever that I am not a terrorist."

Both Marines started laughing. The first Marine said, "Like we haven't heard that one before."

He closed the door and Ames heard the snick of the lock closing.

Ames leaned back against the wall and absently picked at the beard with his fingernail while trying to figure a way out of this mess.

* * * * * * * *

General Manystars tossed the file he had been reading into the basket on his desk. For some reason government offices generated mounds of paperwork and everybody and his buddy had to stick his two cents in just to prove their job was needed. The last report had spent twenty pages on the efficient use of toilet paper as part of the paperwork reduction act. It had take this moron twenty thousand words to say that one sheet should be used instead of two and that one ply was cheaper than two ply.

Considering that this report had been sent to all seventeen thousand four hundred and ninety two government offices, the cost of printing and distributing the report would have kept the entire country in toilet paper for a year. The General was pretty sure this is not what the Paperwork Reduction Act was all about.

As he reached for the next useless report the door to the office opened and his secretary, Miss Pinchpenny, came in holding a sheet of paper. "Sir" she said. "This just came in. It's a report of a request for the finger prints for an Ames Blond that was sent to the FBI."

The General's considerable eyebrows went up creating a slight breeze across his face. "Who the heck would want his finger prints? This isn't some more legal stuff dealing with that Bitz broad is it?"

"Pinchpenny examined the paper. "No, apparently the request comes from the Joint Operations Command in Cuba."

"What the devil does JOC in Gitmo want with Ames' finger prints? Ames is in Iraq."

"I don't think so," said Pinchpenny with a frown. "It seems that the fingerprints came from one Walid Rhamin who is an enemy combatant now incarcerated at Gitmo."

"Don't tell me that doofus twit got himself arrested! What the heck is he doing? This was a simple exercise. Find al Raini and report back. Who did the comparison and are they sure they don't belong to this Ramen noodle character?"

"That's Rhamin without the noodle and our guys did it. The FBI doesn't have Ames' prints. We only got a set of Rhamin's prints as a courtesy from the FBI. We were listed on the distribution. We've also had reports that Walid Rhamin has been active in Iraq since Ames was picked up."

"Well how did they mistake Ames for Rhamin? Why didn't he just take that stupid beard off and show them who he is. Is he that freaking stupid? Scratch that, this is Ames we're talking about." said the General in disgust.

Pinchpenny smiled, imaging Ames sitting in a cell in Cuba wearing a fake beard. "Apparently R has come up with a new type of glue. There's a special procedure for getting the beard off. Until he gets that to Ames and he uses that procedure he's sort of stuck in it." She giggled at her little pun.

"I swear to Baal that bloody screwball R causes more problems," the General said with anger in his voice. "I used his new patented hemorrhoid cream last year and my butt cheeks were stuck together for a month. All right, here's what you do. Send the finger print information to JOC identifying Ames and requesting his release. I want him back in Iraq within twenty-four hours. Al Raini and his wet weather are getting out of hand. What about Hassim? Where's he? In some camp in Somalia?"

"No, he's still in Iraq," said Pinchpenny consulting her paperwork. "It seems the Marines at Irbil remembered him as a local trader in junk jewelry and camel crap. They wanted to arrest him for fraud, but he talked them into believing he was just a guide for Ames."

"Well why the heck didn't he tell them Ames was an agent for us?"

"He didn't want to blow Ames' cover."

"Well I'd say it's blown about as much as President Clinton, wouldn't you say?"

"What about clothes. Ames is either in an orange jumpsuit or that robe R gave him. Should we send some clothes down there for him?"

"Make it so," said the General going back to the report on dust recycling. Pinchpenny rubbed her hands in glee at the prospect of sending Ames a Mickey Mouse costume or some other nasty clothing ensemble.

CHAPTER TWENTY ONE

Ames was sleeping in his cell when the guards came for him. During the two days he had spent in Camp Delta he had been interrogated four times by the Marine Lieutenant. Each time he had been escorted from his cell, across the compound to the little room with two chairs.

Each time the Lieutenant had pressed him to give up information about his "gang" and the "boss" of his operation. Each time Ames had insisted he was an America and that the Lieutenant should contact his boss at DORK. Always he had been derided and had left the room knowing that no contact would be made. The agent was getting seriously depressed.

The remainder of his day would be spent sitting alone in his cell or in the exercise yard pretending to be an Arab. He acted as a deaf-mute, capable of only speaking with his hands. He spent the morning and evening calls to prayer hunched over on his knees listening to the Arab babble around him. To do less could have resulted in his being attacked by Moslem fanatics.

His pretense at a hearing loss came in handy when a new prisoner arrived on the second morning. He was standing near the fence when the new guy started talking to one of the older detainees. At first they whispered together until the new prisoner looked at Ames and the old guy glanced over and said something in Arabic. From there they spoke louder and in French, which Ames understood.

"So there have been changes?" asked the old guy.

"There have been some deaths and damage due to flooding along the Zar, Tigris and Euphrates Rivers, but there have been tremendous changes. The word is that the rains will continue and may even get worse. It may greatly affect the economy and politics of the region. That should stir up those self-righteous buffoons."

The old guy nodded. "And to think this all comes from one mountain and a man with vision."

"Ah," said number one. "But did not the mountain come to Mohammed, may he be blessed, who was also a man of vision? Should not the mountain again come to our aid?"

The new prisoner glanced at Ames and saw him watching. With a frown he drew the old guys shoulder to him and the two moved toward the corner of the containment, out of earshot. Ames was left thinking over what the two had said.

* * * * * * * * *

While the timing did not seem right this time, all of the other interrogations had almost been on a schedule, Ames got up and slipped his feet into his slippers. The guard led him on the usual path across the yard and into the administration building. Here the routine changed. Instead of the small interrogation room, Ames was led into the office of a Marine Colonel.

The Colonel sat behind a gray military desk with a pair of crossed flags behind it, one the US colors, the other the crimson and gold of the Marine Corps. The desk was littered with papers and a large coffee cup with the Marine insignia on it. On the front of the desk were a small flag stand with the Marine colors and a wood and brass nameplate reading "Michael Jewett." The name was flanked on one side by a gold and silver Marine eagle and the silver eagle of a full Colonel on the other.

Colonel Jewett looked Ames over for a moment and then asked, "So who are you?"

Ames looked back at the Colonel and said," I'm Blond, Ames Blond."

"Bull," said the Colonel with a skeptical look. "I thought you were British. MI6 or something?"

"No," said Ames looking at the ceiling. "That's the other guy. I'm an American."

"Hmmph," responded Colonel Jewett. "You know, if you had taken off that stupid beard you could have saved yourself a whole lot of trouble."

"The damned thing won't come off!" cried Ames tugging at the offending hair. "That twit R used some blasted glue he came up with and it sticks worse than crap to a sheep's butt!"

"Simmer down," said the Colonel with a chuckle. "Maybe we can give you some assistance there. We've cleared up the problem with your identity. Apparently some piss ant Army General knows you and vouches for you. Unfortunately the daily flight has already left leeward, so there won't be another plane out until tomorrow afternoon. The Navy here has some people who can probably get that off. I'll have someone take you over to the medical center. Somebody there might have an idea or two."

"Thank you, sir."

"Oh, before you leave, have you heard the latest about Iraq?"

"No, sir, is there something special going on?"

"General Manystars asked me to tell you. It seems the unusual weather over there has had some interesting side effects. There's grass growing in the southern desert. That grass extends southward into Saudi Arabia and westward into Syria and Israel."

"That says there has been a Major shift in weather patterns," said Ames thoughtfully. "I need to get back there as soon as possible."

"First let's get rid of that butt ugly beard."

At the medical center a young doctor decided it would be a good idea to get rid of the fur first so that the base of the beard could be seen more clearly. A corpsman used scissors to trim away the hair and get as close as possible to the cloth underlayment. Ames now looked like a badly shaved pirate with a really horrible skin condition. The cloth made his face look rough and patchy. Tufts of dark hair sprouted at random like ugly moles. Some of the longer hairs gave the impression of random whiskers from a cat.

To make matters worse, Ames' real beard had been growing for a number of days and those hairs seem to have blended in with the false stuff.

The doctor selected an area on Ames' cheek and applied a small amount of witch hazel, rubbing it in and then lightly pulling to see if the cloth would come loose. Ames "ouched" at the pinch, but the cloth remained firmly attached. The doctor then tried alcohol with the same affect.

After attempting ten or so different things with no effect, the doctor called in a second doctor for more ideas. Together they poured, poked and prodded for a number of hours. As the time passed Ames' face became more and more sore and the number of doctors increased until it seemed that every medical person in the center had had a chance at poking at him. It rather reminded Ames of the last HMO he had used. They even brought in a proctologist and a gynecologist. He had some trouble explaining there was nothing wrong with his butt and he wasn't about to become pregnant soon.

One of the doctors suggested doing a skin scraping to remove the beard remnants. This would involve using a very sharp knife to scrape the top layer of skin and the adhering cloth. It would be time consuming and would leave Ames' face raw and red for a number of days. There was also the possibility of facial scarring. Ames suggested he take a sharp stick and place it in his anal orifice.

Eventually the doctors started trying more volatile substances such as gasoline and turpentine. Ames face was becoming very sore from the poking and the chemical reactions. Finally he just told them to stop and asked for a SatCom link to DORK.

Ames dialed the number for the DORK offices after he was shown to the phone.

"Yes?" asked the voice that came on the line.

"Three four seven six five three four nine eight eight two one three four," said Ames.

"What is your security code?" asked the voice.

"Zero zero seven," replied Ames.

"How may I direct your call?"

"Get me that butthole R," said Ames.

"What department is that, sir?" the voice came back.

"He's the butthole in ASSHOLS," said Ames with growing irritation.

"One moment, please."

The sounds of "I Need a Hero" began floating through the phones earpiece. Ames started tapping his foot as he wondered when the song had become musak.

Bonnie Tyler was just reaching a crescendo when there was a click and R came on the line. "Hello?" he asked.

"R, this is Ames."

"Ames old boy. How're things in Iraq?"

"I'm not in Iraq. I'm in Cuba."

"I thought you went to Iraq? That's where you lost my watch and the Pinto."

"I found the Pinto. It's a little the worse for wear, but you'll be able to take that sucker off my bill."

"Worse for wear? I'll take it off after I see how much you damaged that beautiful car. And what about the watch?"

"That car was total junk and you know it! It was sold at an auction for a measly seven bucks. The watch was junk, too."

"Why did you sell it at an auction? That thin is government property and they could prosecute you for selling off government assets. You're not a Congressman you know."

"I didn't sell it at auction, the Baghdad police did. Never mind it's a long story. Just take that twenty two hundred off my account.

"You get the car back here and we'll talk about it. See you later."

"Wait!" yelled Ames as the phone clicked off. "Blasted idiot," muttered the agent.

He redialed the number.

"Yes?" asked the voice that came on the line.

"Three four seven six five three four nine eight eight two one three four," said Ames.

"What is your security code?" asked the voice.

"Zero zero seven," replied Ames.

"How may I direct your call?"

"Get me that butthole R again," said Ames.

"What department is that, sir?" the voice came back.

"He's the same butthole in ASSHOLS that you had on the line before. What are you dyslexic?" said Ames with growing irritation.

"Rudeness will not be tolerated, sir," said the voice and the phone clicked off.

"Damn it!" yelled Ames. The doctor standing beside him backed up a step.

He dialed the number for the third time.

"Yes?" asked the voice that came on the line.

"Three four seven six five three four nine eight eight two one three four," said Ames through gritted teeth.

"What is your security code?" asked the voice.

"Zero zero seven," replied Ames.

"How may I direct your call?"

"I would like to speak to R in ASSHOLS," said Ames.

"One moment, please."

Bonnie Tyler came back on the line warbling about her need for someone on a white horse.

Ten minutes later Bonnie had crooned her need three times and was starting on the fourth when the line clicked and a voice said, "Hello?"

"R, this is Ames again. I need some information from you."

"Hold on a minute," said the voice. "He's tied up in an experiment at the moment."

"Well tell him to drop it for now, this is important."

"No," said the voice. "I mean he's really tied up. He was experimenting with some memory rope and it tied him up. We're trying to cut him loose now. Hang on."

Bonnie came back again. Ames was really beginning to hate the song.

Five minutes later R came on the line. "What is it now?" he asked, his breathing heavy.

"R this is Ames again. I need some information."

"You lost the car again?" R asked slightly petulantly.

"Forget the car. How do I get this damn beard off?"

"You still have the beard on?"

"Yeah, I still have the beard on! I can't get the damn thing off. I've tried everything, gasoline, turpentine, witch hazel, milk, Tabasco sauce. Everything!"

"Didn't you read the operators manual before you put it on?" asked R.

"What operator manual?"

"Wait a minute," said R. Ames heard the phone thump down and Bonnie came back again. "I'm gon'na shoot that woman," muttered Ames.

There was a click and Bonnie shut up. "Sorry," said R. "I've got the instructions here. I guess I forgot to give them to you."

"You forgot! So how the heck do I get this thing of?"

"Did you try soap and water?" asked R.

"Uh, no," stammered Ames.

"Really Ames," R came back. "You really ought to take a shower now and then. Soap and water releases the chemical bonds in the glue and the beard just falls off."

"Soap and water. Well, I guess that makes sense. Is there anything else I need to do?"

"Yeah," said R. "You might want to use some after shave."

"So what does that do, react with the glue or something?"

"No, stupid," cackled R. "If you haven't taken a shower in a week I imagine you smell pretty ripe. The after shave will make you smell better!"

"Thank you very much," Ames muttered as he slammed down the phone. He turned to the doctor. "Where do I find a shower?"

Twenty minutes later Ames was clean, freshly shaved and denuded of the beard remnants. The hospital had provided him with a pair of jeans, a shirt and some sneakers that were just a hair too large. They didn't have any underwear or socks, but Ames figured he could live without them for a while.

He got into a Hummer with the Marine PFC who had brought him to the hospital. They left the hospital and followed the access road to Sherman Boulevard, the main road through the base. Unlike the ride to the hospital Ames now felt human enough to examine his surroundings. He had never been to the isolated Naval Base before and found it interesting.

The hospital and, for that matter, most of the habitable areas of the base were built on small fingers of land extending out into Guantanamo Bay. This provided the building inhabitants with a wonderful view of the blue waters of the bay.

The land was rolling with scrub grass, brush and various forms of cactus scattered around. Where a building sat, the scrub had been cleared away and green grass tried to flourish, sometimes with success. In others areas the heat and lack of water made the grass look somewhat sickly and brown.

The base had no fresh water supply since Castro had ordered the water line cut back in the late sixties. To compensate the Navy had built a huge fresh water desalination plant near the ferry landing. However, this did not mean unlimited water. It meant strict rationing with people coming before plants. From his driver Ames learned that most of the time Cuba was sunny and hot with temperatures up to 110 degrees, except for the winter rainy seasons when the rain could come in deluges. The driver said that recent hurricanes had been a problem, but the base residents coped pretty well by using hurricane shelters.

The driver stopped at the bottom of the hill and turned right onto Sherman Boulevard. On the left were number of metal warehouses and a large white building. On the right they past a sign that read, "Marine Corps Security Forces Company" with the obligatory Marine Corps insignia.

As the Marine driver started the HUMMV forward Ames heard a crunching sound, rather like a bag of potato chips being crushed. "What was that?" he asked looking out at the road beside the vehicle.

The young Private smiled. "Crabs, sir. Crabs here have a tendency to cross the road and when you hit them it sounds like crunching potato chips. If you go up the road toward the rear gate during, I guess mating season or something, there are like, thousands of crabs in the road.

You can't miss hitting them. Crunch, crunch, crunch all the way down the road."

Ames started laughing at the thought of all those crabs. The Private laughed along with him. Finally his laugh subsided to a few snickers and he went back to looking out the window.

As they rode Ames noticed that a number of the buildings seemed to be pretty new. The Marine explained that most of the older buildings had been replaced during a base expansion period from 1984 to 2000. The powers that be had even removed the minefields.

"Minefields?" asked Ames."

"Oh, yes sir," said the Marine. "From nineteen sixty five until two thousand the base was ringed by over twenty thousand land mines, antitank and anti-personnel. Between nineteen ninety-nine and two thousand one the mines were removed to comply with some treaty or other. As a matter of fact, where Camp X-ray up by the rear gate used to sit was on ground that used to have a minefield in it."

Ames glanced over at the Private, "What did they do with all that stuff when they removed it?"

"Some of them they blew up here. The rest they shipped out to somewhere, I'm not sure where."

"So they put them in the ground and left them there for over forty years? That seems like an awful long time for them to be any good anymore."

The Marine gave Ames a quick look. "No sir. They had a special group of Marines here called the Minefield Maintenance team. They had the job of removing old mines and putting in new ones. I heard it was really dangerous and they lost a number of people over the years. I'm not sure I would have been able to do that job. Those were some special guys with large brass ones."

"But they're all cleaned up now?" asked Ames with a worried look.

"Oh, yes sir," said the young man. "Not a one left. The certification team came in and pronounced us clean as a whistle."

They had just passed through a Major intersection and a group of buildings, one of which had a sign indicating it was the Guantanamo Naval Base Navy Exchange. The exchange was a long white and brown building with a group of arches in the center and across the street Ames spotted something he did not expect, the golden arches of a McDonald's.

The friendly yellow curves reminded him that the only thing he had eaten that day was a bagel and some cream cheese, standard breakfast issue for prisoners.

He almost told the driver to pull in when he realized he had no money. For that matter he had no identification, no driver's license, nothing. The only thing he had, somewhere, was an Iraqi identity card. And that had been confiscated when he was arrested.

The promise of food disappeared behind them as the Humvee went around a curve in the road and passed the fleet area. They then passed an open-air theater and went up the hill toward the old airfield and Camp Delta.

Back in the Colonel's office, the senior Gyrene looked Ames up and down. "Well, that's a definite improvement!

You look more like a human being than a goat herder. Now we can feed you, bed you down and get you out of here tomorrow on the NATS flight to Norfolk. Can I get you a coffee or something?"

Ames nodded and the Colonel yelled for the clerk to get a couple of cups.

While they were waiting Ames had a thought.

"I happened to think of one problem," said Ames. "We passed the McDonalds and I realized I don't have any identification or money. The money's not a problem, but how do I get back into the States without ID?"

The clerk, a Marine Sergeant came in and handed Ames a cup and filled it with coffee from a carafe. He then lifted it toward the Colonel, "Sir?" The Colonel nodded and the Marine filled the cup on the desk. He turned back to Ames, "Would you like cream and sugar, sir?"

"Not milk and sugar," said Ames, "But if you have some of that brown unrefined sugar I'll take that, and maybe some half and half with a touch of chocolate."

"We only have milk and sugar, sir"

"How about some honey then. I always like a little honey in my coffee."

"No, sir. Just sugar and milk."

"How about . . . "

"Ames!" yelled the Colonel. "Just take the God damned milk and sugar. This isn't Starbucks!"

Ames winced as the Sergeant handed him a couple of sugar packets and a container of milk.

"As I was saying," said the Colonel as if he had never yelled. "No problem about the ID. I'll have my people make you up a Federal employee's ID card. It won't take but a few minutes. And I can arrange some vouchers for the officer's mess."

"As a matter of fact," he continued, "that should be your next stop. I'll have Corporal Michaels take you over there so you can check in, unless you'd rather spend another night in your cage?"

"No, thank you, sir. Clean sheets and a real bed for me."

The Colonel laughed and stood up to take Ames' hand. "Alright, go get some sleep and I'll see you in the morning."

CHAPTER TWENTY TWO

For the third time Ames watched Iraq slide past the wing of an airplane. Watching the ground below, he noted significant differences in the view. The country was definitely greener looking. Where before there had been brown and tan, now the brilliant green of young plants lit the terrain.

The trip from Guantanamo had been long and Ames felt dirty and tired. He had left Gitmo on the two o'clock NATS flight to Norfolk. There a courier from DORK had provided him with new identification, credit cards and tickets from Washington to Paris, then on to Baghdad and finally to Irbil. He had been traveling for over thirty-six hours. He was sick of airports and airline food. He could not sleep in the cramped second-class seats. His bottom hurt and he had already seen the in-flight movies, so his boredom threshold was way beyond normal.

The only exciting part had been at Orly Field in Paris when a Jamaican midget had been accused of being a

Chinese terrorist. The plane had been delayed until a quick thinking security officer noticed that the Jamaican had been eating Mandarin instead of Szechwan and therefore could not be from Tsing Tau like his passport said. He was released without the heels of his shoes and no belt. He had boarded the plane holding a briefcase in one hand and pulling his pants up with the other. Although he walked funny he made it to his seat with no problem, other than emitting a stream of curses in Chinese.

Fortunately the midget had gotten off the plane in Baghdad where he was met by a fat Arab, wearing a robe and turban, who had a strange blocky looking body. The two had gotten into a blue car with really bad springs; the car was low to the ground, and driven off toward Fallujah. Ames dismissed the short person from his mind and headed for the plane to Mosul and Irbil.

The plane was another of the pre-dinosaur twin propeller things that seemed to be held together with string and duct tape. Experiencing a feeling of déjà-vu, Ames mounted the stairs to the passenger cabin where he was met by a smiling stewardess who handed him a roll of tape and a packet of goat cheese.

Taking this as a sign of acceptance Blond pushed into a seat next to an old man with a goat. In an act of kindness Ames presented the man with the goat cheese. The old man frowned and handed it back. He then reached into a bag and pulled out a cheeseburger and offered it. Ames accepted gladly. The man pulled out a second burger and the two munched happily as the plane took off.

As the plane climbed away from the airfield Ames spotted an explosion on the road a short distance from the terminal. The blast appeared to come from a blue car with one tall and one short person in it but he could not be sure because the car disappeared in smoke and flame.

In Mosul the pilot asked for their assistance and everyone deplaned to wrap the tail wings in duct tape. They were presented with new rolls when they reboarded. The agent was sorry to find that his companion was staying in Mosul.

Upon arriving in Irbil Ames found a Marine Staff Sergeant in desert ACU's waiting for him. Since he was the only westerner getting off the plane the Sergeant headed right for him.

"Are you Mister Blond?" asked the Sergeant.

"Yes," said Ames. "Are you from the Eighth Marines?"

"Yes, sir. I'm here to take you out to the base. I'm Sergeant Sergeant."

"I'm sorry," said Ames. "I didn't know that the Marines took people with speech impediments."

"What are you talking about?" asked the Sergeant.

"You mean no one has noticed that you have a slight stutter?"

"I don't stutter!" said the Marine indignantly. "I have perfect English!"

"Okay, have it your way," said Ames giving the Sergeant an odd look. "Let's get out of here."

As they started out the door a second Marine in MARPAt's joined them.

"Mister Ames," said the Sergeant gesturing toward the second Marine. "This is Major Major. He will be riding with us to the base."

Ames glanced sideways at the Sergeant as he took the Major's hand. "You did it again, Sergeant."

"Did what again?" asked the Sergeant as they headed for a Hummer parked at the curb.

"Stuttered," said Ames. "You said Major twice just like you said Sergeant twice."

"Of course I did," said the Sergeant. "My name is Sergeant Gunner Sergeant and this is Major Minor Major. He's the battalion operations officer."

The Major looked at Ames. "I didn't catch your name."

"I'm Blond. Ames Blond."

"Oh, you're English," said the Major with a bright smile.

"No, I'm an American."

"But I thought you were British, MI6 or something." Said the Major as they entered the Humvee.

"No," exclaimed Ames through grated teeth. "I'm an American with DORK."

"You're a dork?" asked the Sergeant looking back at the two. "Isn't that like a nerd or a geek or something? Why would they send you out here? Have we got a problem with our computers?"

"No, I'm not a dork," hissed Ames. "I work for DORK and the people in ASSHOLS!"

"So you're an asshole?" The Major asked. "How come they sent an asshole dork to Iraq? This place is screwed up enough as it is."

"Oh, shut to heck up, both of you!" cried Ames turning to the side to look out the window.

The rest of the trip to the Marine base was done in confusion and silence.

Passing through the gate into the base Ames noted a guard on the camel enclosure. When Ames mentioned the guard Major Major pointed out that just after Ames had left for Cuba there had been a major terrorist attack and the camels had been badly corked. The resulting mess had been horrible and had resulted in six WIAs - four camels, one Marine and a local worker who had the misfortune to be at the back of a camel when the cork was removed.

Sergeant Sergeant dropped him at the headquarters building along with Major Major. The Sergeant went to park the vehicle while Ames and the Major went inside to speak to the Colonel. They met Colonel Round in the Admin area.

"So you made it back Mister Ames," said the Colonel with a smile as he offered Ames his hand. "How did you enjoy your R and R in sunny Cuba?"

Taking the officers hand, Ames replied, "The accommodations left something to be desired, as did the cuisine. Bagels, cream cheese and cereal can get old real quick."

"Well, the accommodations aren't meant for four stars. Most of those people there are real bad apples who have killed with no care at all for the people, the families or the country. Most of them don't even come from Iraq or Afghanistan. They've just come here to cause as much hate and discontent as possible."

"The ones I had to be with didn't seem all that bad. I couldn't talk to them, but they weren't rowdy or anything. They actually seemed very subdued."

"People tend to get that way when they're put into cages and watched by armed guards. Those assholes are real brave when they're attacking defenseless people," said the Colonel. "Not so when confronting armed men. So I understand you have a line on al Raini? I gather he's somewhere in our area."

"Yes sir. We have information that indicates he's somewhere near Ghunda Zhar, the large mountain to the east of here, just north of Rayat. I plan to go up there and snoop around. There are some people in a village close to there who might help me out."

"If you'd like I can loan you a couple of Marines as support."

"No, sir," said Ames thoughtfully. "I don't want to spook the natives or al Raini. One American showing up should be tolerable. Armed Marines are something else. What I'd like to do is set up some kind of communications with you in case I need assistance, and possibly a ride into Rayat."

"Sure we can do that. We have a random patrol convoy that goes between here and Rayat. We can fit you in with that. As it happens they're leaving tomorrow morning. We have a small sat-com unit that you can use.

225

It's small and battery powered. I'll just need you to sign for it."

"I have to sign for it?"

"Certainly, those suckers are expensive."

"Exactly how expensive? I mean what if I lose it or something?"

"Come on, you know how the government works. You sign for it, you lose it, and you pay for it."

"Yeah, but I'm already in hock for a car and a watch – although we found the car, so maybe I can get that off the books."

"Fat chance of that. It'll take fifteen years for the paperwork to catch up."

"Yeah, well maybe I'll get lucky. "

"Well anyways," the Colonel continued. "I'll send you out with Lieutenant Commander's convoy in the morning. In . . "

Ames interrupted, "Did you say Lieutenant Commander?"

The Colonel nodded. "Yeah. Pretty good man. We alternate convoy commanders each week. This week the Commander is commander."

"You have Navy guys here?" asked Ames dubiously

"No, except for the corpsmen. Why do you ask?"

"Isn't Lieutenant Commander a Navy rank?"

"Not here. Lieutenant Commander is an African American kid from Pennsylvania someplace. I don't think he's ever been to sea."

"You seem to have a lot of that. Sergeant Sergeant, Major Major, Lieutenant Commander. Is there some reason for all the military names?"

"I see your point. Let me ask you, if you had a name like Sergeant, Major or Commander, could you see yourself working at Picway Shoes stuffing size eleven feet into size eight shoes?"

At that moment a large black man entered the Colonel's office. The Colonel grinned and said, "Mister Ames I would like you to meet Sergeant Major Private. He's the head enlisted man around here."

Ames groaned as he took the Sergeant Major's hand. "Pleased to meet you," said Private. "I understand you found Guantanamo to be the jewel of the Caribbean at government expense."

"Oh, yeah," replied Ames. "A thoroughly enjoyable experience. Almost as much fun as having my feet cut off. But I did learn something useful there. I overheard a couple of the prisoners talking about Ghunda Zhar. I couldn't follow the entire conversation, my Arabic isn't all that good, but I caught the words kahrabaii and gabal. Those mean electrician and mountain. The one guy said gabal and Ghunda Zhar and mentioned Al Raini's name. There was also something about Saudi Arabia. Then they saw me listening and shut up."

"So you think the mountain they were discussing is Ghunda Zhar?" asked the Colonel thoughtfully.

Ames nodded. "With the information provided by a drawing we found, this gives us a real clue to the possible, likely, could be whereabouts of Al Raini. I think

227

a few days snooping around in the mountains has at least a ten percent shot at locating him. And if the mention of Saudi Arabia means Al Raini is moving, then I'd better do it as soon as possible."

"Well, with odds like that I think you should go for it," said the Sergeant Major. "I've bet on horses that looked a lot worse. Course I lost all those bets but all you need is one win right?"

"I have no idea I don't play the ponies. Big Ball lotto for me. Anyway if the information does mean he's moving toward Saudi Arabia, then you need to get started," added the Colonel. "You lost a bit of time fooling around in Gitmo and then getting back here."

"I wasn't fooling around," said Ames indignantly. "I was sent there by mistake and used the time to get useful information!"

"Yeah, through dumb luck," chortled the Sergeant Major.

Ames bristled at the comment. "It wasn't dumb luck! I am a highly trained and observant agent for the United States government. I'm trained to pay attention and to notice things that other people would ignore. For example I notice that you're insignia is wrong Sergeant Major. What are those stripy things? You should have Sergeant on one side of your collar and Major on the other!"

The Sergeant Major glanced down at his collar. "What the hell are you talking about?"

"If you were a Sergeant Major you'd have two different insignia, Sergeant and Major. All you have is a bunch of stripes, so you're like, what, a zebra Sergeant?"

The Colonel had been sipping his coffee at the start of the exchange. He now started to laugh so hard coffee spurted out of his nose and sprayed onto Ames and the Sergeant Major. They both stopped arguing and looked at the Colonel while wiping at the mess on their shirts.

The Colonel started to choke on the coffee and his laugh turned into a croaking gasp. He bent over and started hacking and coughing.

The Sergeant started pounding the Colonel on the back as the senior officer's hacking turned into a wheeze. After a moment the Colonel started waving his hand and the Sergeant Major stopped pounding. Both junior men looked at the Colonel with concern.

The Colonel coughed once more and said with a croak, "Damn it Sergeant Major, I knew you wanted to do me in, but you could have picked a better way."

The Sergeant smiled. "Well sir, I have always figured I could run the battalion better than you. What the heck, I do most of the work as it is. Getting you out of the way would make things just a little easier."

"Well next time pick a better way. Good Grief! Can you see the epitaph on my tombstone – here lies Colonel Round, done in by coffee by the pound?"

They all started laughing at the joke until the Colonel started coughing again. After a minute the coughing subsided again and the Colonel said, "One of these days I'm going to learn how to breath that stuff." Everybody smiled again.

The Colonel walked back to his desk and sat down. "Sergeant Major, have Sergeant Jenkins find our Mister

Ames a place to sleep until tomorrow morning but not in the officer's quarters. Then get a hold of commo and get him a SatCom. Make sure he signs for it."

"I won't need a SatCom," said Ames. "I've got my cellphone."

"Most places around here cellphones don't work. No cell towers, no bars."

"Guess I'll take the SatCom," muttered the agent in resignation.

"Oh, and Sergeant Major you might want to get him a rucksack or something with some MREs and a camelback or a canteen or two. Do you need a weapon, Ames?"

Ames thought that one over for a minute. "No, sir, I'm qualified with one, but in my line of work I've found that a gun can get in the way. Its better I don't have one. I'm pretty good at living on my wits."

The Sergeant Major chuckled. "If I had your wits I'd still be a Lance Corporal."

"Don't get me started again, zebra Sergeant," said Ames.

The Sergeant Major was laughing hard enough to disturb the admin people in the outer office as they left the Colonel's office to find Sergeant Jenkins.

CHAPTER TWENTY-THREE

Driving into Rayat was a lot like riding into confusion. The city, although small was a mixture of ancient and modern. There were adobe looking homes built of compressed mud brick mingled with brick and concrete block stores and shops. Along the main road there were open-air bazaars with fruits and vegetables mingling with silver and gold jewelry. There were squawks from chickens and the bleat of goats. Camels hawked and spit. People hawked and spit.

The people were dressed in a mix as well. Some wore traditional abaya robes in various colors, with earth tones predominate, while others wore the suits and ties of the west. Turbans abounded, but here and there a red or blue baseball hat stuck out proclaiming allegiance to the Yankees or the Bears. Occasionally a woman in chador moved mysteriously from house to house.

The streets were crowded with life. People wandered from building to building, some dragging goats, camels or sheep. Chickens ran around freely. Dogs barked and snapped. Strange and sometimes unknown odors assailed the nose. Camel and sheep dung blended with exotic spices, the smell of roasting meat and unwashed bodies.

Auto exhaust permeated the area. If a vehicle had four wheels and an engine, somebody was driving it regardless of the condition of the body.

The convoy, composed of three Hummers with pedestal mounted machine guns, a squat wheeled vehicle with a heavy machine gun poking out its front called a LAV, two five ton trucks and a monster truck called an MRAP, entered Rayat by the main road. They had made good time from Irbil to the outskirts of the city. The road was macadam that was reasonably well maintained and in good shape.

The patrol had cruised up the highway, stopping now and then to check culverts and bridges for bombs and mines. Every once in a while they would stop and an engineer would move carefully forward, a mine detector leading the way.

For Ames the eight-hour trip had been boring. Sergeant Jenkins was busy with his duties and the driver, a young Private First Class, was annoying. He persisted in telling Ames all about his high school football team, drinking parties in his dad's motor home and some bull about hitch hiking through the mountains during a snow storm. He also threw in anecdotes about some girl names Roseanne or Rosalie, most of which involved dark nights and lots of wine. Ames pretended to sleep to keep from having to listen to it. The kid droned on anyway.

On entering the city, the convoy slowed to a crawl. The people and animals seemed to have no idea that the road was for vehicle traffic. They walked in the middle of the road or stopped to chat until a blaring horn required them to step to the side and that included the animals. Then they would give the offender a dirty look and step out of the way. There were a lot of blaring horns.

The Hummers went part way into town before stopping in a small open square. They were ignored for the most part, except for the usual panoply of kids with their hands out for candy, gum, chocolate and cigarettes.

Sergeant Jenkins and Ames dismounted from one of the Hummers and walked over to Lieutenant Commander's Hummer. The Lieutenant was just climbing out of his vehicle when they arrived. "Mister Blond," he said as he turned to face the two. "I've been thinking this over as we drove here. What I would like to do is send you with Sergeant Jenkins and the other two Hummers up the road to As'al Quarba. I'd send the LAV with you but looking at the map, there are places where it would not get through. Without it you'll get there faster and you'll still have some security during the trip. There are still some insurgents running around in these hills and it'll give my people a chance to scout around for them a bit."

"That sounds good to me if the Sergeant is up for it," said Ames looking at Jenkins. "It'll save me a lot of walking."

Jenkins shrugged. "Makes no never mind to me. I go where to Corps tells me to go."

At that moment Ames was grabbed from the back and a bushy face yelled in his ear. Almost instantly the barrels of six M-4's poked into a turbaned face. Ames dropped loose and spun around. "Hassim, you son of a bitch," yelled Ames as he recognized the erstwhile camel crap dealer. You scared ten years off my life. Where the heck did you come from?"

Hassim had a huge smile on his face as the Marines lowered their rifles. "When they took you away to send you to Cuba, they let me go because everyone knows I am the finest jewelry dealer in the Middle East." He was interrupted by Sergeant Jenkins, who butt in with, "You mean the biggest purveyor of garbage."

Hassim gave the Sergeant a dirty look as he continued. "Since I suspected you would be back to hunt for Al Raini I picked the best spot to wait for you, right here in Rayat. And my nose was right, here you are." It was a big nose. "So you are going back into the mountains?"

Ames nodded. "Yeah, I'm headed back to As'al Quarba. That should be a good starting point for my search. Are you going with me?"

"Of course, my friend. As'al Quarba has many good points including one that has long hair and beautiful eyes!"

"Are you talking about Fatima? She's only a kid. I think she's only about sixteen years old."

"Ah, but she is a woman to the Kurds," said Hassim with a wink. "At sixteen she is an old maid. They get married here at twelve. They do not believe that it is good for a woman to grow too old alone and lonely women get into mischief. Besides, I think that one liked you."

Ames shook his head and turned to Sergeant Jenkins. "It looks like we'll have one more for the trip. Could you add in some extra MREs for the fat guy here? Considering his size you might think about double rations."

Everybody looked at Hassim who stepped back while putting his hands on his stomach. "Hey, this is all muscle! There's not an ounce of fat here, except for what I have saved up for hard times."

"Must be a lot of hard times coming up," muttered Ames. "Okay Sergeant. Funs over. Let's get packed up and headed for As'al Quarba."

As the Sergeant selected two other Humvees to go with them, Ames and Hassim climbed into Jenkins vehicle. Within minutes the three Hummers had been loaded with extra chow and other needed equipment from the trucks. They turned around and followed the street back out of town.

Two miles past the last house the machines turned right and started up a winding dirt track heading north into the mountains. They had been on the road for half an hour when the rain started again. Unlike the other times when Ames had been caught by a deluge, this was a fine drizzle that soaked into the ground. Unfortunately it seemed to be non-stop and within a few minutes the road had become a muddy trail.

While a versatile machine that usually had no trouble with any kind of terrain or weather, the HUMMV's soon became bogged down in the growing mud. Unable to progress further up the steep track, Sergeant Jenkins called a halt and suggested they eat the evening meal while waiting for the rain to stop. He had the drivers pull up onto rock outcrops so they would not have any problems getting the tires loose later.

The machine gunners on the other two vehicles gratefully got out of the rain and climbed into the closed cabs with their drivers while everyone dug into the tan colored boxes and started pulling out brown plastic packages of food. Ames looked at the package in his hand.

Meal Ready to Eat
Pressed Goat w/Goat Cheese
Accessory Pack A
For Indigenous Personnel.

"Hey, somebody grabbed the wrong box. This is stuff for the locals!" He started to hand the package back to Hassim, who was passing out the meals.

Jenkins grabbed his hand. "No, it's okay. I got these for something different. I got tired of beanie weenies and spaghetti with turds. Go ahead and try it. Some of this local food is pretty good."

Reluctantly Ames borrowed the Sergeant's knife and slit the package open. He dumped the contents into his lap. He had a brown cardboard box that said "Pressed Goat w/Goat Cheese", two foil packs, one that read "Unleavened Crackers" and one marked "Strawberries Dehydrated." There was also a brown package marked with "Accessory Pack A" on it. He first opened the accessory pack and out dropped a compressed roll of toilet paper, a package of matches, a small box of two Chiclets, a plastic spork and a brown cube of something.

Holding up the cube he looked at Jenkins. "What the hell is this?"

"Oh, that's hashish. Some of the locals chew it. They say it gives them a religious experience. I forgot that was in there. US forces are not allowed to partake of those experiences. Just chuck it out the window."

Ames reached for the widow, thought twice about it and stuck the brown cube into his pocket. Opening the brown box he pulled out the foil package that contained the pressed goat. Inside he found a compressed brown blob overlaid with a yellowish substance. The whole thing looked vaguely like something that came out of the south end of a northbound camel. Gingerly biting into it and chewing he decided his estimate was right on the money. He stuffed it back into the package and opened the dehydrated strawberries and took a nip only to find his mouth instantly as dry as the Sahara. The strawberries had sucked every drop of water from his throat. He figured if he ate the whole thing his body would shrivel up to nothing. As a last resort he tried the crackers. Cardboard would have been preferable and more tasty. In desperation he tossed the Chiclets in his mouth and called it dinner.

The sky had darkened and the moon had come up while Jenkins and Hassim munched happily on the goat or whatever they had. Ames assumed that the men in the other vehicles were doing the same. Eventually Jenkins

237

waded up his trash and stuffed it under the seat, took a pull of water from his canteen and said, "We'll spend the night here and start off in the morning. There's about another hour and a half along this path to the village and I'd rather not roll in the dark."

"So we stay here?" asked Ames.

"Sure, hunker down in the seat and grab some zees. And don't worry, I'll put some of my people out on guard." The Sergeant climbed out of the vehicle and disappeared into the darkness.

Ames leaned his head against the door and closed his eyes. He immediately started to get a headache from the hard Kevlar wall and his legs began to ache from being cramped into a two inch by two inch space. Within minutes his butt felt like it had been soaked in lead. Just as he started to doze off, the door slammed open and Jenkins climbed back in. He fussed around with his flak jacket for a minute or two before settling in. Finally the cab became quite again. Ames went back to feeling miserable. Jenkins and Hassim started snoring like pigs rooting for truffles. This was going to be a long night.

It seemed only minutes after Ames had finally gotten to sleep, after what could have been hours of listening to the pigs, when someone banged a gong directly into his ear, disturbed his fitful slumber. His head snapped up causing a massive crick in his neck. In the moonlight he could see Jenkins and Hassim looking around dazedly. Then the gong sounded again.

"What the heck is that?" Hassim muttered.

"Damn," yelled Jenkins as he pulled the door open and fell out of the vehicle and into the mud. "Incoming!" His hand reached up and pawed at the floor, grabbed his rifle and jerked it out.

Ames and Hassim popped open their respective doors and dropped onto the ground. The agent could now hear the pop of M-4's and the rattle of a squad automatic weapon. A louder roar came from the two M-60's mounted on the Hummers. With a "whoosh" a flare rocketed into the air and burst with a loud pop. The area was instantly awash in glaring white light that flickered as the flare parachuted slowly to the ground.

Ames spotted turbaned figures in the rocks around them. Sergeant Jenkins yelled. "Everybody back into the vehicles! Let's move!"

Armor clad Marines and two frightened agents jumped back into the Hummers. The machine gunners on the other two vehicles sprayed the area with 7.62mm rounds. Jenkins jerked the starter and all three vehicles raced up the track away from the firefight. Bullets and an occasional mortar round followed them. Ames cringed as something spanged against the back wall of the Hummer.

Two fast and bumpy miles up the road Jenkins jerked the Hummer to a halt and jumped out. "Anybody hurt? Any WIA's," he yelled as the other machines stopped behind him. When he received a negative, he continued. "Anderson, get on the radio and tell battalion about the ambush and give them the GPS. The rest of you set up a perimeter. Those characters might try to follow."

The Marines scrambled to create a protective cordon around the three vehicles, while Ames and Sergeant Jenkins looked off to the south for signs of pursuit. Hassim peered fearfully out the window of the machine.

Minutes later, as they watched for enemy movement, they heard a whoosh as two AV-8B Harriers flew over followed by two Apache gunships. Within seconds the aircraft were launching missiles and directing Gatling gun fire on the ambush sight. This was followed by the express train sound of incoming artillery as Marine 155 batteries opened up. The assault ended with a tremendous crash as a B-52 bomber unloaded its bomb bay on what remained of the target area. Smoke drifted up into the moon lit night.

Just as suddenly as it began the night became still and quiet.

"Kind of overkill, wasn't it?" Ames whispered to Jenkins.

Jenkins nodded grimly, "Nothing is too good for our local friendly terrorists."

"Well, the light show was pretty," expressed Ames. "Do you think they got them?"

"Probably not," answered the Sergeant with a shrug. "More than likely the ragheads were across the border into Iran before the planes showed up."

"Over the mountains? That quick? That seems unlikely."

"Oh, our Arab friends can beat feet real quick when they're outnumbered. Let's get some sleep with what's left of the night."

The Sergeant rounded up his men and set a watch, telling the rest to grab some sleep. Ames crawled back into the uncomfortable seat and leaned his head against the wall. It was still hard as a rock. Things got worse when Hassim switched positions and found that Ames made a good pillow. The agent tried pushing the bulky Arab away, but it was like trying to move a tank. Reluctantly he closed his eyes and tried to sleep.

CHAPTER TWENTY-FOUR

The following morning the troops unfolded themselves from the vehicles and climbed out into the morning sunlight. They were a ragged bunch with bleary eyes and mud stained clothing. Ames looked around in the morning light. They were at the beginning of a defile between two huge rock outcroppings. To the south the trail led downward along a flat track with rocks and boulders on the left side. To the north the trail entered the defile and disappeared around a corner.

On both sides of the track green grass sprouted and bushes with bright green leaves made the area look like Vermont in the summer. A few trees provided patches of shade. Everywhere hues of green shown where there should have been brown and tan scrub grass and gnarled bushes. The trail itself, while covered with a light coat of damp earth had sprouting grass partially hiding it.

The Marines milled around, stretching and talking in low murmurs. A couple of the men had pulled out hoses on their camelbacks and were slurping down some water. A few were brushing at the semi-dried mud on their clothes trying to neaten their appearance. Ames looked

242

down at himself and found he was mud spattered as well. His black cotton slacks and the tan bush jacket were streaked with dark stains. Using his hand he tried to brush the dirt off. Were it had dried the mud crumbled away leaving light colored patches. Were it was still damp his hand smeared it. He gave it up as a lost cause and looked over at Hassim.

Hassim was looking around, completely ignoring the dirt on his striped robe. His beard had clumps of dried mud in it. He ignored that as well.

Jenkins waved the other Marines over. When everyone was assembled he said, "Grab an MRE and we'll fix something to eat. The village should be about a mile or so further on. I want to get in, drop Mister Blond and Hassim and head back out before noon. I want to try to get back to Rayat before nightfall. Anybody got anything to say?"

The troops all shook their heads. The Sergeant added, "Anderson, contact the Lieutenant and give him our position and our intentions. Tell him we'll contact him in the village and again when we start back."

Anderson nodded and headed for the Hummer that had the radio. Everyone else started poking into the vehicles for the meal packs. Jenkins reached into the box and pulled out an MRE. He then grabbed an odd looking plastic bag. After opening the MRE pack he pulled out the main meal and set it aside. Using his canteen he opened the plastic bag and poured some water into it. He then slid the main meal in and closed the top. He put the whole thing on the hood leaning against the windshield.

Ames watched as other Marines copied the process. "What's that?" he asked.

Sergeant Jenkins grinned. "New technology. It's a heater for MRE's. When you add water the chemicals inside gets hot and heats the food. Just don't drink the water unless your life insurance is paid up. Here let me show you."

Ames squeezed back in beside Hassim who was already digging through the MRE box. He passed Ames a package that read, "Lamb w/Rice Pilaf."

With trepidation Ames opened the package and followed Jenkins instruction. Within minutes Ames and Hassim were watching their meals heat up. Then the Sergeant showed them another trick.

He emptied the foil accessory pack and filled it with water. He then added water to a heater and carefully lowered the accessory pack into it. He set the bag down on the ground, held up straight with his rifle. Within minutes the water was steaming.

When the water was steaming he pulled the accessory pack out and wiped off the outside with a handkerchief. He then proceeded to open the coffee packet into the water. He grinned as he took a sip of the hot liquid.

Ames and Hassim hurried to follow his example, borrowing the handkerchief when it was needed. By then the main meal was done as well and the agent used a spork to take a bite of the brown and white mass. Oddly, it tasted fine. He started stuffing the concoction into his mouth while wondering if he had been in this dippy country so long that food was starting to taste good. He decided not. He had just gotten lucky.

After getting fat and happy with a hot breakfast everybody starting piling into vehicles. With a roar of engines the HUMMV's started up the track and through the defile. The enclosing rock made the motors sound loud and precluded any conversation. However it did not last long. After passing around the bend the machines roared into the open and they could see the tops of buildings poking up over a rise about a mile ahead.

A few minutes later they topped the hill and roared down into the village scaring goats, sheep, chickens and people. They came to a stop near the center of the village and Ames was just getting out of the Hummer when Shaykh Muhammad al Quddus and some of his men came out of the mosque and headed toward them. Ames recognized Abdel as one of them.

Walking to the head of the group of Marines, the agent held his hand in the air and said, "Assalam Alaykim, sadikie." The aged Shaykh stopped in front of Ames and immediately slapped him hard and started yelling in Arabic.

Abdel began a running translation. "My father says you are a pig and should get your goat-like self out of his village. How dare you shown your swinish face here after what you have done. You are the offspring of a pig who has mated with a snake. May your children be born with two-heads. May your winkie rot and fall off. May your balls shrivel to pebbles and dry up. Allah grant that your parents have no more children for the world cannot afford any more of such an ugly beast as you. You are lower than camel turds, lower than sheep dung, lower than lizard droppings. May Allah bless this village by taking your butt the hell out of here!" The old man ran down and stood glaring at Ames.

The agent looked back and forth between the two men. "Okay, I understand you're not too happy to see me again. You want to tell me what that was all about?" he said resting his gaze on Abdel.

Abdel stared into Ames' eyes. "Because of you Fatima will not marry Rojyar. She says she cannot marry a sheep dipper after she has met someone as worldly as you. This has seriously angered my father. He has lost the dowry of twenty goats, fifty sheep, six camels and a partridge in a pear tree. He was counting on the dowry to help pay off his Visa bill. Now that is all screwed up. He blames you for filling her head with heretical ideas. He has even considered a fatwa against you."

"Hey, wait a minute!" cried Ames. "I barely spoke to the girl. And I certainly didn't fill her head with any nonsense. Yeah, she's a pretty girl, but my culture wouldn't accept me hanging with a teeny bopper."

Jenkins tapped Ames on the shoulder. "Sorry to butt in here, but is this going to take long? I need to get back on the road again and I need to know if you're going or staying."

Ames waved his hand, "Hang on a few minutes while I try and straighten this out." He looked back at Abdel. "Tell your father, I did not meddle with his daughter's feelings. If there is a misunderstanding here, I apologize.

246

If need be, I will speak to the girl and find out what the problem is."

Abdel put his hand on his chin. "That could be a problem. She has locked herself in her room and won't talk to anyone. Father is very upset by the whole thing."

Abdel quietly began talking to his father and Ames turned to Jenkins. "You guys go ahead. We'll work this out, just be sure to leave me some MRE's and the SatCom."

"You sure you're going to be okay?" asked Jenkins. "These guys have a bad habit of cutting off hands and other body parts when they get angry."

"No," said Ames, "You have a long drive. You'd best get started."

With an, "Okay, you're the boss," Jenkins waved to his men to load up. Anderson pulled the SatCom out of the Hummer and set it at the agent's feet, while another Marine dropped two boxes of MRE's.

Ames looked back in time to see Hassim climbing back into a Hummer. "Whoa, big guy," he said as he grabbed the Arab's arm. "Where the devil are you going?"

Hassim continued trying to get into the machine while pulling on Ames' hand. "Hey, these people are royally dissed, and you heard what Jenkins said about chopping off hands. I have a real use for my hands. It's tough to sell camel patties without hands."

Ames pulled hard and succeeded in getting Hassim out of the vehicle. Hassim dropped backward on his butt in the dirt. "Your job is to stay here and help me. I can handle these people. We've gone through this before. Just relax. It's me they're mad at." Hassim sat in the dirt and glared at the agent.

With Hassim taken care of Jenkins tapped Ames on the shoulder and handed him a form with a pen. "Just sign here and we'll get going."

"What's this?" he asked looking at the form.

"You have to sign for the SatCom. Just put your John Hancock on that line there."

With resignation Ames signed the form and handed it back. He had hoped the Colonel had forgotten about signing for stuff. Jenkins tore off a copy and handed it to the agent and turned back to his vehicle.

With waves and cheery good-byes the three Hummers circled the people, drove out of the village and disappeared over the rise. Ames watched them go and secretly hoped he hadn't just screwed up again.

His reverie was broken when Abdel touched him on the arm and waved for him to follow. The agent trailed behind the Kurd while watching the Shaykh walk back to the mosque. The old man still did not look happy.

Abdel led him to one of the pressed mud brick homes, probably the same one he had woke up in for what seemed like a long time ago. They entered the front door and were in the meeting room with the rugs and pillows on the floor. They crossed the room and Abel tapped on a closed door. There was a moment of silence and then something crashed against the door. "Go away!" Ames heard, muffled by the door and the walls. "I will not marry Rojyar and you cannot make me!" Something else hit the door.

"Fatima," implored Abdel, "Open the door. There is someone here to see you."

"I don't want to see anyone!" the girl shouted. Another something hit the door. Ames could imagine the pile of rubble on the other side.

"You might want to see him," said Abdel in a raised voice. "Ames is out here."

There was a loud shriek followed by the sound of many objects being scooted across a floor and the click of a bolt being thrown. Abdel was knocked to the side as the door flew open and Ames almost fell over as a blur of red and blue swarmed over him.

He felt soft arms grip his shoulders and a tangle of dark hair against his face as Fatima hugged him. A flea crawled across his face. "Ames," she purred into his shoulder. "I knew you would come back. You came to rescue me from these horrible people and to take me away from that nasty sheep dipper."

Carefully Blond disentangled the girl and held her by the shoulders while looking into her sparkling eyes. "Fatima, we really need to talk about this. Come over here and sit down." He led her to a pillow and pushed her down. Abdel watched as Ames sat cross-legged facing the girl.

The agent took the girls hand and said, "Fatima, you think you want me, but you're wrong. You would never fit into my culture. In my society a girl of fifteen does not hang around a man of thirty-eight. If we tried the police would lock me up for being some kind of nasty pervert."

"But you could stay here," she said with tears in her eyes. "You could be a goat herder or even learn to be an imam, or maybe be like Hassim and sell crappy jewelry."

"Fatima," he said gently, "I'm not cut out to be a farmer or jewelry salesman. My job takes me away from home for months at a time. You would never see me."

Her eyes flashed. "But I could be with you when you are home, and when you're not I could fool around with salesmen and the pool guy."

"Sorry, but there wouldn't be a pool," said Ames, hanging his head. "I don't make very much money."

"You are a great secret agent." She said with a surprised look. "You must make lots of money!"

"Not really. I get about the same as an Army PFC, and I don't get the benefits that PFC gets. I have to pay for my own health insurance."

"PFC? But that other guy is a commander in the navy. You mean to say you're not even an officer?" she asked suspiciously.

"No, but that guy is the Royal Navy. They treat their people better than we do, at least the officers. Listen. Someday you'll meet the right guy. You see me as freedom, a paycheck, bennies, but you have all the freedom you need right here. You have the freedom of the mountains, the freedom of the goats and sheep, the freedom to be treated like a chattel, the freedom to die young from overwork. You have a wonderful life. Just tell your father how you feel about Rojyar. I'm sure he'll understand. Come on, let's go talk to him."

Standing, he helped Fatima to her feet and waved for Abdel to come on. Together the three of them crossed the yard and entered the mosque. At the sight of his daughter the Shaykh's eyes lit up.

Fatima went over to her father and sat down beside him. She took his hand and started speaking quietly to him in Arabic. Occasionally, the Imam would look at Ames and giggle. After a few minutes, the holy man looked at Ames and spoke.

Abdel translated, "My father says he is grateful to you for speaking to Fatima. He will be more than happy to help you in any way possible. However he is a little annoyed that he has to tell the kids to put the marshmallows away again."

Ames sat down on a pillow in front of the Shaykh and Fatima. The old man scowled. Ames crossed his feet. The old man stopped scowling.

Abdel continued translating. "My father apologizes for the remarks about your wiener and balls. He would never heap such curses on a man who is so badly paid. However, he still thinks you have as swinish face."

Ames bit his lip to keep back his own curse. "We believe that the nefarious terrorist Al Raini is hiding somewhere around Ghunda Zhar. Tomorrow Hassim and I are going to the mountain and look around to see if we can find any evidence that he's there. I would like to use one of your villagers who knows the area as a guide."

Fatima translated. "My father says if you are going after Al Raini he will help. He's tired of that piece of donkey turd sending kids around to shake their cans. Certainly he will help. You can use Abdel, my brother. He knows that mountain like the back of his camel. We will also provide you with an Abaya so that you do not stick out so much. There are not too many villagers who wear safari jackets. I suppose it would be too much to ask for you to grow a beard by tomorrow?"

Ames remembered the last beard and shook his head emphatically.

Hassim, who had been standing and listening to the conversation, butt in, "Ames, I do not think this body of mine is designed to climb mountains. I believe I should wait here for news."

Ames looked at the big Arab. "Can you use a SatCom?" The Arab nodded. "Good, you stay here. If I find anything I'll send Abdel back and you can get reinforcements from the Marines, if we need them." The Arab nodded his head with obvious relief.

"Just leave the girls alone and stay out of the kitchen," admonished the agent. Hassim looked stricken, then bit into the leg of lamb he had found somewhere. "And if you lose that SatCom I will personally skin you with a dull fork," continued the poorly paid government employee.

Hassim tried to pout while chewing, but the result looked like the results from an overworked food grinder.

The Shaykh was grinning by this time. Fatima said, "My father is very happy. He would like to have a feast

252

tonight to celebrate your adventure. He has decided we will have spaghetti with garlic bread and a nice tossed salad. Your choice of dressing. We have ranch, blue cheese, Italian and a very nice house dressing. Please make your selection before being seated."

CHAPTER TWENTY-FIVE

They started out the next morning, Ames, Abdel, a villager named Jiwan and a donkey carrying a supply of MRE's, water and some local foods. There was also a small tent, a Coleman stove and a couple of lanterns. Three folding chairs, a television, a stereo, three rolled mattresses, six rugs and 14 pillows completed the list of needs. The donkey walked on wobbly legs as the pile swung back and forth on his back.

Most of the village had turned out to see them off. Someone had set up some tables and there was a flea market and an outdoor barbeque. Ames picked up two Beanie Babies and a barbequed goat sandwich. Arabic music played over a loudspeaker and troop of native dancers, in traditional costume, whirled around in the village square. Fatima hugged Ames under the disapproving eye of her father. Abdel looked slightly bemused. Hassim slept in.

Ames had pulled a red and yellow striped robe over his slacks and bush jacket to hide his un-Arabic appearance. A gray turban sat on his head. Fatima had fashioned a beard from a piece of black cloth cut into strips. The contraption hung from his ears by a cord and smelled slightly of sheep. From a distance it looked like a cloth cut into strips. She thought it looked terrific.

While the peak of Ghunda Zhar looked close, the mountain was almost fifteen miles away. Because of the location of the village they were already on the lower skirt of the mountain and their path took them through the foothills in a slow climb up the slope. There progress was good, except for having to chase the local kids back home. The kids apparently thought this was a Boy Scout outing and it took some doing to talk them into going back. They were disappointed when they found there were no merit badges to be had.

The land around them was rocky and hard to travel through. The mountain was straight in front of them, but they were constantly forced to travel around large rock outcroppings and through defiles that did not go in their direction. Where there should have been sparse grass and scrub trees, there was an abundance of greenery. It seemed that the grass was growing even as they walked over it.

They had been moving for about five hours when they noticed that the sky above Ghunda Zhar was darkening very rapidly. Ames stopped and watched it for a few minutes and then called to Abdel. "We might want to consider setting up the tent or finding some shelter. I think it's going to rain again."

Abdel looked at the sky and nodded assent. They traveled forward another ten minutes when they found a natural cave. The entryway was big enough for all of them to fit inside, including the donkey. Ames and Jiwan unloaded the donkey and set up the chairs and the Coleman stove. Abdel set about preparing lunch while Ames watched the sky.

The clouds had become darker and more threatening. Suddenly raindrops started pattering on the rock. The agent stepped back within the shelter of the cave. "Here it comes," he said rather unnecessarily. Jiwan put his hands together over his head and muttered something in Arabic.

Abdel looked up from the ravioli he was cooking and glanced outside. He stood up and walked over to Ames. The donkey took the opportunity to stick his nose into the pot and munch on the lunch Abdel was preparing.

Abdel looked at the sky and the rain. "Is this what Al Raini is causing?" he asked.

"Yeah," said Ames. "I think so. The information we have is that he has built some kind of machine that controls the weather. If that's true, he can dump rain or snow or whatever wherever he wants. That could cause real harm to the economies of the world."

Abdel thought for a moment. "Yes, but are there not good things that can come from it? Look at the plants here. They should be brown and dead looking, yet they are alive and growing like weeds, which they are. If those were real crops we would have an abundance of food, like your Midwest."

"Sure, it seems like maybe a good thing here, but what if they dumped this much rain down by Basra? Can you imagine the problems the oil fields would experience if they were inundated with water? Pumps would jam.

Transportation wouldn't be able to move. They'd have to shut down. Look at the lost revenue and the people's lives that would be impacted. It would make a hell of a terrorist weapon."

At that moment there was a clatter as the donkey knocked the pan off the stove to get the last of the ravioli from the pan. Abdel started to chase the animal away, but Ames stopped him. It was kind of pointless to stop the donkey now. The ravioli was gone.

The three men ended up sitting and watching the rain while eating bologna and cheese sandwiches, followed by Twinkies. Ames wasn't about to tell them the ingredients in the meat. And he damn sure wasn't going to tell them what was in the cakes. They sipped at some really bad tea that Jiwan had prepared.

Eventually the rain let up and they loaded up the donkey and started out again. Ames figured it would take a couple of days to find the entrance into the mountain. He was sure that Al Raini was in a cave somewhere and there had to be an entrance. It was probably well hidden and had guards posted all over. He suspected their hunt would be much like the one for Usama bin Laden.

They had been walking about four hours from the lunch break when they accidentally stumbled across the cave entrance hidden in the side of the mountain. They did not see any guards.

A two-lane macadam road led up from the base of the mountain, passed through a chain link fence and disappeared through a ten-foot concrete arch into the hill. A yellow and black striped guard post with a flagpole sat astride the road at the opening in the fence. A bright red flag flew over the guard post. The flag had a large yellow "R" emblazoned on it. Two more flags flew over the end of the arch.

A helicopter sat inside a hanger on a concrete pad to the north of the road. A red flag with an R flew over the hanger. A line of high-tension power lines marched down the hill and off to the northeast.

The three men hunkered down behind a large boulder to watch the entrance. They lay there for a few minutes before Abdel said, "Do you think if we moved around to the side of this thing we might be able to see something besides the rock?"

They shifted position and could now see a bright blue golf cart emerge from the cave entrance and drive over to the helicopter. Ames pulled a pair of binoculars from thin air and focused them on the cart. "Rats," exclaimed the agent, "That's Al Raini. I'd recognize him anywhere. Well maybe not anywhere. I mean, if he got a haircut and shaved off the beard and put on a suit, I'd probably not know him from Adam. But, hey that's him. I don't know who the other bozo is, but he must be another terrorist."

"Looks to me like the other guy has a suit on," Abdel put in. "The only terrorist I know who wears a suit is Arafat, and that ain't him. He's dead and I don't think he pulled an Elvis."

Ames shifted the binoculars and scanned the entrance to the tunnel and the hillside around it. A black opening caught his attention. He pulled the glasses from his face and peered closely at the mountain. He dropped the binoculars down and squinted to see the spot.

Above and to the right of the archway a small dark spot wavered in the heat. The agent pulled the binoculars back up and looked at the spot, his thumb playing with the focus wheel. The spot resolved into an opening partially covered by a bush, the green leaves hiding it from all angles except from where the three lay.

He pulled the glasses back down again and pointed. "I think there's another entrance over there hidden by that bush." Abdel peered at the hole. "Let's work our way over there and take a closer look. Tie the donkey up and we'll leave him here."

Staying low behind the ridge, they worked their way over to the side of the mountain. Everyone ran hunched over except Jiwan who strolled along near the crest of the ridge, peering over it from time to time. Suddenly he turned and yelled something to Abdel.

"Get down!" the Kurd yelled at Ames. "The helicopter is taking off!"

All three dropped down and scooted under the closest bush. Moments later they could hear the clatter of helicopter blades and Ames looked up in time to see the turquoise machine fly over the ridge and turn west. Within moments it was out of sight.

Twenty minutes later Ames brushed the bush aside and, using a pencil flashlight he obtained from the same source as the binoculars, peered into the black hole. It was about three feet in diameter and extended into the mountain through a rock passage.

Ames snapped off the light and turned to Abdel. "I'm going to go in here and see where it leads. You head back to As'al Quarba and tell Hassim what we've found. Have him contact the Marines and ask them to stand by for some back up if I need it. Leave Jiwan here. He can bring you a message if I need help."

Abdel looked at Jiwan and back at Ames. "But Jiwan does not speak English. How will he know if you are in trouble?"

Grimly Ames said, "Oh, he'll know."

Abdel nodded and spoke to the second Kurd. Jiwan nodded and slipped down the mountain headed back for the donkey. Abdel shook Ames' hand and handed him a can of spray paint. "May Allah bless you and guide you sadikie. Use this paint to mark your trail. If you get lost you can follow the paint trail back out. If you die we can use the trail to set up a tourist attraction. We will call it the Blond Caverns in your honor." He pulled his hand loose and followed Jiwan down the hill.

With some trepidation Ames relit the light and eased his way into the hole. Immediately it became apparent that the robe would be a problem. He backed out and pulled the robe of and unstuck pulled of the cloth beard, shivering as he thought about R'as beard. He squeezed back into the hole again.

The tunnel went straight for about fifteen feet, then angled up and became narrower. Holding the flashlight in his teeth, the agent clawed his way upward until the passage suddenly leveled off and opened into a large room. He spray painted the side of the hole he had just come through.

Stalagmites and stalactites extended from the floor and ceiling, giving the space the look of gnarled teeth. Carefully he moved forward into the room skirting the extending spires and ducked to miss the hanging fangs. He carefully searched until he found a second tunnel leading deeper into the mountain. Behind him he left splotches of red paint on the ground.

This passage was bigger than the first and Ames could walk stooped over, the flashlight guiding his way. The walls were hard granite and moist. Tiny trails of water seeped from the walls and dribbled down the center of the tunnel making the floor slightly slippery. The flashlight dimmed and went out.

The agent banged the instrument against his palm a few times and clicked the switch off and on. The light remained out. He stuffed the light into his pocket in disgust and inched his way forward using his hands to feel the cave wall.

Without warning the passage dipped downward and the agent lost his footing. He fell with an "oomph" that knocked his breath away. He started sliding downward and scrabbled at the floor and walls to stop the slide.

Suddenly he sailed out into space and his frantic hands grabbed at the nearest object. He found himself dangling from a stalactite thirty feet in the air. The flashlight flew from his pocket and skittered through space and landed on top of an odd looking machine. Looking up he could see that the roof domed upward another seventy or so feet. There was a hole in the center and Ames could see daylight reflected off the stone.

Holding on tight he looked down. Below him were strange machines, wires and pipes. A large machine with a huge dish sat in the middle of the floor. All the wires and pipes seemed to lead to it. Floodlights mounted in the ceiling lit the area. People in white coats moved from machine to machine or stood in front of panels writing on clipboards. A fat Arab in a chartreuse robe and yellow turban seemed to be overseeing things. Every once in a while one of the white coats would come up to him and speak for a few seconds before walking away.

As Ames hung suspended another man in a robe walked up to the fat one and started talking. Ames recognized him as Al Raini.

* * * * * * * * *

Abu reentered the cave after sending Salim on his way with instructions for further funding, a list of needed spare parts and an order for Chinese takeout. Inside the large cave the Arab walked over to Sidi.

"Well, that butt head is on his way again," he said to his partner with a shake of his head. "Every time that twit shows up my ulcers start acting up. Get me a couple of Tums."

Sidi reached into his robe and pulled out a box. "Here try these. They are supposed to take effect immediately and they last for twenty-four hours, something your Tums do not do. Four doctors out of five recommend them." He started to open the box.

With a stunned look Abu stared at Sidi, then reached out and swatted him knocking the turban off. "When I need a commercial I'll turn on the bloody boob tube! Just give me the Tums!" Abu seemed unaware that he had just done a Tums commercial himself.

With a sigh, Sidi put the package back into his pocket and pulled two tablets out. He handed them to Abu and then reached down and snagged his turban.

The head terrorist grabbed the pills and popped them into his mouth. Instantly he gave a strange expression and began spitting. The tablets popped back out and hit the floor in a glob of saliva. Abu dug into his mouth and swiped around with his finger. He pulled it out and looked at the wet gray mass.

Abu sputtered and yelled, "Blast it, haven't I told you to carry the whole bottle! I really didn't need a mouthful of pocket lint." Abu spat again. Sidi looked downcast and ashamed.

Abu grabbed the clipboard from Sidi. "Where are we at with the transitional move? I want to start on the southern areas tomorrow. And I want a boost in power to see if we can cover both areas at once." He looked over the figures on the board.

"The dish alignment can handle another twenty degrees of shift," answered the heavy Arab. "By tuning . . ." There was a loud crack and pebbles started dropping on them.

They both ducked and looked up in time to see a stalactite with a strange hump drop towards them. Abu pushed Sidi and then jumped backward. The stalactite hit the ground with a crash and both men looked at the crumpled figure of a man partially covered by the debris.

CHAPTER TWENTY-SIX

Ames opened his eyes and saw a rock ceiling over him. Sitting up and looking around he found he was lying in a rough bed with a thin mattress in a rock-hewn room with a metal door. Holding his aching head he muttered, "I really have to stop waking up in strange weird places. Better yet, I need to stop getting my silly head knocked out."

He then noticed a fat Arab in a chartreuse robe sitting in a chair by the door. He also noticed that he was in his underwear. Pulling the blanket up, he asked, "Who the devil are you and where are my clothes?"

"I am Sidi al Down, assistant to the great Abu Al Raini." Sidi leered at Ames. "I took off your clothes so that you could sleep better. They are right beside you on the floor. Nice butt you've got there."

Ames pulled the blanket more tightly around himself.

At that moment the door opened and his arch nemesis walked in carrying a tray. Abu was dressed in a dirty brown robe with a red and blue striped turban. He set the tray on a small table. With a wave he dismissed his underling and Sidi reluctantly left the room, glancing back at Ames while wiggling his eyebrows. Ames stuck his tongue out. Abu closed the door and pulled the chair close to the bed and sat down.

"Would you like some tea?" asked Abu with typical Arab courtesy. When Ames nodded yes, the genius poured two cups and offered one to Ames. He sipped at his own and set Ames' cup on the bed.

As Ames sipped the hot beverage the Arab looked at Ames for a moment and said, "Okay, who the devil are you and why are you falling from my ceiling?"

Ames lowered the cup and said, "I'm Blond, Ames Blond."

Abu scowled and asked, "What the seven stages of Hades did I do to the British that they've got secret agents hanging from my ceiling like bats? What's with that anyway? Don't you people believe in doors?"

"No, no," stammered Ames. "I'm not British, I'm an American. My name is Ames Blond. That other guy works for the British."

"Okay, so I've got American bats hanging from my ceiling. Are you a tourist, an investor, what the heck are you? What do you want here?"

"I'm a secret agent working for the American government. I'm here to find out about your weather control experiments."

Abu looked confused. "What does the CIA want with my weather machine? Don't they have enough oddball stuff on their plate with talking dolphins, bad breath bombs and trying to assassinate Castro?"

Wait a minute," said Ames, turning and putting his legs over the side of the cot. "I don't work for the CIA. I'm an agent with the Department of Reconnaissance and Knowledge."

"So you're a dork who's come to spy on me?"

"Yeah that's right," answered the agent. "We need to know what you're up to."

"So what's a dork want with my weather machine? You get plenty of rain in Kansas. You get too much rain in Florida, but I guess old people like to be soggy."

"No we don't want to use it on Kansas or Florida. We want to know what you're going to do with it."

"But you should already know what I'm doing with it. It has been in operation for over two weeks now. Is there some problem with your National Weather Service? You can predict hurricanes, but lose a rainstorm in Iraq?"

"No, that's not it. I'm just here to collect information."

"Okay, Brunette," said Abu. "I'll accept that for now."

"It's Blond," said Ames with a grating voice.

"Yeah, whatever," muttered Abu standing up. "Well, get your clothes on and come on then. We'll have some lunch and I'll show you around." Ames looked and found his stuff sitting on the floor by the head of the bed. When he pulled on his pants and shirt a small brown cube fell out of the pocket. Thinking quickly he palmed it and dropped it into Abu's cup. He then sat down and slipped on his socks and started putting on his shoes. He could only find one.

"Where's my other shoe?" he asked looking under the bed.

"Oh, that got swept up with the rest of the stalactite. By the time we noticed it was missing the trash had gone out. If it had not been a Tuesday we could have found it, but on Tuesday's the trash goes out first thing in the morning. Sorry." Abu raised his cup and drained the tea. He made an odd face and looked into the cup before setting it back on the table.

After he was dressed, minus one shoe, and they passed out the door, Ames looked at Al Raini. "Lunch? How long have I been here?"

They walked down a passage through the rock, with Ames rocking back and forth from shod foot to unshod, as Abu answered. "You hit your head pretty hard when you landed. You slept through the night and part of the morning. It's now eleven o'clock."

Ames looked at Abu, who was weaving slightly from side to side bumping into the rock walls, and thought to himself, "It's been almost twenty-four hours since Abdel left. By now Jiwan should have noticed something was wrong and went back to get help. All he need do was stall this crazy raghead until the Marines arrived."

With that thought the two men left the passageway and entered Al Raini's unimpressive office. Abu staggered across the room, staring at the desk lamp with a silly grin on his face. Ames seated himself on a sixteenth century French divan while Abu almost fell into an American west style bench sofa. Facing each other across a glass coffee table Ames looked around and noticed a picture on the wall. "Kind of roughing it here aren't you?"

Sidi entered before Abu could answer. He placed a tray of tuna fish sandwiches with watercress and glasses of chocolate milk on the table. With a bow he walked back out the door.

Abu selected a sandwich and followed the agent's gaze to the picture. "Yes, it is rough, but what is one to do?" he said with slightly slurred speech. "Money is tight and everything must go into my creation." He pointed to a picture on the wall. It was Gainesborough's "Blue Boy." "That is the only decent picture I have," said the terrorist mournfully, tears dribbling down his cheek." I obtained it last year. I wanted "Pinky" too, but she was not available." He looked sadly at the blank spot next to the painting and tried to wipe his face. His hand plowed a track through the unkempt hair across his forehead.

Ames looked at Abu in puzzlement while taking a bite. "I thought "Blue Boy" was in the Louvre in Paris?" he said through bread crust.

"It was, but the French premier needed some money to bail out the economy." He sipped at his chocolate. A brown swirl dribbled from his mouth, down his beard and onto his robe. He looked down and poked at the spreading stain.

"So why didn't you get "Pinkie" at the same time?" He noticed that Abu was slowly sliding off the bench.

"He had what he needed. I guess I'll just have to wait until he needs more money for his mistress, er, for economic problems, before she becomes available." With a thump he landed on the floor. He shook his head a few times and fell asleep.

Ames sat and watched him for a moment, then crept over to shake the terrorist. Abu smiled and muttered something about Samantha. The agent smiled and ran over to the desk.

Taking his time he opened each of the drawers and examined the contents. With disgust all he found were some old Playboy magazines, a bottle of rum and a stack of credit card receipts from Wal-Mart. Finally, in the last drawer he found a leather bound address book.

Scanning quickly through the book Ames noted that there were hundreds of girl's names and addresses from various places in Massachusetts. With a sly look the agent stuck the book in his pocket. He then scuttled back to the couch to wait for Al Raini to wake up.

Two hours later the Arab woke up and looked blearily around. He absentmindedly wiped dried chocolate and spittle from his beard. "Why am I on the floor?" he asked somewhat dreamily.

"I guess you can't handle your chocolate," said Ames

The Arab slowly pulled himself to his feet using the bench for support. "Is lunch over?"

"I would say so."

"Then come with me, I must show you my dream." He hobbled unsteadily to the door with Ames in tow. He seemed to gain strength with each step until he was walking almost normal. He glanced back suspiciously at the agent.

Abu led Ames out to the main cave. With a wave of his hand the Arab said, "Behold the wonder of the age. With this I can provide rain to anywhere within a thousand mile radius. At least, I think I will when I get the fershlinging thing to work right."

Ames looked out at the vast array of machinery and equipment that he had seen from above. The sidewalls were covered with flashing lights and panels with buttons and switches. There were odd-looking things connected by pipes, wires and string. A heavy hum filled the space. In the center of the room Ames could see the big dish moving upward into position.

"Oh good," exclaimed Abu. "A test is about to start!"

As they watched the dish moved up to the roof and through the opening. The scissor legs stretched upward until they melded into a solid support. Ames could see massive electrical conduits connected to the dish.

Men at various points were furiously pushing buttons and switching switches. Dials that had been idle snapped to life. Sparks flew from huge insulators. The hum increased until it was almost painful. Abu reached out to a wall hanging and handed Ames a set of earplugs.

Abu pointed around the room while yelling at Ames. "We get power from the grid that is connected into the hydroelectric plant on the Great Zab River. Those huge condensers over there collect the electricity and convert it into millions of watts. That power is directed to the dish that uses the ionization to collect and focus hydrogen and oxygen atoms. Those atoms are sent through the Hydrogen Ovulator that I invented and sent back out through the dish into the atmosphere. We can control the direction and force of the electron beam much as you control the beam in a television."

Ames watched as the sparks grew in power and heard the hum increase until it was inaudible.

Al Raini continued in a more normal voice. "Once the beam is focused it begins coalescing the ion stream into individual water molecules. When enough molecules collect to overcome the weight of the atmosphere, it starts to rain. The test we are conducting now is to see if we can reach southern Saudi Arabia with the beam without impacting the ozone layer."

Abu smile smugly at Ames until, with a loud crack, the sparks stopped and the dish started back down. The terrorist's smile disappeared and he yelled at Sidi who had been standing at one of the control panels. The heavy Arab hustled over to his master.

"What the devil just happened?" Abu yelled as he took off his earplugs. "This test was scheduled for two hours duration!"

Sidi shrugged. "It looks like the number two power transformer couldn't handle the output. The breaker tripped and pulled it out of the circuit. When that happened the power levels cascaded and more transformers kicked out. Pretty soon the entire eastern grid was off-line. At that point the computer terminated the test and we had a massive power failure."

Abu scratched his head. "I thought we changed that transformer the last time that happened. There were supposed to be protocols put in place to prevent this from happening. We calculated the power levels and the new transformer should have handled it." He glanced over at Ames, who now had the smug smile.

Sidi shrugged again, "The transformer didn't get changed. Samir was supposed to have ordered one from GE but they were backlogged."

"So why the did you run the test?" yelled Abu. "You could have blown the entire system! It would have taken us weeks to repair the damage!"

Sidi looked at the floor. "I told them to go ahead." He backed up quickly as Abu raised his hand. "I didn't want you getting petulant when the test didn't go forward! You know how you get when things don't go the way you want! Don't hit me!" Sidi cowered as Abu glared at him.

"Having a little trouble with the help?" asked Ames watching the exchange.

"You stay out of this, Brunette!" shouted Al Raini.

"It's Blond," hissed the agent.

"Blond, Brunette, Redhead, whatever! Who gives a fart! Stay the heck out of this!"

"Got a bit of a temper there, Rainhead?" said a smirking Ames.

"Rainhead!" Abu's eyes grew large. "You dumb doofuss dork, I could have you locked up forever for butting in! This is my baby. Don't mess with it!"

"Okay, Thunderbutt, have it your way."

The terrorists face grew bright red and he started panting hard. He raised his hand to hit the agent, but Ames ducked and Abu spun around and fell to the floor. He lay there screaming and kicking his heels up and down. Sidi shook his head and took Ames by the arm.

"I'm sorry, but my master gets like this sometimes. He hates it when things go wrong." The chartreuse terrorist guided Ames back through the passageway to the small room. As Ames entered the room Sidi said, "Oh and thank you. By butting in you kept Abu from hitting me. My face was getting sore."

Ames looked at the obese Arab. "If he hits you all the time why don't you leave?"

Sidi looked at the floor. "Because he needs me. He has to have someone around him to demean. If I weren't here he would not be able to think and this great project would not be completed. It is as much mine as it is his." Sidi looked up into Ames' eyes searching for understanding.

Ames turned and looked at the room, not understanding. He went over and sat on the bed looking at his feet. "Do you think you could find me some shoes?" he asked Sidi.

Sidi shook his head, "No, I don't think you will need them. I'm pretty sure Abu is going to leave you locked in here for a long time."

"Well, I suppose I can get some more sleep," said Ames rolling onto the bed.

"Can I help you get undressed?" asked Sidi hopefully.

"No," shouted Ames as he took off the shoe and threw it at the big Arab. Sidi ducked and ran out the door, slamming it shut.

CHAPTER TWENTY-SEVEN

Ames was sitting in the sparse room playing with his thumbs when there was a tap on the door. Getting up he walked to the opening and whispered, "Who's there?" He heard a vague noise from the other side, followed by another tap.

Raising his voice slightly he called again, "Who's there? I can't hear you."

He could barely hear the unintelligible reply. He's raised his voice some more. Again the answer was distorted. Finally he shouted, "Who the bloody armpit is out there? Answer me blast it!"

"Ames, is that you?" he heard through the door.

"Yes," shouted Ames. "Who is it?"

He was knocked backward as the door flew open and a crowd of people jammed into the small room. Sitting on the floor he looked up and saw Salim and his six PRICKS, all clad in tiger stripe uniforms with bandoleers across their chests. Which was odd since none of them had a gun.

Behind them were Abdel and Jiwan and three or four others he recognized from the village. At the back he spotted Fatima dressed in a tight brown shirt and dark Capri pants. Her hair was tucked into a French kepi. Hassim stood at the back wearing a bright yellow robe. "What's all this," Ames asked as he stood up. He heard a snick as the door was closed.

Salim grinned and said, "When you did not come out of the tunnel, Jiwan came to the village to get help. Hassim tried to contact the Marines, but kept getting an answering machine. I was in the village and offered my services. Then everyone pitched in and here we are."

"So you decided it would take fifteen people to sneak me out of here." Ames said with a grimace. "Good thought. I'm sure no one will notice. And what is Fatima doing here?"

The girl pushed forward eliciting smiles from the men she pushed passed. She slapped at a roving hand. "I am here because I am your friend too!" she said defiantly. "And do not tell me this is for men only, I don't need any more of that chauvinistic crap. I get enough of that in the village."

"Fine, fine," exclaimed Ames hiding behind his hands. "If you want to fool around with terrorists don't let me stop you!" The girl crossed her arms, accentuating her bosom, and looked smug. The men looked at her, ah, arms.

"So what's the plan?" asked Ames tearing his eyes away.

Salim looked around and said, "We will sneak out of here through the main tunnel using the path we used to get in. We go out through the tunnel to the main cave, then hang a left at the first generator. We go two power panels over and turn right to the cross tunnel. We'll go down that to the fork and take the left hand fork, then back to the main cave. We cross the cave to the second tunnel on the right and go through it to the power generator room. We go in the front door and out the back, cross the tunnel and enter the storeroom. We come back out of the storeroom and renter the power room and back out the tunnel to the main cave. From there we dash to a third tunnel and go into Al Raini's office. After stealing some stuff, we go back into the tunnel and back to the main cave. After that we make a dash to the front entrance and out onto the road. We can overpower the guards at the gate and get away into the hills. Good plan, huh?"

"What's with all the backtracking and going in and out of rooms? There must be an easier way to get out of here."

Salim looked at the floor. "I'm sorry but I only remember how we got in here and we have to take the same route back out."

"Yeah, great," said Ames. "How about we just confront Al Raini and shut down his operation here? Do you think that might work better?"

"But there are a lot of people out there," added Hassim. "They might start shooting or something. I would not look good with holes." He poked at his massive bulk with a sausage finger as though bullets were impacting.

Ames shook his head. "Those are a bunch of techies out there. I don't think there's a gun in the whole place. Even the guards aren't armed. I remember seeing a patch that said Pinkerton Security Services. The guards look to average about seventy years old. You could probably take them out with a whisk broom."

Salim smiled at the idea. "Sure, we could be heroes! The first real action of the Patriotic Rebellion for an Independent Central Kurdistan!" He started rubbing his hands together. "We will be famous. We might even make some money off this deal." He hurriedly started speaking to his PRICKS in Arabic. The PRICKs started cheering.

After a minute of breathless speech he waved his hands and the cheering stopped. He turned back to Ames. "They agree! We will do it. You lead," he said pointing at Ames.

Ames sighed and wiped sweat from his forehead, "Okay, let's go. Hassim, open the door and let's get out of here. It's getting a tad warm and close with all these bodies."

Hassim yanked on the door. It would not open. He yanked again with the same results. Sheepishly he looked at the others. "I think it locked when it closed."

"Well that figures," muttered Ames. He pushed through the crowd and examined the lock. "Anybody got a knife or something." People started patting their clothes and digging into pockets. Finally they all stood with their empty hands showing. The white innards of pockets drooped like dog's ears. The agent slumped his head and banged it on the door.

Then he heard a bright, "Wait a minute," from Fatima. She reached under the kepi and handed Ames a hairpin. "Here," she said. Ames took it and frowned, "Who uses hairpins anymore?"

Using the pin he had the door opened in a mere half hour of poking and prodding. Most of them had sweat dripping from their foreheads and the air in the room was getting very stale. Two PRICKs made gurgling noises and fell on the floor, reducing the foot room for everyone else.

When the door opened there was a mad dash out into the corridor. After the initial rush the group tip-toed a few feet down the corridor before someone remembered the two missing PRICKs. They all waited anxiously while Salim went back to collect them.

Finally everybody was back together and the cluster of people snuck down the hallway. It sounded like a herd of elephants.

Ames had planned to stop and look over the main cave before herding his troop out of harm's way. He stopped at the entrance and was immediately pushed out into the open as the crowd behind him rushed forward to see. Across the room Abu and Sidi looked up to see what the commotion was. They both looked startled at seeing the mass of people spill out of the tunnel.

Abu screamed, "Now what the heck is going on here?" and headed for the mob. Sidi waddled along behind him.

Ames regained his footing and headed for Abu. Things were under control until Salim yelled, "Let's get em!" He grabbed a nearby sledgehammer and took off across the cave. The rest of the crowd of armed themselves and took off after him waving hammers, ball bats, sticks, iron bars and a bicycle frame.

Hassim brought up the rear carrying a Wiffle bat that he started banging into machinery with absolutely no results. The rest did not have that problem and were happily beating the stuffing out of machines, tearing at wires and pulling down pipes. White coated technicians ran screaming for the entrance.

Abu stopped in his tracks with his eyes popping out. He could not believe the carnage these people were committing. "Stop it!" he screamed. "What are you mad people doing?" He ran over and grabbed the Wiffle bat from Hassim. Hassim released the bat and ran after Jiwan who was wielding an iron bar and the bicycle frame. Hassim grabbed the frame, yanking it from the Kurd's hands and started swinging it a control panel.

The door popped open and sparks started flying. Abandoning the bicycle, Hassim reached in to grab a handful of wires. There was a loud snap of electricity followed by a very bright blue spark. Hassim flew across the room with his hair and beard smoking. He landed against the big machine and blew a smoke ring.

Sidi was trying to pull a metal bar from Salim and a tug of war started with Sidi pulling Salim across the floor. Finally Salim gave up and ran across the room to grab a wooden beam. Sidi chased after him with the bar.

Ames caught up with Abu and grabbed him, pinning his arms behind his back. "Look's like your nefarious scheme is over, "cried the agent.

Abu looked over his shoulder and screamed, "What the devil are you talking about, this isn't nefarious! Let me go you moron. Those idiots are destroying everything!"

At that moment ropes dropping through the opening in the roof interrupted them. Looking up they could hear the sound of helicopters reverberating off the rock walls. The ropes were followed by hordes of black and white clad men who came sliding down with rifles on their shoulders.

As they hit the floor one of them broke away from the rest and ran towards Ames and Abu. The rest took off after Ames' troop, breaking wires and pipes as they went.

As the man closed on him Ames recognized the bulk of Colonel Round. The Marine skidded to a stop in front of the agent as the rest of the Marines went to work helping Salim and his crew tear the machine up. One platoon tore into a bright red Prius with a vengeance, ripping off doors, smashing the windshield and flattening tires. They looked like a Detroit street gang on bargain day.

"So you caught him," said the Colonel poking Al Raini with the barrel of his rifle. "Good work. That's one less terrorist to worry about."

"What are you talking about?" yelled Abu, struggling to get free from Blond. "I'm going to sue the crap out of the whole bunch of you! You have no idea of the dung storm you're in for!"

Ames and the Marine both laughed. "That's the funniest thing I've ever heard of," said Ames. "A terrorist suing somebody." They laughed even harder.

"You'll stop laughing soon enough when the lawyers for GE get done with you," said Abu in a low grating voice. "You'll be sitting your fanny in Federal court from now to forever. They'll make sure you never own anything ever in your life. They'll get your house, your car, your furniture, your dog, your cat and your kids out to ten generations!"

Ames stopped laughing and turned the terrorist around. Looking him in the face Ames asked, "What do you mean by GE?"

"I mean General Electric you dumb retard," hissed Abu. "GE is part of the consortium financing this project. They and a half a dozen American firms are involved."

"American?" asked Ames in disbelief. "But you're part of NERDS!"

"What the heck do you think the Non-European Resources Development Society stands for? You didn't think Non-European meant Arab did you."

"Well actually I did," muttered Ames.

"This is a multi-billion dollar project to develop the Middle East so it can function when the oil revenues are gone," said Abu while rubbing his arms, tears starting to fall from his eyes. "The objective was to make the land green and fertile so everyone could have a home site or farm. Right now everyone is crowded into the sparse lands around the rivers. If we could make the rest bloom, there would be more than enough for everyone. No more hatred, no more rivalry. And you and that bunch of idiots are ruining the whole thing!" He waved his hand at the carnage around them.

"But you were collecting pennies from the people in the villages. How could you be part of a huge consortium when you're pinching pennies?"

"We had to start that way. We didn't have any money and venture capitalist won't back you until you prove you don't actually need the money. They don't want to risk money until there's no risk. So we had to fund our start up with pennies from kids. After that it was a piece of cake to get the biggies involved."

A group of Marines ran past them headed for the cave entrance to start collecting the scattered technicians. A second group chased after a screaming Fatima who disappeared behind the big machine. The Marines reappeared a moment later, running in the opposite direction. Abdel and Fatima came running after them. Abdel had a massive curved sword and Fatima had the Wiffle bat. They watched them until they were gone.

Salim and company were still banging away at stuff. Fatima reappeared again dancing around with a bundle of wires waving over her head. Salim went toward her and got slapped to the floor by the wires before she could stop. She dropped the wires and bent over the small PRICK.

"So who was the suit I saw out by the helicopter?" Ames asked looking at the Colonel who had a very sour expression on his face.

"That was Salim," said Abu wiping at the tears.

"But Salim is an Arab name! That means you had Arabs involved in this," exclaimed Ames triumphantly.

"Wrong again dippy." Al Raini said. "Salim is just a code name to throw off the French and Germans who would love to get their hooks into this and the billions of dollars from the eventual land development. Salim is actually the Vice President of procurement for Arab Enterprises, the front organization for the consortium. We almost had it licked and you destroyed it. Years of work and struggle and it's all gone." He fell to the ground and started crying.

The Colonel looked from Abu to Ames and back again. He grabbed the agent's shirt front in two massive hands. "You son of a bitch. There goes my star! There goes my pension! Damn you, you dork!"

He turned with a snort and yelled for Sergeant Jenkins to collect the troops. The Sergeant took a final swing at a condenser, turning it into glass shards, before dropping his hammer and blowing a whistle. He had a big grin on his face. The grin disappeared when he saw the look on the Colonel's face.

EPILOG

Ames sat in a booth at the McDonalds in Baghdad munching on a Big Mac with Hassim. It was good to be able to relax after the trying events of the last few weeks, and even better to chew on something that wasn't made from goat.

Hassim took a sip of his Coke and said, "So you have lost your job. If there is not going to be any prison time, possibly I could use you over here. You could start small, maybe pushing camel patties or something. After a while, if you show promise, I could move you up to fake jewelry. Maybe you could even join the CIA like me."

Ames smiled at the big Arab as he swallowed the bite he had been working on. "No thanks, Hassim, although I appreciate the offer. No, I still have my job. The General was really pissed with me until he found out I didn't actually give the order for Salim and his bunch to destroy the rain machine. Those nuts just took it upon themselves to put Al Raini out of business."

He took a swig of his Coke and continued. "I was doing the job I was supposed to and that was to find Al

Raini. It wasn't my fault that a bunch of fanatics went ape shit in the cave."

"So Salim is in trouble?" asked Hassim picking at his American fries. "What are they going to do to him?"

"Nothing. As it turns out, Salim is a national hero. The Kurds needed a national hero to unite them and the higher ups have chosen him. Sort of like a latter day Bolivar, living in the hills, living off the land and opposing the evil regime in Baghdad. They're even going to put his picture on the new Iraqi currency."

"I can't imagine that little twerp as a hero," muttered Hassim while looking out the window.

"Yep, he's a hero. The story they've put together is that Salim was instrumental in ensuring Kurdistan is properly represented in the national council and that he is going to make it possible for a Kurd to run for, and maybe even get, the position of Prime Minister. Quit a guy is our Salim."

"So, a national hero who lives in a ragged tent in the hills."

"Nope, not even close. The NERDS are backing Salim to start a chain of fast food joints in the Middle East. He's going to open a string of McGoat burger restaurants. They plan on using the Falling Arches as their logo. He'll be a millionaire in six months."

"So all the blame falls on the villagers from As'al Quarba," said Hassim a little sadly. "That'll really mess up those poor people."

"Wrong again. It seems the headman, Fatima's father Shaykh Muhammad al Quddus is going to be the next mullah for all of Kurdistan. If they blame the villagers and the Shaykh it will cause all kinds of anti-American feelings. So instead, they're going to provide twenty million in aid for the village, you know, new school, upgrade the mosque, and improve the streets, buy toilet paper, stuff like that. Make everybody happy."

"So nobody gets blamed. The story has a happy ending. What about the rain machine? It seems kind of sad that the Middle East won't be green."

"Yes it will. The bureaucrats had a choice of letting the NERDS rebuild and repair the damage to the project for 10 million dollars or having the Federal government finance it for five billion. In the interest of forestalling lawsuits the government is kicking in the money and the rain machine should be back in operation within six months barring cost overruns, project delays, and bureaucratic meddling. Washington has even hired Halliburton to provide any assistance that Al Raini needs."

"So that just leaves you and Fatima," Hassim said with a leer. "Are you going to get together with her?"

"No, Fatima is marrying Salim. She likes the idea of being with a national hero, particularly one who's going to be a millionaire. She can be really liberated with that much money."

"But he's kind of ugly isn't he," Hassim tossed out. "The guys got bad teeth, bad breath and looks like a short camel. How's she going to put up with him?"

"No problem. He's getting a full makeover - dental care, hairstyling, new clothes, lifts in his shoes, a bath, and lessons in how to be one of the rich and famous. By the time the specialists are done Salim will be gorgeous and you nor he will ever recognize him again."

Hassim leaned back in the chair. "So everything is over and you're ready to get on with another mission."

"Not quite," said Ames leaning across the table toward Hassim. "Do you remember that car we drove to Irbil in? The blue Pinto?"

"Sure," said Hassim nodding his head. "I think the Marines impounded it. Why?"

"Do you think you could find it?" Ames said with a pleading look.

"Yeah, I think so. Why? It was a pretty crappy car."

Ames snorted. "Because that butthole R is driving me crazy about the darn thing! He's docking my pay twenty two hundred dollars for that piece of crap and I'd really like to get it back to him!"

"So you want me to find it? What do I get out of it?"

"Maybe I'll help you to really join the CIA, or at least make you an agent for DORK."

"And do what you do?"

"Sure," said Ames.

"Not on you're life," muttered Hassim. "I have enough problems with passing junk jewelry to tourists. I don't need screwballs chasing me around. And I darn sure don't want to chase them. You never get anything out of it."

"Yeah, but I did get something out of it," said Ames, pulling out a leather book and tossing it on the table with a look of disgust.

Hassim picked it up and looked through the pages. "But this is full of women's names and addresses? This is terrific! You will never be without a date. Where did you get it?"

"I stole it from Al Raini's desk, like a dummy."

"Why would you be a dummy? This is great!"

"No it's not. I forgot how old Al Raini is. Most of the broads in that book have kids my age. A lot of them are grandmothers. Some of them are in nursing homes." He took a sip of coffee and stared down at the table.

Hassim glanced from Ames to the book and back. With a grin and a flip of his eyebrows he slipped the book into his pocket.

Characters Represented in the Book "A Roar in the East"

Characters do not represent any real person, living or dead even though it may seem like it.

Abdel	Son of Al Quddas
Abu al Raini	Head of Al Shamute
Alan Mohamet	Lawyer for Sheila Bitz
Ali Baba	Iraqi businessman
Al Jazeera	Not a person. An Islamic newsrag (translated "The Island") published in Qatar
Allah	Muslim deity, creator of all things. I'd say more but I dislike fatwas
Al Quddas	Head man of the village As'al Quarba. Fatima's father
Ames Blond	Agent for the Department of Reconnaissance and Knowledge
Ashe Blond	Ames Blonds father and government bureaucrat
Ayatollah	Fanatical Arab religious leader who

Khomein screwed up Iran

Bonnie Tyler   Singer

Bush   George H or HW both former presidents of the United States

Carla Hooker   Guest at Mrs. Jacob's soiree

Dick Cheney   Former Vice-president of the United States

Farah Fawcett   American actress. Known notably for the TV show "Charlie's Angels"

Fatima   Daughter of Al Quddas

Fidel   Fidel Castro, president for life of Cuba

Frank Nitti   Al Capone's second in command and enforcer

Gamil   Son of Al Quddas. Taxi driver in New York City

General Manystars Tenstars   Code name N, head of DORK, see N

George Bush   Former President of the United States

Harold Hardimann	Ambassador for the United States in Iraq
Hassim Abdul-Aziz ibn Najidal Mustafah	Ames' contact in Baghdad
Hassim Mustafah	See Hassim Abdul-Aziz ibn Najid al Mustafah
Ibrihim al Rashid	Another name for Abu al Raini
Kong	A donkey. Also last name of large gorilla named King Kong and video game named Donkey King
Jenkins	Sergeant with 2/8 Marines in Irbil
Jiwan	Arab from As'al Quarba
Lawrence Arabia	British agent supporting the Arab of Revolt against the Ottoman Turks in 1916 to 1918.
Lieutenant Commander	A lieutenant with 8th Marines in Irbil
Madonna	Rock music artist
Major Minor Major	A major with the 8th Marines in Irbil

MARPAT	Marine Pattern. The digital design of Marine utility uniforms
Michael Jewett	Colonel, commander of the Joint Operations Command in Cuba
Muhammad	Guy who wrote the Koran; the name of every other Arab
Mumar Raini	Libyan engineer working for Abu al
N	General Manystars Tenstars' code name
Obama	President of the United States from Hawaii or possibly Kenya with British or Kenyan or Indonesian or something citizenship
Osama bin Laden	Nasty evil Islamic cleric. Purportedly the mastermind behind the attack on the World Trade Center and the Pentagon on 9/11/2001
Otario Uther Tenstar	Same guy as N, different name
Pierce Brosnan	Irish-American actor, played the other guy but not as well as

	Connery
Pinchpenny	General Tenstars' secretary
R	Very odd inventor for DORK
Rojyar	Fatima's arranged fiancé
Sally	Secretary at BITCH
Salim Muhamet al Jabar	Leader of the Patriotic Rebellion for an Independent Central Kurdistan
Samir	Abu's contact with Arab Enterprises
Sadaam Hussein	Former President for life of Iraq
Samantha	Abu al Raini's girlfriend in America or he thought she was. She didn't have a clue
Sean Connery	Scottish-American Actor, played the other guy in movies
Sergeant Gunner Sergeant	A staff sergeant with 8th Marines in Irbil
Sergeant Major Private	The sergeant major of 8th Marines in Irbil

Scooby Doo	Cartoon dog from Hanna-Barbera television productions
Shiela Bitz	Secretary at DORK. Filed suit against Ames for sexual harassment
Sidi al Down	Abu al Raini's somewhat chubby assistant, patsy and fall guy
Summer Blond	Ames Blonds mother and a former special education teacher
T	Lawyer with the DORK Legal Information and Rehabilitation Department
Walid Rhamin	Terrorist. Ames is arrest because he looked like him

AAOAS
Acronyms, Abbreviations and Other Assorted Stuff

155	155 mm M777 howitzer used by the US Marines
747	Boeing 747 widebody commercial cargo/passenger jet
AK-47	Russian assault rifle now made in almost every country in the world and given to anybody who wants one – children, teenagers, terrorists, idiots
AN-24	Anatov 10 Aircraft, Russian. Fielded in 1962, it was an outstanding cargo/passenger hauler
ASSHOLS	Advanced Special Sciences and Hidden Office of Laboratory Studies (Fictitious)
ATF	Bureau of Alcohol, Tobacco, Firearms and Explosives
AV-8B	Vertical takeoff and landing attack/fighter used primarily by the US Marines and the British who originally designed it.
Base-X	Tent system that is easy to put up and take

	down. There are various designs and uses
BDU	Battle Dress Uniform, used prior to Army ACUs
BITCH	British Intelligence, Technology and Communications Heralding (Fictitious)
BOP	Bureau of Prisons (I didn't make it up!)
C-141	Starlifter cargo plane with 4 engines, workhorse of the USAF
CHRIST	Communications Handling, Reporting, Information Specialization and Training (Fictitious)
CIA	Central Intelligence Agency
CP	Command Post, generally the heart and operating center of a military unit
DAMN	Defense Ammunition Maintenance and Nomenclature (Fictitious)
DDT	Department of Dirty Tricks (Fictitious)
DEA	Drug Enforcement Agency

DIA	Defense Intelligence Agency
DORK	Department of Reconnaissance and Knowledge (Fictitious)
F-16	US Air Force Fighting Falcon multi-task jet fighter
FAX	A facsimile machine to transmit documents over telephone lines. Mostly replaced by pdf formatted documents and email
FBI	Federal Bureau of Investigation
FBP	Federal Bureau of Prisons
FFRD	Federal Fraudulent Recipes Division, FBI (Fictitious)
G-2	Intelligence section of a unit's staff. There are also G-1 (personnel), G-3 (operations), G-4 (supply) and G-5 (humanitarian operations)
GE	General Electric
GOD)	General of Defense (Fictitious

GPA	Grade Point Average
GPS	Global Positioning System
HE	High Explosives
HMO	Health Maintenance Organization
HMMWV	High Mobility Multi-purpose Wheeled Vehicle. Replaced the "Jeep." It has multi-roles as a passenger/cargo carrier, ambulance
ICE	Immigration and Customs Enforcement
ID	Identification
IRS	Internal Revenue Service
JESUS	Jet Engine Special Usage Section (Fictitious)
JOC	Joint Operations Command
LAV	Light Armored Vehicle – large beasty with 8 wheels, primarily used by the US Marines
LCD	Liquid Crystal Display, also called a television

LIAR	Legal Information and Rehabilitation department of DORK (fictitious)
LT	Lieutenant
M240	Medium machine gun
MFM	Minefield Maintenance in Guantanamo Bay, Cuba, No longer exists
MIT	Massachusetts Institute of Technology
M1	Advanced heavy tank named the "Abrams"
MRAP	Mine Resistant Ambush Protected
MRE	Meals Ready to Eat, some good, some really bad
NATS	Naval Air Transport Service
NERDS	Non-European Resources and Development Society (Fictitious)
NCO	Non-commissioned Officer – Corporals and above
NSA	National Security Agency

PMS	Premenstraual Syndrome. Do NOT be around women with this condition!
POL	Petroleum, Oil and Lubricants
PRICK	Nationalist organization – Patriotic Rebellion for an Independent Central Kurdistan (fictitious)
R and R	Rest and Recover
SatCom	Satellite Communications, a type of radio
SAW machine gun	Squad Automatic Weapon. A light
SHIT	Special Habits Intelligence Training (Fictitious)
TSA	Transportation Security Administration
TV	Television
USFSEI	US Forest Service Enforcement and Investigations
USMC	United States Marine Corps
USMS	United States Marshals Service

| WPPA | West Point Protective Association (Fictitious) |
| WIA | Wounded in Action |

www.ingramcontent.com/pod-product-compliance
Lightning Source LLC
Chambersburg PA
CBHW062113170626
46813CB00002B/431